PRAISI
JUI

TROPHY

"Fast-paced international thriller that details the inter-workings of fighter pilots and their equipment. Savarin demonstrates keen insight into the complex lives of his Europilots."

—Mark Berent,
Author of *Rolling Thunder*

LYNX

"The flying sequences are terrific."

—*The New York Times*

"Plenty of treachery and hairy high-tech dog fights. . . . Plenty of agreeable tension."

—*Kirkus Reviews*

"Fast-paced action."

—*Library Journal*

WATER HOLE

"First-rate."

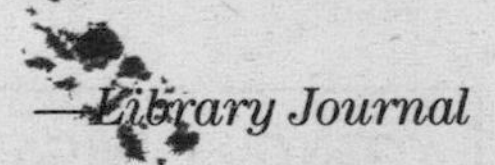

—*Library Journal*

"Savarin keeps his story rolling at a terrific clip."

—*Publishers Weekly*

BOOKS BY JULIAN JAY SAVARIN

Horsemen in the Shadows
MacAllister's Run
Pale Flyer
Trophy
Target Down!
Wolf Run
Windshear
Naja
The Quiraing List
Villiger
Water Hole
The Queensland File

Published by HarperPaperbacks

HORSEMEN IN THE SHADOWS

JULIAN JAY SAVARIN

HarperPaperbacks
A Division of HarperCollins*Publishers*

HarperPaperbacks *A Division of* HarperCollins*Publishers*
10 East 53rd Street, New York, N.Y. 10022

Cover illustration by Danilo Ducak

First printing: January 1996

Printed in the United States of America

HarperPaperbacks and colophon are trademarks of HarperCollins*Publishers*

❖ 10 9 8 7 6 5 4 3 2 1

COURIER

Life had, Jordan Blish decided, despite everything, been exceedingly good to him. Life, he could not realize, was about to rectify that serious mistake. And soon.

The bullet seemed to have a mind of its own. But the man fought it, refusing to die. It was a one-sided contest. The bullet plowed through, trailing a vortex of blood, tissue, and bone. It left the shattered head to embed itself in a wall, but by then, he knew little of it. As life faded, he had no way of knowing that the circumstances that ended it had begun in several places, a long time and a long way from where he died.

■ ■ ■

The man in the Moscow hotel was smartly dressed; smart in a discreet way that seemed at odds with his physical presence. He looked more like a slimmed-down version of a bouncer from one of the many dubious clubs that had sprung up all over the former Soviet capital, as the new eras of a bizarre kind of capitalism and unaccustomed freedoms took hold. Yet for all that, he did not seem as large as would have been expected. There was, however, an air about him that gave that impression.

He looked as if he had little faith in the developing state of affairs within the former Union and, quite clearly, expected it all to end very nastily indeed. The expression of world-weary cynicism, which appeared to have been stamped upon his features since birth, openly telegraphed that belief. He was a man whose demeanor unashamedly said he expected the worst of behavior from his fellowman, and that his trust was not easily earned.

There was a companion in the hotel room. The man, with precisely cropped steel gray hair, almost rake-thin and very tall at six-foot-three, was just as smartly dressed. Dead eyes stared out of a hollow-cheeked face. But there was a telling difference between them: *he* wore his clothes with the air of someone accustomed to good tailoring. When he walked, he dragged his right leg barely perceptibly, and his right foot was turned outward just slightly more than the left. He disguised this so well, only the very observant would notice.

The man who looked like a bouncer knew that particular gait very well, and its history.

A shot fired by a drunken soldier on a lonely desert

outpost on the southeastern border of the old Soviet Union, though only grazing the knee, had given the taller one the draggy leg. The soldier had subsequently died for such an act of suicidal folly. The outwardly turned right foot had been the legacy of a difficult birth.

Both men were staring at the gleaming, leather-bound briefcase that lay unopened upon the bed.

"It's all in there?" The bouncer surveyed the case uneasily. There was a coarseness to his voice that fitted his appearance.

"It is," the other replied with curt brevity.

"I still can't believe it."

"Scared?"

The rough-looking man was in fact an army lieutenant who had been promoted late from a noncommissioned rank. He did not appear to be someone who was easily frightened and, unlike his colleague, was not a Moscovite.

"Who in his right mind wouldn't be?" he now countered.

"Don't worry," the tall one said with a hint of superciliousness. "You're quite safe."

"I'll feel safe when I've got rid of it."

"Don't look so worried," the other repeated. "The stuff in there is well shielded."

"Like Chernobyl?"

"Your sarcasm is not appreciated." The tall one's eyes were cold.

The lieutenant had a stubborn expression upon his face. "Pulling rank?"

"Of course not."

"Good. I'm the one who has to travel with this piece of hell."

"Unlike your sarcasm, your effort is fully appreciated. It will be noted in the highest places."

"I don't care about being noted. Just doing my duty for the Motherland."

The lieutenant was singularly disinterested in flattery. His years in uniform, his combat experience, and other, lesser-known services for his homeland had created within him a healthy distrust of people who said nice things when they were sending you out to risk your neck. Only the fact that he still believed in the army prevented him from being one of the many gangsters plaguing his increasingly turbulent country. But even the army was being betrayed.

"You have your weapon?" the tall one asked.

"Naturally. Loaded and ready for use."

"Good. When you get to Leningrad—"

"You mean St. Petersburg—"

"When you get to Leningrad," the tall one repeated, emphasizing, in a hard voice that was several degrees colder, the old Soviet name for the Baltic city. "It will always be Leningrad. Let's not have any of that Czarist crap."

"Petrograd, then. Let's compromise."

The dead eyes surveyed the lieutenant unblinkingly. "One day, that warped sense of humor will be your undoing." The tall one paused to let the remark sink in. "You will be met," he continued evenly, "in a park on Krestovskij. Take a circuitous route from the station. Use whatever form of travel suits you to get there, but *be on time*. The briefcase will be exchanged for an identical one. You will not ask questions of the person who exchanges it, and you will not check its contents. You will not be able to open it without betraying yourself. Go to the hotel as arranged and stay the night, then return the next day with the new case. I will see you back here. Do you wish me to repeat these instructions?"

The lieutenant stared at his companion. "Do I need to be tucked in bed? I'll manage to remember. I do know the Kirov islands, and I do know Petro—Leningrad, considering I was born there."

"You have a questionable attitude, Comrade. You're being insolent."

"And I thought you weren't going to pull rank."

The lieutenant was on the train to Leningrad when the tall man spoke into a public phone near Moscow station.

"When the switch has been made," he said to the person at the other end, "kill him. Use your own discretion and timing. But be careful. He's armed."

There was no acknowledgment before the phone went dead. There'd been no need for one.

The journey to Leningrad was without incident. On the alert in case of trouble, the lieutenant walked slowly away from the station. As instructed, he began his elaborate roundabout route to the exchange point on the stadium island on the Nevka delta. It suited him to do so. He had his own reasons.

When he'd decided he'd walked long enough and was satisfied no one was following, he hopped aboard a tram, checking once more for pursuit. He was still in the clear. He got off on the island itself, at the junction of Petrogradskaja and Morskoj Prospekt, and did some more walking. But he did not continue along the wide avenue toward the World War II monument and the stadium. Instead, he turned off it, spent some more time laying a false trail, then doubled back to head toward the small square named in his instructions.

He was sauntering along, close now to his destination, when he became aware of being followed. He did not alter his deliberately measured stride, and remained outwardly calm. He gave no sign that he knew he was being tailed. When at last he began to hear footsteps, he did not quicken his own pace.

Presently, the footsteps caught up with him. A man, smartly dressed and wearing a lightweight coat despite the warmth of the day, matched his steps precisely. Their heels struck the ground in exact unison. The stranger carried an identical briefcase.

He glanced down at the man's footwear. They were of real leather. Foreign shoes. A man with money, or at least with access to expensive Western goods.

They were approaching a small park.

"If you forget the history of the wars and the revolutions, and the crime that's going on, this is not a bad city," the man with the shoes said, speaking for the first time. "You were born here, I believe." The accent was east Siberian.

The lieutenant did not reply.

"What's the matter?" the newcomer inquired.

"I wasn't told I had to give you my personal history as well."

"Touchy."

There was a watchful silence between them as they walked.

"There's a bench," foreign shoes eventually said. He glanced casually about him, with seeming disinterest. "No inquisitive people around. Let's sit for a while."

They went to the bench and sat down. They put their briefcases next to each other.

Anyone interested in watching would have seen them begin to converse animatedly; and anyone choosing to do a bit of eavesdropping would have heard nothing more than two harassed fathers discussing their troublesome teenage offspring. Neither was married, nor were they fathers. After a while they stood up, embraced briefly, then parted. They picked up their briefcases and went in opposite directions.

The lieutenant entered the basic hotel room that had been booked for him and placed the briefcase on the threadbare carpet next to the single bed. He sat down on the bed to wait. Just five minutes later, a knock sounded on the door.

"It's open," he said.

Even as he spoke he had risen swiftly to cross the room, drawing his automatic as he did so. From a pocket, he took out a silencer and quickly fitted it to the weapon. He then flattened himself against the wall next to the door.

It opened suddenly and two men, guns drawn, rushed in on eerily silent feet. Neither was the man who had caught up with him in the square. The intruders, in long army greatcoats that bore no markings of rank and were worn over civilian clothes, paused uncertainly when they saw the unattended briefcase. Puzzled expressions began to form upon their faces.

Then consternation turned to self-preservation as they rapidly became aware of their very immediate danger. Moving swiftly despite having been caught completely off guard, they began to whirl round to face this unexpected and unknown threat. They need not have bothered, for all the good it did them.

The lieutenant was much, much faster.

He shot them before they had fully turned. He was quick, and economical. One shot each as the automatic coughed. They fell with strange, soft thuds as their dying, puzzled expressions changed into fixed grimaces of pain, and of utter surprise.

The lieutenant did not waste time. He removed the silencer, placed it back in his pocket, and returned the automatic to its holster. He then picked up the briefcase and, stepping calmly over the bodies, went out. He even shut the door carefully.

There was a lot of money in that briefcase.

In a far country two men, in a room guarded by heavily armed soldiers posted outside, shook hands on the completion of a deal. The buyer had just purchased, on behalf of his principals, a minisubmarine.

OCTOBER

1

"We are," the speaker began, "the Four Horsemen—waiting unseen, astride our horses in the shadows. Our task—to manipulate, to influence, but most importantly, to *regain* the ground lost by those incompetents whose political myopia has brought our great nation to its knees. They are that worst of all things: fools in positions of power. Despite this, we must continue to exercise great patience; for we possess the real power base, and time is on our side."

Feliks Alexandrovitch Kurinin, recently promoted general in the federal security services, still considered himself a member of the old KGB. As far as he was concerned, his former service continued to exist. He had no time for newfangled, politically acceptable semantics. KGB was KGB. Period. He took a deep breath of the cold Siberian air and felt a perverse pleasure as the sharpness hit his lungs. He exhaled slowly, and twin plumes of heated air came from his nostrils, giving the impression of a furnace raging within him. He stared across the vast waters of the Baikal, upon whose shores the October snow had already settled. Over 660 kilometers from end to end and nearly seventy wide, the lake was a special place to him. At a maximum depth of just over one and a half kilometers, it was the greatest body of fresh water on the planet.

He stared at the low-lying shrouds of mist suspended over the deceptively still surface of the lake.

"The local people don't like to hear Baikal called a lake," he continued, speaking as if to himself. "To them it's a sea, and an entity, with its own spirit, a source of myth and legend that can rage into sudden storms at will. It is fatal to anger Baikal." He seemed to give a brief shiver though, in the thick greatcoat he wore, he was snugly warm. "I understand how they feel. My grandfather, one of the first Russians who came to live among the Buryat people, used to fish for omul. My father was born here on Olk'hon. Of course, like many of his generation, he headed for Moscow; but he brought us back to the island from time to time, during the holidays. For that, I will thank him forever."

At last, Kurinin turned from the lake to regard each of his three companions in turn. Wispy tendrils hung about their heads in the stillness as they breathed.

"Apart from the obvious reasons of security, choosing this location for this meeting and those in the future has an additional purpose. I wanted you to get close to Baikal, since none of you has before. Of course, you've all flown over it on at least one occasion, and I know you've briefly visited the south shore, Viktor. But none of you have got truly close, spiritually. Baikal symbolizes everything about our Motherland. It is majestic, it is precious, it is vital. Much has been said about the threat to Baikal—caused by the abuse of its environment—and its need for protection. We are told if Baikal's ecological balance is destroyed, this will be of detriment to the entire planet.

"Comrades, you do not need me to tell you about what is happening to our people. You have eyes and ears. Our soldiers, highly trained and dedicated, have returned to hovels and tents in muddy fields. Our superbly skilled fighter pilots are being demoralized when they discover the kind of accommodation *they* have returned to. There are wars on our borders, and the West is thinking of spreading its influence eastward. All this is making us seem weak. Our lifeblood is being drained, drop by debilitating drop.

"The Motherland, *our* Motherland, needs protection from the vandals that are both within and without. If *its* equilibrium is destroyed, then, I assure you, the entire planet *will* indeed suffer. We have done well since those idiots mounted their abortive coup in '91, but still, no one outside our inner circle knows what we truly are about. This is as it should be." Kurinin gave a sudden, brief smile as he came to the end of his speech, as if at a private joke. "We, the Horsemen in the shadows, will continue to watch and wait for the time to strike."

The island of Olk'hon, situated almost exactly midway along the lake and close to its western shore, was said to be its oldest landmass. More than seventy kilometers long, it gave Kurinin all the security he needed. The helicopters that had brought his companions and him—with their combat-ready escort troops—had landed in the secure compound that had been in construction even before the failed coup. None of the Horsemen had been stupid enough to be associated with that mistake.

The compound itself was an intruder-sanitized zone about six kilometers across, with a solid building at its center deep within the *taiga*, the island's ancient forest. It was well away from the once-thriving fishing settlement to the north and had been built with minimum disturbance to the *taiga*. The secure perimeter was full of trees, with no clearly defined open spaces to excite interested eyes. Excellent camouflaging ensured that the location was invisible from the air and even prying, space-borne satellites would be none the wiser. The helicopters, in civilian markings, had found their landing pads by the pilots' precise knowledge of the coordinates, and acceptance by the ground staff of the secure landing codes. The aircraft had been placed out of sight, and it was as if they had never existed.

Kurinin took no chances. It was the first time he had brought the others.

His face had now hardened. "We have a serious problem that must be resolved quickly, before we take our plans further. About two months ago, people I had trusted chose to go into business for themselves. A quantity of weapons-grade nuclear material—small, but sufficient to give us all nightmares—has gone missing, as has the very large sum of money that was paid for it, *and* an enterprising army lieutenant. The lieutenant has the money, and someone else the plutonium. This incident is entirely separate from those that have been making the international news and it must *not* be allowed to."

They were all staring at him in varying degrees of shock. He briefly wondered whether any of them had felt tempted to do likewise. Everybody—soldiers, disaffected scientists and the like—seemed to be in the business of smuggling nuclear material, or selling it for a relative pittance to those who did. He discarded the thought. Not the Horsemen. Like him, they were playing for far higher stakes.

"The lieutenant," he went on, "was meant to exchange the material in Leningrad for the money, which he was then to bring back to Moscow. This was supposed to be a good faith payment, with more material to follow. But he was never intended to make the return journey, and no more material was going to be delivered to that particular buyer. He had been set up to be double-crossed.

"Our lieutenant, however, was clever. *He* double-crossed the double-crossers. He shot and killed two men sent to assassinate him in his hotel room, where he was expected to be innocently waiting like a lamb led to the slaughter. One has to admire that, if nothing else," Kurinin finished grimly.

"And where is he now?" the one called Viktor demanded.

"I have not yet been able to find out. Our informant does not, for the time being, have that piece of intelligence. I suspect, however, that our enterprising lieutenant has gone to the West; or he may be lying low in some forsaken hole, prepared to wait for weeks, perhaps months, before surfacing.

"He will know that even in the near-abroad, he would not be safe. He *must* be found, no matter what it takes, or how long. He must feel no safer in the West. I don't care about the money. I'm more worried about that lieutenant, and the damage he may do to us. He knows our group exists, though not our real purpose."

"Then there's no real danger—" another began.

But Kurinin cut him short. "There is *always* danger. As military men, you all know that. At least, I sincerely hope you do. Your lives may depend upon it one day."

"And the plutonium?" Viktor asked.

"Gone to its buyer."

"And do we know the identity of this buyer?"

"As yet . . . no."

Their silence spoke volumes.

"I told you the situation was dangerous," Kurinin said. He was not apologetic.

"The name of this insane lieutenant?" Igor Garadze, a Georgian with strong Russian ancestry, was an army general. Deep-set dark eyes stared out from beneath brows that looked like a cliff face. He was as formidable as he appeared, a man who was ruthlessly unforgiving.

"Mikhail Mikhailovitch Diryov," Kurinin answered. "His motor rifle regiment was stationed in Germany."

"So he used to sneak into the West in the old days and got a taste for the life?"

"He used to sneak into the West . . . but under orders, and of course he got a taste for the life. That's always a risk with field agents—more so when someone like that sees what glorious democracy has to offer our returning soldier heroes," Kurinin went on sourly. "He has scant regard for superior rank, which is probably why he was promoted so slowly, because he *is* good. Let's not forget he was able to fool his playmates most effectively. He must have planned all of it, a long time ago. He looked into the future, and didn't like what he saw."

"Rather like us."

"Not like us, Igor Leonidovitch," Kurinin retorted coldly. "Not like us at all. Perhaps he holds a grudge for the slow promotion. *He's* doing it for the money, but he won't live to enjoy it for long. He will not like what he sees in his own future. You can count on that."

"And those who bungled that transaction?" It was Garadze again, refusing to let go.

"They're being attended to. Except for the one Diryov tricked. His sole mission in life now is revenge. This means finding the man who made such a complete fool of him. He is a perfect weapon for our use. If Diryov does not kill him first, we shall—eventually. He is finished, and knows it. This will make him even more implacable in the hunt for our fortune-stealing lieutenant, the man who blew his little operation into the open."

The manner in which Kurinin spoke made even his hardened companions shiver involuntarily, as tendrils of the warmed lakeside air sneaked from their nostrils.

APRIL

1

On a bright and mild morning in Chelsea, London, Jordan Blish kissed his wife and two young children good-bye as he went out to his car. He climbed into the silver-blue, six-week-old Rover Vitesse Sport, waved to them, and set off on his journey to the Foreign Office in Whitehall.

He had picked the time well, slotting in neatly between the two phases of the morning rush hour. As a result, the Kings Road traffic, frequently balked by what seemed to be permanent roadworks, appeared to have temporarily ceased to exist. He got through what would normally have been the snarl-up nightmare of Sloan Square within minutes. Once, when he'd gauged it badly, he'd been caught in a jam that had immobilized him for an hour. One hour to travel a few feet. Today, however, he was making good time.

He cut through the back streets, heading for the other choke point of the Hyde Park roundabout. Hopefully, he would get through that just as easily, then it would be the homestretch run down the Mall and then through St. James's Park to where he normally left the car in a secure compound. Finally it would be the short walk to the office.

As he drove, Blish reflected upon the turn of fate that had brought him this far, albeit to a relatively junior post in the Foreign Service. It still meant he was more fortunate than a lot of other people.

And it could all have been so very different.

Thirty-two years before, he had been born in Trinidad to a very young and besotted Carib girl—daughter of a minor chief of what was left of her tribe—and an itinerant Trinidadian sailor. Mianna, herself from Dominica, and a descendant of one of the very few real Caribs to have survived down the ages since the arrival of Columbus, had fallen for the sailor, who worked aboard one of the interisland schooners. In her innocence, she had looked upon him as exciting, an exotic breath from an outside world she was eager to see. Against the strong opposition of her family, who lived on the euphemistically named Carib "reserve," she had succumbed to the call of the bright lights and had run away with him.

In Trinidad, and far from the security of her home, the exciting lover had become less so. She soon discovered she was not the love of his life, and when she inevitably became pregnant, he left her. She grew up very quickly after that.

Too ashamed to return home even if she could have managed the fare, she gave birth to the child among strangers, and later took any job to enable her to survive and care for the baby, for whom she had a great love. She named the boy Jordan, taken from the half-remembered religious teachings of her childhood. As a pretty young woman, she was prey to a great deal of unwanted attention, and many tried to entice her into prostitution. Good money, they said. She steadfastly resisted. Her shame was great enough.

But her heart was broken. She eventually lost the will to live and one day, she asked the then three-year-old to wait for her near a police station. She never returned. Her body was later found washed up on a beach. She had simply walked into the sea. The sharks had not touched her.

The boy was put into care, but, not unsurprisingly, he was a difficult child, prone to long periods of brooding and a total distrust of anyone. By the age of six he was absconding regularly, living off the streets and frequenting the harbor where the schooners came in. He was looking for a father he never found.

Then one day, fate took the first of the steps that would change his life forever. He saw an English couple, James and Harriet Blish, walking in one of the tourist areas and boldly went up to them to offer his services as a guide. As they looked down at the beautiful ragged boy with his smooth, pale brown skin and slightly almond-shaped eyes that stared back at them unwaveringly, Harriet Blish was overwhelmed by maternal love. The boy could not know that his future benefactors, in their thirties, could not have children of their own; neither could he know that the husband and wife team worked for the Foreign Office's Commonwealth Development Agency.

The Blishes inquired about and pieced together such details as were available of Jordan's history, adopted him, and took him with them to England. They gave him their surname, but sensitively retained the one his mother had given him. The transformation of his life had begun.

He was sent to a public school, where he proved to be academically gifted. University followed, and it was there that he met the woman who would eventually become his wife. Charlotte Durleigh, a tall natural blonde with striking, but unusual, dark brown eyes was immediately fascinated by the quietly confident undergraduate to whom she was introduced at a party; more so when, totally unlike the other young men who were trying to impress her, he appeared to ignore her completely. It was only after they'd become intimate that he finally admitted to her that he had been smitten on sight, but had been too scared to talk to her.

The first time she'd introduced him to her parents had been a disaster. They had not bothered to hide the shock on their faces or, subsequently, their feelings. A marriage and two children later had not wiped that particular memory away. The wedding had been a happy affair, marred only by the absence of her parents. His own adopted parents, true to form, had treated Charlotte as if *they'd* been giving her away to be married.

Though he would never dream of voicing such thoughts to them, Blish felt certain his path to the Foreign Office had been made less hard because of their own past service. But they had sensed his uncertainty and had assured him he'd got there on merit alone. At a dinner, when they'd proudly announced that Jordan was going to be something at the Foreign Office, he'd drily countered he was going to be nothing at the Foreign Office. He had no illusions. His was a dark face, but it did not worry him.

Though his was a junior post, he'd long decided he could not complain. His parents, reasonably well-off, had always ensured he'd never been short of money. It was as if they'd been compensating for the circumstances of his early years. Ever since he'd started earning his own, he'd asked them to stop. They had already done so much for him. But his pleas had fallen upon deaf ears. Charlotte's father, a man much richer, had cut her off since the marriage, and the Blishes had decided their son needed their assistance, especially now that they had two grandchildren upon whom to dote. He hadn't the heart to continue refusing.

As he stopped at a traffic light, Blish pondered his good fortune. It was something he'd done on countless occasions over the years, throughout all the periods of his life. He kept reminding himself how it could have been all so different. He could have ended his days on a Trinidadian beach as yet another statistic of the world's young, his brains addled by a lethal cocktail of rum and cocaine, or in some street fight somewhere. Just like one of those kids in the documentaries on the television.

The conscience games, Charlotte once described them. The new Roman arena. The kids were the doomed Christians, and three of the Horsemen of the Apocalypse—famine, war, and pestilence—the lions waiting for the next meal. And the world watched.

Something more than the Band-Aid of assistance programs was needed, she'd insisted.

But he was one who'd escaped. And so, here he was, public school and university educated, on his way in a smart car to his job at the Foreign Office. Behind was a Chelsea home, a beautiful wife, and two lovely children.

"I am," he said to himself, "a very lucky man."

Then fate decided to call in the debt.

The passenger door of the car was yanked open with shocking suddenness. Blish jumped with shock as a man got in. The Rover rocked slightly.

"Why don't you lock your doors, Jordan?" the unexpected passenger demanded. "Haven't you heard of carjacking?"

Blish stared at the man, the shocked surprise giving way to dawning recognition.

"Jesus! Branko! What a thing to do! Where the hell did you spring from?"

Horns began to blare.

"I think you'd better move," Branko suggested mildly. "The citizens are getting irate. The light's green."

"Shit."

Blish pulled away, found a side street, and parked. "My God, Branko. That was some start you gave me."

There was a faint smile upon Branko's face as he looked at Blish, eyes scrutinizing. "Very prosperous." He looked around the car and made a great show of sniffing it. "Leather upholstery. *Car* phone. You have done well."

"My God," Blish repeated, staring at his companion. "How many years?"

"A good ten . . . maybe twelve. Who's counting?"

"You've been in Czechoslovakia . . . sorry. Force of habit. I mean the Czech Republic, for all that time?"

"Don't worry," Branko said airily. "These days, countries don't know what to call themselves. Today, the Czech Republic. Tomorrow . . . who knows?"

"And no more use for dissidents."

"Don't believe that, my friend. The day of the dissident is not over. The playing fields have changed a little. That is all. And you? Did you go into the Foreign Office? Or are you something rich in the City?"

"What do you think?"

Branko made another show of looking round the car. "The Foreign Office, I think. It's still a nice car, of course—"

"Why thank you—"

"No need to be sarcastic. You must still be in shock. In the City," Branko went on calmly, "you would have had a Porsche, or maybe a Mercedes. So? What is it like being a nonwhite face in there?"

"I'm not the only one—"

"Perhaps . . . but I think your position is a little different. I do not think you make the tea."

Blish studied the face that had come so suddenly out of the past. "You don't sound like someone who's asking. You sound like someone who already knows. I've always wondered about the Czech dissident who came to our student parties."

"Ah . . . Cambridge. Such memories. I remember Charlotte. So beautiful. All the men were after her and you, so quiet and already in love, would not talk to her. What happened?"

"I married her. Her father's a Tory MP. He hated the idea. Still does."

Branko nodded, a man who expected the answer. "Of course. The whole thing was inevitable. The marriage, and the father."

"As if you didn't already know."

"What are you saying, Jordan?" Branko was smiling again.

"Were you really a dissident? Or even a student? Your English, I see, is as good as ever."

Branko looked thoughtful for a moment, then brightened. "The quiet ones are always the sharpest. So you think I was not a true dissident?"

"I've given it some thought over the years."

Branko patted his stomach. "I've grown fatter, hmm?"

"Not fatter." Blish paused. "Harder. You've still got that big frame, but the student face is long gone. It's as if it never existed. Many of us from that time simply look like older versions of ourselves, but you . . ."

"I did . . . different things," Branko said vaguely, then went on another tack. "There was always something about you that the others did not have. You had a kind of . . . wariness. You did not take things at face value." He seemed amused by something. "Not one to swallow slogans whole, you once said to me. You didn't go on many marches."

"Call it a natural suspicion of other people's motives."

Branko peered at him, as if looking for something hidden deep within his eyes. "There's something in there. Something you keep to yourself. When I first met you, I thought you had come from the East. But of course, some of your genes have. The people who became Caribs are descendants of those who crossed the top of the world to populate the Americas, long before the Europeans." Branko paused. "You are a little like me. That is why I have chosen you, after all these years."

"*Chosen* me. What are you talking about?"

"I thought of Giles Mackillen," Branko went on, ignoring Blish's words. "Now *he* is something in the City, and he does have a Porsche. Too predictable, and is still as sly a shit as I remember him. Someone like that can never be trusted. He is not the kind of person to whom I would leave my back exposed. He would also sell me to the highest bidder, just like the commodities he deals in. I'm equally certain he still envies you over Charlotte.

"I have also considered Henry Tamblin. Unfortunately, he's still fighting his radical wars. Too unstable and also incapable of accepting that the world he knew has long changed into something he cannot recognize. There are the others, but they all fell at the first barrier. So you see? You are the only possible choice. I have been following your progress with great interest, you know. Beautiful blond wife. Beautiful kids. Impressive. I've always believed that mixing the genes makes for greater beauty. You are in the right place, and this is the right time."

"I didn't marry Charlotte because she's blond. A lot of people try to interpret this according to their own prejudices. I married her because I love her. End of story."

"Hey, hey! I'm not one of those types of people."

"Then what exactly are you, Branko, and what choice am I supposed to be? What do you mean when you say you've been following my progress?"

"So many questions!" Branko had the look of someone who knew that what he was about to say would shock, and would enjoy doing so. "I'm going to make you very big at the Foreign Office," he announced mysteriously. "October is the month of revolution, after all. Something started last October. To begin with, my name is not Branko, and I am not Czech. I am Russian. I am about to give you a scoop that, if you were a journalist, you'd kill for. I'm about to give you information about a coming rebellion, about the movement of weapons-grade nuclear material . . . and about a lot of money which I received in return.

"I am going to tell you about new dangers; about nightmares. I am also going to tell you about a psycho case we shall call the major. If he ever finds me, he will try to kill me. I will also try to kill him; but he has many friends, powerful people. I have double-crossed him; therefore, in a way, I've double-crossed them, too."

Blish stared at him openmouthed.

"Your chin's about to hit the floor," Branko said. "Close your mouth. You'll get a fly in it."

Blish gave a single blink, as if suddenly coming awake, and shut his mouth slowly.

"What's the lesson of history?" Branko demanded.

"Is that a trick question? You sound like one of my old professors."

The man who called himself Branko smiled. "The lesson of history is that no one ever learns from it. I'll be in touch," he added as he opened the door.

"*Hey!* You can't just—"

"I'll be in touch," Branko, the man who looked

like a bouncer, repeated. He started getting out of he car, then paused. "Do you think she married you to spite her father?" He got out quickly, before Blish could say anything, and walked away.

Blish twisted round to look, but Branko seemed to have vanished into thin air. He settled back in his seat once more and gripped the steering wheel hard with both hands, the skin stretching tightly across the knuckles as he did so.

He heard a strange knocking. He tracked his head round the car, searching out the cause. It was only when he looked down that he noticed his right leg was shaking uncontrollably and banging against the side of the car.

Suddenly, the snug foundations upon which his cosy world was built seemed no longer secure, and a shiver of dread went through him as he thought of Charlotte and the children.

"My God!" he cried. "*Charlie and the kids!*"

He turned the car quickly round and headed back.

Despite the fact that he was traveling in the opposite direction to the rush hour, the traffic had suddenly worsened. It took a great deal of self-control to keep his hand off the horn button. Making other drivers irate would not get him there any faster. He crept along, fantasizing about having a police siren to clear the way.

He rang the office to say he would be late, citing bad traffic as the cause. Strictly speaking, it was not a lie. He was being held up. But those who knew his habits would be mildly surprised. He was known as the traffic-buster who *always* made it on time.

Many would choose to believe it was trouble at home. The attitude of Charlotte's parents to the marriage, especially that of her father, was no secret. While he wouldn't swear to it, Blish had always harbored the suspicion that there were a few private bets about how long it would last. The fact that there were now two children did not seem to change the minds of those waiting for the disaster to happen. Someone had once told him that a particular colleague could barely contain his sense of anticipation. *Schadenfreude* would reign supreme.

He also knew that the man in question had a strong fancy for Charlotte and clearly thought she could have done better by choosing him instead. The jealous colleague, Montgomery Allardyne, was the epitome of correctness, but Blish did not trust him for a second.

Giles, and Monty. Friend, and colleague. Two people who would like to see him fall. Now Branko had tried to plant a seed of doubt about Charlotte. To what purpose?

"Damn you, Branko!" Blish whispered savagely. "Why did you have to come back into my life?"

When he'd at last made it to the Sloane Square roundabout, the place was choked with stationary cars. He turned on the radio and selected Radio 3 for some classical music. A harpsichord sonata of one of his favorite composers filled the car, calming him as he waited with the string of cars trapped behind the lorry that was causing the problem.

"Thank God for Scarlatti," he muttered.

He could see a totally empty road over to his left. Going that way would enable him to use the back streets to get home. Unfortunately, he was now hemmed in by an outside ring of cars, all trying to feed into the bottleneck.

Scarlatti continued to soothe him.

It took a good half hour to clear the mess, requiring what had seemed like a regiment of traffic wardens, and three motorcycle policemen, who looked extremely irate. The lorry driver was not their favorite person for the day.

As he drove along the Kings Road with the now relatively free-flowing traffic, Blish came to the chilling realization that he would have been much too late to affect anything if Charlotte and the children were already in danger. The traffic jam had seen to that.

He cut into a side street that was close to where he lived and finally came to a halt outside his house. The tires gave a brief, sharp squeal in response to the force of his braking. The door of the integral garage was closed; but that didn't necessarily mean anything. Without checking to see, there was no way of knowing whether she'd gone out with the kids, the youngest of whom was just over a year old.

He hurried to the front door of the white, double-fronted house with its columned porch, anxiously put the key in the lock, turned it, pushed the solid white door open. The burglar alarm was not armed. She was still in.

But he could hear nothing. No sounds of children.

"Charlie?" The first call was tentative. "*Charlie?*"

When there was no reply he began to rush through the house, first checking every room on the ground floor, then the garden, trying to quell, not very successfully, a rising panic.

"*Charlie?*" He was shouting now. "*Charlie?*"

Nothing. No kids.

He ran upstairs to the first floor, heart in mouth, calling out her name. There was still no reply. He searched every room, including his study. Emptiness greeted him.

The top floor. They must be on the top floor. The kids were with her, playing in the master bedroom. They hadn't heard him because the door was closed. Of course. That was it. So obvious. But the thought didn't make him feel any better.

He hurried up to the last floor, now adding the children's names to his increasingly worried calls, while he tried hard to curb the dread that was rapidly growing within him. There was a perfectly rational explanation, he tried to persuade himself. There had to be. On any other day, if he hadn't seen Branko . . .

But he *had* seen Branko, and this was not just any other day. Not anymore.

Again, he checked every room. The bedrooms were empty, including the master.

"*Charlie? Amanda! Mianna!*"

The silence mocked him. Oh God, oh God! What had happened to them? Had Branko—

"Jordan?" the blissfully familiar voice called from below. "What are you doing home? And what's that racket all about?"

He shut his eyes briefly with relief and told himself to be calm as he hurried back down. No point in alarming her needlessly.

But her instincts were razor-sharp. Though he looked unruffled by the time he reached her, he could not keep his anxiety totally hidden. It was all there in his eyes for her to see.

"Jordan? What's going on? And why all the shouting? I was down in the cellar."

The cellar!

Why hadn't he thought of that? He had allowed the sudden appearance of Branko to so disrupt him, he'd gone off in all directions, barely under control.

He embraced her, giving her a tight squeeze.

Charlotte Blish was one of those women whose beauty sneaked up on you when you weren't looking. She was not someone who would be unnoticed in a crowd. Her gleaming blond hair would see to that; but once past the blond hair an observer, on first scrutiny, would think: nice hair, so what? But there was an astonishing amount left in reserve.

The subtleties of her features would begin to make an impression just as interest was starting to wane, leading to a feeling of confusion. How could such beauty have possibly been missed during that first glance?

This was the aspect of her that had captivated Blish from the very beginning. He had seen past the blond hair to the real beauty and had been hooked, despite feeling very much the underdog, and deciding there was no chance of his ever getting past the gaggle of attentive males that had always seemed to be tagging along wherever she went.

But she had become his wife and mother of his two children, to the chagrin and envy of many. Now, an old friend from the student days might well have put them all in danger.

Charlotte's startling brown eyes, with their tinge of blue, searched his face as she inclined her head slightly backward to study him closely. He'd always found those eyes a marvelous contrast to that blond hair and derived a continuing pleasure every time he looked at her.

"Much as I like your version of tight dancing and you . . . feel quite excited to see me . . . "

"Oh!" he said. "Um . . . um . . . "

"Don't you 'um' at me, Jordan Blish," she interrupted, holding on to him firmly so that he was pressed hard against her. "You're supposed to be excited to see me, no matter what state you might be in. And as that seems to be happening, why don't we discuss this afterward?" She licked her lips sensuously and gave him a smile that needed little interpretation.

"The kids!" he said. "Where are the kids?"

Her smile vanished slowly, and she frowned at him. "I don't believe you've just turned me down. Jordan? What is the matter with you? Have you forgotten Mother's having them today?"

Then he remembered. "Oh hell, yes. I'm sorry. I—"

"You know how she likes seeing them." She was still frowning at him, trying to understand the reasons for his strange jumpiness. "Daddy was coming up to town and she decided to accompany him for a day or two. So she's taken them to the house for a few hours. But you knew this already." Her eyes continued to search his face.

He nodded. "I know. I just seem to have forgotten."

The large town house, with its extensive, walled garden, was perfect and safe for the children, and was a welcome break for Charlotte, who stubbornly refused to employ a nanny, or an *au pair*. Unlike many of her peers, she did not agree with the practice. She allowed a cleaning lady, but that was it.

She gently moved his hands from her waist and stood back, still holding on to them.

"I don't see how you could have." The eyes maintained their close scrutiny. "All right," she said. "Give."

"Branko's back," he said after a while.

She let go of his hands. "*What? The* Branko? Our resident Czech dissident? After all these years of silence?"

If only she knew!

"Where did you see him?" she went on. "I mean—how did this happen? And why would meeting up with Branko after such a long time send you scurrying back here . . ." Her voice faded.

"Jordan?" she continued. "Is Branko in trouble? Is it to do with something he did when we were at Cambridge? You know . . . being involved with other dissidents against the Czech government, as he was. Now his past has caught up with him so he's come to you for help. That's it, isn't it?"

It was quite astonishing, he thought. She'd hit most of the targets first time out. Problem was, she'd have a fit if she knew the true nature of the trouble.

"But hang on," she continued. "They wouldn't be chasing dissidents these days, unless—" She stared at him. "What exactly has he been doing?"

He would have to tell her, but not just yet. He'd wait to see what Branko was really about.

"I don't really know, and I'm not sure what to think," he said. "I'll just have to wait and see. Meanwhile—"

"You were worried about the children. You were worried about me. Why? Should I be worried too?"

It was going to be very hard to keep the truth from her, but for the time being, he had to. Until he knew precisely what Branko was about.

"I'm just being cautious. God knows what Branko's really been up to. Eastern Europe is an unholy mess at the moment and seems to be getting worse. Conventional wisdom has it that it will get much worse, before it gets better—"

"And your own feeling?"

"It will get a lot worse. Period."

"Does anyone at the office agree with you?"

"Charlie, you know I'm not in a position to give advice to anybody. And who would listen? I have no illusions about my status."

"They'll wake up one day." She came close and kissed him.

"You're just a loyal wife."

"*Just* a loyal wife?"

"A very special, loyal wife."

"That's much better. And don't you forget it." She kissed him again.

"I'd better be going," he said, "or I'll drag you up stairs and who knows how long I might stay? Then they'll be sending the dogs out after me."

Her expression changed suddenly and became very serious as she looked at him. She reached upward to gently hold his face in her hands. "I don't like it when you say things like that. I know you're making one of those jokes of yours, but this has connotations of runaways and overseers with bloodhounds. I know and understand what you're saying, even if most other people don't.

"And I know Daddy gives you a terrible time. But that's his problem, not ours. I want you to remember one thing . . . *always.* I'm your wife, and the mother of our two lovely children. No one is going to change that. Ever. I will be with you for as long as you want me. You, me, and the children. Our team. It comes first. Always. And I love you. Never forget that. Do you hear me?" She leaned toward him and, still holding his face in her hands and rising on the balls of her feet, kissed him once more. "Never forget," she finished against his lips.

"I won't," he said.

Allardyne saw him come in.

"My, my," Allardyne began, smiling to coat the barb. "Little woman won't let you leave the house?"

"Something like that," Blish said, and walked on.

He told no one about Branko, the Czech who had become a Russian.

MAY

I

Moscow, 0800. Tuesday, 23rd.

Kurinin paced his office slowly. This was not a display of agitation. It was more like the slow, metronomic certainty of the sweep of a tiger's tail, while it waited alertly for its prey to fall into the ambush it had laid for it.

There was still no news of Diryov, or the money, or the plutonium. As he'd told his fellow Horsemen on Olk'hon, he cared little about the fate of the money, or the nuclear material. He wanted Diryov.

Kurinin stopped his pacing before a large window. He looked down upon the wide thoroughfare. A big black Mercedes swept along it. So-called democracy, capitalism, freedom, elections; all had come. But nothing had really changed, except the cars. Democracy was tank shells in Moscow's White House. The chaos was growing almost by the hour while, on the borders, the republics were igniting like a sequence of bonfires. Georgia, Abkhazia, Armenia, Azerbaijan, Ukraine, Crimea, Chechnya . . . The list was growing. The fire would eventually spread to the Baltics. He was sure of it.

As for the Western powers, who continued to delude themselves that they had permanently won the Cold War, they had failed disastrously to capitalize upon the advantage they had gained, and, in time, this would begin to look decidedly temporary.

The disaster they were making of the Bosnian crisis proved his point while suiting his intentions perfectly. Having a virtually pointless United Nations force hamstringing an organization like NATO was an insane joke. Their totally confused command structure, with its squabbling and factional power plays, conspired to make them dig themselves into an impossible hole.

Had he been on the Western side, he would have had none of this ludicrous posturing. A massive, swift, and punitive action right at the very beginning, over two years before, would have prevented the very mess that was now occurring. Despite the fact that this debacle fitted neatly into his own strategies, he could well understand the frustrations of those military commanders out there who knew how to use their brains properly. The political incompetence would have enraged him, just as it did on his side of the fence. This sympathy for the Western commanders' predicament was a very private thought, which he would never admit to anyone.

One had to show some solidarity with the Slavic brothers, after all, he thought with cynical expediency. And besides, after Chechnya, the Motherland could hardly be said to have been covered with glory.

The disintegration of NATO, the EC, and the so-called Western European Union was inevitable as long as the squabbling continued. With a little judicious prodding in the right quarters, helped by the snarling-up from time to time of the diplomatic process—like blocking Security Council resolutions, for example—this downward process would continue, and gather momentum as matters got worse. There were nightmares on the horizon, and so busy were they with their own vested interests, they were oblivious to them.

He smiled grimly. It was all happening as he had predicted since the days of the ludicrous and abortive coup that had changed everything forever, but not for the better. The time was coming to put matters right once more, but Diryov's continuing survival could seriously jeopardize the well-planned agenda.

"Standing as you are," a voice said from behind him, "you remind me of someone from history."

"As long as you don't say it's Napoleon."

"I won't."

Kurinin turned to look at his visitor, who sat in the gleaming, pale brown leather armchair, patiently waiting.

"Diryov must be found!" he said to her fiercely. He had switched to English, sounding almost like an Englishman, with an ease that betrayed long experience with the language. "It's been seven months now. He can't stay under forever. He's got to come up somewhere."

"We've gotten our people well spread out in many countries, particularly in Western Europe. In the States, too. We're also activating those who never thought they would be called." Her English carried an American accent. Clipped, Boston tones.

She smiled coldly as she went on, "Many now have families. They have become soft and cosy, even persuading themselves to believe that this New World Order the West bleats on about stands a chance of becoming reality. They have forgotten a most-important factor: how quickly human nature can drag everything back to its basest level once you give it the chance. Everyone should use Yugoslavia as a blackboard upon which that warning is written, for all to see. As for Diryov . . . we'll find him."

"Once, time was on our side, Comrade. Now, it is our enemy. Diryov's actions, along with those of the others involved in this affair, have seen to that. You can also see for yourself that the Motherland continues to deteriorate daily."

She nodded slightly. "I do. It is—"

"Obscene!" he interrupted with unexpected savagery. "And now we've got that traitor Diryov to deal with," he went on with barely less intensity. "He could jeopardize our agenda for the rebirth of the Union. Have you targeted his old contacts in Britain as I ordered? He might choose to put in an appearance there."

Again, she nodded. "If he's already made any contact, it must have been before we set up full surveillance. Since then, there have been no attempts. We're covering Giles Mackillen, Henry Tamblin, and a few others. Mackillen is a loathsome creature who deals in finance, and is exceptionally greedy. There's a climate of greed in some quarters over there, and Mackillen is one of its most passionate practitioners.

"The man has no morality. His only true loyalty is to the numbers in a bank account. He can certainly be paid to betray a former friend. We have identified that as a high-priority route to take if the situation requires it."

"And after he has betrayed Diryov?" Kurinin inquired softly.

"That would depend upon the operational requirement at the time."

They both knew what she really meant.

"Of course. Go on."

"Tamblin is one of those political dreamers who was once good fodder, but is now merely tedious. If Diryov is crazy enough to involve him—which I strongly doubt—Tamblin's rose-tinted stupidity would soon point us toward our absconding lieutenant. So we're keeping a close watch on him, too. There are the others whom we can use, if the need arises. One or two have become drug users and dealers, with a taste for violence." She smiled without humor. "Ironic, when you consider in the bad old days they were vociferous pacifists."

"And the other one . . . ?"

"Blish? He's also targeted. Now Blish is a totally different proposition." She smiled again. This time, there appeared to be some genuine humor. "We call him the Black Prince, although in reality he looks as if he has a heavy tan. He's done well for himself, considering the obstacles. Married into the British Establishment, and with an Establishment job. The

Foreign Office, of all things! He has a beautiful wife and two very pretty children.

"This makes him exceptionally vulnerable. In Diryov's place, this is the one I would approach, and, of course, the Foreign Office connection is perfect for what Diryov probably has in mind, *if* he decides to break cover. Blish is the only truly stable and incorruptible one among them."

"No one is incorruptible."

"He comes close. He's really an innocent."

"That won't last long," Kurinin growled ominously. "Especially when the vengeful major arrives on the scene."

He went back to the window and looked out.

"There are those," he continued, speaking so quietly it seemed like a confession to himself, "who believe we are witnessing the last thrashings of mankind, and come the millennium it will all be over. I do not personally subscribe to that view. History tells us there have always been such fears at the approach of the millennium. Humanity's perpetual superstitions. I do believe, however, that a bad time *is* coming—unless we do something to contain it." He turned, eyes burning at her. "That is why we *must* not fail in what we are about to do."

The cavern was a remarkable testament to the awesome repertoire at nature's command. Formed thousands of years before, its entrance was thirty meters beneath the surface; a long, narrow-necked channel that eventually widened into the high dome of the vast cavern itself. The great natural chamber was part of a thousand-meter-high mountain. No one, except the people who had searched for and found it, knew of its existence.

Created during the eruption of a mud volcano which had itself been caused by the explosive force of rising methane gases from the bowels of the earth, the ground above the cavern had long since solidified, shielding it from even the most advanced sensors of the many satellites that prowled the heavens. Despite the fact that the geological phenomena that had been the genesis of its construction had been dormant for several centuries, and though the nearest center of activity was a good hundred kilometers away, the region was itself still very much alive with the continuous, innumerable bubblings of mud that rose to the surface. The terrain above, looking more desolate than any imagined moonscape, was punctuated by alien structures of great rising mounds and mud towers, and with steaming, liquefied earth that hissed and oozed from every available fissure.

The scientists and engineers who worked within the cavern were very much aware that the eruption that had created the cavern could, at any time, be followed by one that would boil upward through the water to destroy it and all within, irrespective of the passage of centuries. Many of them felt that this extended period of inactivity made a repeat performance even more likely in the short term and were thus galvanized into ensuring that their business was concluded as quickly as possible.

During even the lowest of tidal ebbs, the entrance remained hidden, and thus no one, except those responsible for the presence of the submarine within the cavern, knew the vessel was there, or of the work being done on it.

The minisubmarine was 23.5 meters long and 2.0 wide. Powered by a single diesel motor, its six-bladed propeller could drive it at just under nine knots submerged. Its operational range was twelve hundred kilometers.

But the submarine was not intended for long patrols. To carry out the mission for which it was being prepared, it would need to travel the merest fraction of that distance.

Over the past months, within the cavern beneath the remote coastal mountain of fossilized mud, the vessel had been undergoing an extensive refit and modification. Changes in its armament would reduce its normal crew of eight to six, but its control and monitoring systems were being upgraded with the latest technology, all acquired clandestinely.

The two weapons it would eventually take aboard would give it a destructive power out of all proportion to its size.

It was owned by no government, but the people who were preparing it for its terrible mission saw themselves as a government-in-waiting . . .

London, 25th. 1230 hours.

Jordan Blish walked along the left side of Whitehall, toward the Houses of Parliament. Allardyne was with him.

Blish did not particularly like Allardyne, but tolerated his company. There was little point, he felt, in being hostile. He was perfectly aware of Allardyne's calculated slyness, so carefully shielded by overt displays of bonhomie. The joke was, Allardyne actually believed this subterfuge worked. It suited Blish's purposes to leave matters that way. A smug Allardyne, though envious, was still less dangerous than one who felt his own position within the pecking order was under threat. So when Allardyne had made one of his periodic offers of lunch, Blish had accepted. He wondered what his competitive colleague really wanted.

Allardyne was tall and almost gangly at six-foot-two, but exhibited no appearance of awkwardness. His dark blond hair was precisely cut in such a way that it flopped about his ears as he moved. There was a looseness about his dark gray suit that spoke of deliberate styling rather than of one that might have been slightly too big.

Blish's own attire was a classically cut, lightweight dark blue with stripes that were virtually invisible. Both men wore black shoes that gleamed.

They walked past Parliament buildings and crossed the road, heading for a place where they tended to lunch from time to time.

Out of the corner of his left eye, just as they were about to enter, Blish caught a glimpse of a familiar figure sitting on a park bench across the road on the Embankment side. He paused, turning more fully to check. There was no one on the bench.

He looked beyond the bench to the Thames, where the superstructure of a tour boat was gliding past, going upriver. The amplified voice of the guide came across indistinctly, seeming to float upon the very air, above the noise of the road traffic.

Strange, he thought, as he turned to follow

Allardyne down a flight of steps and into the atrium restaurant. *I'm seeing things.*

He did not see the man in the blue Vauxhall Astra that had cruised slowly past, going toward Millbank. The car was now parked a short distance away.

There had indeed been a man on the bench, but he was not the man in the Astra.

"Seen someone you know?" Allardyne asked mildly as they were shown to their table on the raised, gallery-like crescent of the restaurant. It was like sitting outside, but without the traffic noise, or pollution.

"More like phantoms," Blish replied as they sat down. "I saw a man who wasn't there."

"How very odd," Allardyne said with a tiny smile of lofty indulgence. "Working too hard, old boy."

The waiter, who knew them, handed over the menus and wine lists.

"Thank you," Blish said to him.

"Sir."

Allardyne simply nodded and began to study the dishes on offer. He made his choices, then picked up the wine list.

The waiter stood by patiently, ignoring Allardyne's rudeness. He was accustomed to it.

Allardyne muttered softly to himself as he checked out the list, then came to a decision.

He looked up at Blish. "Would you like a stiff drink before the wine?"

Blish shook his head. "I'll have some mineral water."

"I'll follow suit, I think. Choose the wine, shall I?"

"Be my guest." Blish knew Allardyne liked to show off his knowledge of wines.

"Right. Order, shall we?"

They gave their orders and when the waiter had gone, Allardyne said, "And what phantom did you think you saw out there?"

"Must have been my imagination," Blish replied. "I thought there was someone on the bench. Seemed as if he was watching us. He looked like one of the many homeless we've got decorating our streets these days. But of course, there wasn't anyone."

"Lazy beggars," Allardyne said with cold brutality.

Blish did not bother to argue the point with him. Allardyne had a worldview that was peculiarly Allardyne's. Anything outside his preferred frames of reference got short shrift. The homeless were lazy, and that was that.

"As I've just said," Allardyne went on, "you're working too hard."

But Blish's thoughts were upon the figure he was certain he'd seen. The "homeless" man had reminded him of Branko, although it had been a very different figure from the one that had so unceremoniously entered his car all those weeks ago.

Then, after giving him that fright . . . silence.

He'd neither seen, nor heard from Branko since that time. It was as if the former Czech "student," who had suddenly become a Russian, had vanished off the face of the earth. Blish had begun to wonder whether the incident had occurred at all.

Until today.

If the man on the bench had indeed been Branko.

"Dab hand at languages, aren't you?" Allardyne was saying offhandedly as they ate their way through beautifully prepared trout. "Let's see . . . German, French, Italian, and *Danish*, of all things. Who speaks Danish outside Denmark?"

Allardyne, himself quite a linguist, was, paradoxically, unashamedly jingoistic. But being Allardyne, perhaps that was not so surprising. Speaking other people's languages was a necessary chore in order to converse with the lesser orders. Blish could never understand what he was doing in the Foreign Office. On the other hand—

"No East European, I note," Allardyne went on. Allardyne had two Slavic languages under his belt. "Up and coming region, Eastern Europe. Money to be made."

"Explosive would be more accurate. I would personally think three times before putting any serious money into any of those countries, considering the general state of affairs out there, beyond the old Iron Curtain. Habits will take a long time dying and some might even spring, newly formed, from the ashes of the old. Someone recently said to me no one learns from history. Look at Yugoslavia. They're using history to justify prolonging their own version of a centuries-old vendetta.

"We can help in other ways. Build up an evolutionary process of trading and political links, and so on. But instant heavy investment? Forget it. It's not as if we don't know what happens when some demented nationalist grabs power. God knows there's enough of those to go around."

"Not to reason why, old boy," Allardyne said smoothly. "Our brief—drag them kicking and screaming into the happy world of capitalism. As I said—

money to be made. Lots of it, before things get sour again."

"I don't know which is worse." Blish began looking directly at Allardyne. "Putting money in and risking losing it all through misinterpretation of the prevailing political winds, or putting it in, making as much as possible, then getting out before the shit hits the fan."

Allardyne grinned. "Spoken like a true diplomat on the second point. To quote Wotton 'an honest man to lie abroad for the good of the state.' Making hay, I'd call it."

"I wasn't agreeing with you. I thought we weren't supposed to be like that anymore."

Allardyne laughed out loud so suddenly that some of the other diners turned to look.

"Sometimes, Jordan," he said, ignoring them as the tremors of his laughter made his shoulders vibrate as if with a life of their own. The laughter faded away in dying chuckles. "Sometimes, I do wonder about you. You sound like a first-day man. Don't you want to rise to the top echelons of the Service?"

"I don't think it's humanly possible," Blish answered pragmatically.

"Selling yourself short? Or do you know something I don't?" Allardyne was being disingenuous.

"No. Realistic. I know I'm capable. But can you see me, say . . . as a future Political Director?"

Allardyne dodged the question. "I can see you as Head of News."

"A spokesperson."

"Don't knock it."

"I'm certain you didn't invite me to lunch to talk

about my prospects, Monty. Is Eastern Europe the reason?"

"Among other things."

"What does that mean, exactly?"

Allardyne appeared to find his wine of sudden interest. He picked up the glass, stared at it, brought his nose to the rim, inhaled gently before putting it down again.

Blish was familiar with the theatrics. Allardyne was about to drop a bombshell and liked to create the right atmosphere.

Blish concentrated on eating.

"Does the name Branko ring a bell anywhere?" Allardyne dropped his bomb softly, making the impact even more effective.

Despite himself, Blish was forced to pause. He stared at his colleague.

"Student days," he replied calmly. It was all there in his files. "Well into my past."

"Czech, wasn't he?"

"He was a dissident. You know, the kind we used to like having over here. Refugees from communism and all that."

What was this? Blish thought. Allardyne carrying out an unofficial positive vetting exercise? He did not have the rank, or authority.

"Are you vetting me, Monty?" Blish added.

"Good lord, no. I haven't any such authority. And besides, you're gilt-edged. Spotless. Everybody knows that."

"That's a relief," Blish commented drily. "So what's the real meaning behind your question?"

"A little bird asked me to mention it. He wanted to

know whether you'd seen your dissident Czech recently."

"Branko is now *my* dissident Czech?"

"Manner of speaking." Allardyne took a mouthful of wine, held it for some moments before swallowing. "Good choice that," he added. "If I say so myself."

"Cut out the pantomime with the wine, Monty. What are you really getting at? Who's the 'little bird' who wants you to do his interrogation for him?"

"No interrogation, Jordan. I assure you. It seems your friend . . . er—all right, all right—it seems this Branko may be in some sort of trouble. Very bad by the sound of it."

"And?"

"He's gone walkabout. All sorts of people are interested in where—"

"So we were being watched," Blish cut in, turning the thing on its head. "I was right. Was that your 'little bird' on the bench?"

"The man who wasn't there? I doubt it. You said yourself there was no one on the bench when you looked."

"Well I haven't seen him," Blish lied, wondering why he did. "Tell your friend."

"Not my friend, old boy. He's one of those rather shadowy people one does not like talking to in public."

"And in private?"

"Different thing altogether." Allardyne picked up his glass, gave it another of his studied sniffs before taking a precise mouthful. "I'm really quite enjoying this wine," he continued with satisfaction when he'd swallowed it. He looked at Blish. "You?"

"Yes," Blish said, his mind on Branko.

After lunch they sauntered back, talking about the minutiae of work. Neither brought up the subject of their lunchtime conversation, but each knew the other had it on his own mind, though for very different reasons.

Neither paid particular attention to the blue Astra. It was just one more car making its slow way in the traffic that went up Whitehall, toward Trafalgar Square.

The man who looked like one of the homeless slouched, apparently without purpose, in their wake. His dark hair, streaked with gray, was long and worn in a ponytail. His beard and moustache were really overgrown stubble, and were similarly streaked. Despite the warmth of the day he wore a long, khaki-colored coat over faded blue jeans that had seen better days and a denim shirt. There were rips about the knees of the jeans.

Upon his feet were Cuban-heeled, light brown boots that would not have been out of place upon a horse on some Texas ranch, or perhaps upon a Harley-Davidson motorcycle. They were in surprisingly good shape. His tall frame was hunched, and his manner of walking suggested he'd long ago given up his fight with the vicissitudes of life.

But there were anomalies that existed beyond the casual, or even the mildly interested glance.

His eyes, almost hidden beneath what seemed like permanently furrowed brows, told a story that was at variance with his slouching gait. From time to time, he would look up to check the positions of both the two men ahead of him, and of the blue Astra. They were not the eyes of a man beaten into submission by the pressures of modern life.

Almost invisible within his hair and the stubble of his sideburns was a tiny disc clipped to his right ear. It looked like a miniature hearing aid, scarcely bigger in circumference than the base of a fiber pen. It was not a hearing aid but an extremely powerful, cordless headphone. A receiving unit, about the size of a standard matchbox, was in the right, flap-secured breast pocket of his denim shirt.

The two items were together a highly sophisticated radio eavesdropping device, complete with an automatic frequency-hopping receive facility. It could also unscramble codes, and was able to remain undetected by the simple expedient of never broadcasting its presence. All it had to do was lie in wait for a transmission to activate it. If the incoming, clear-speech signal proved of interest to its operator, a light touch of the main unit would cause it to focus upon that particular conversation. If no touch was forthcoming, it would return to standby until it was again triggered. Its effective range was more than a hundred meters.

The man in the cowboy boots listened to a series of brief conversations between policemen, both on the beat and in their cars; people making calls on their car phones; security guards in a passing armored van carrying a large sum of banknotes; two lovers, married to different people, making arrangements to see each other; a man in one office building chatting up a woman he could obviously see in another building. The trawl went on, but the "down-and-out" wasn't interested in anything that came through.

Then a sudden, electronic screech came on the headphone. His sole outward reaction was to touch his right pocket briefly. The device went into its decoding routine until clear speech filled his ear. An unidentified intelligence officer was conferring with a senior policeman about the route of a forthcoming demonstration.

The man's brief, ironic smile was hidden by his facial hair. The more a nation needed to control its citizens, the weaker it was. The problem was that few political leaders were wise enough to realize it, as he knew only too well.

He touched his pocket once more. He was not interested in demonstrations. At least, not yet. The unit went back to standby.

He watched as the two men up ahead went their separate ways. One turned left, to be let through the tall gates that sealed off Downing Street. The other kept on for a short while before hailing a taxi.

The man in the cowboy boots looked at the Astra. It could not follow into Downing Street, so it slid in behind the taxi. "A lot of good that will do you," the man said softly. He did not speak English.

Then another screech assaulted his ear.

He tapped unobtrusively at his pocket once more, and presently a conversation sounded clearly as the unit broke through the scrambler.

" . . . Blish has turned into Downing Street—" the man in the blue Astra was saying. He was not using English.

"And . . . ?" came an imperious query.

"Allardyne has taken a taxi. I'm following."

"Any sign of Diryov?"

"Nothing." The man in the Astra sounded as if he'd never expected a sighting in the first place. "I don't believe he's in this country at all—"

"What you do or do not believe is not at issue," the second voice interrupted sharply. "Follow your instructions, and keep up your surveillance until told otherwise. Is that clear?"

"Loud and clear," the man in the Astra acknowledged sourly.

The other person cut transmission without another word.

The man in the cowboy boots pressed for an extended moment at his pocket. This switched the unit completely off. He'd heard all he'd wanted to for the time being.

The conversation had drawn another brief smile out of him, though this was not only because of the language spoken between the person in the Astra and the controller, which he'd understood perfectly.

Hands in the pockets of his long coat, he continued to slouch his way up Whitehall.

Those who did bother to look in his direction saw only another of life's victims and unconsciously shied away, as if afraid he would contaminate them with his misfortune.

At three-thirty that afternoon, Blish walked across the Italianate-marbled tiles on the ground floor of the building. He'd been summoned to the permanent undersecretary of state's office. What, he wondered, could the PUS want with him, a mere cog in the machine? The permanent undersecretary was *the* Olympian in the universe of the Foreign Office.

There were those who insisted that benign attention from the PUS meant the gods were indeed looking favorably down upon you. Promotions became supercharged. Blish doubted this was what the unexpected, first-time summons meant.

He reached the hallowed door, did not knock, and went straight in. It was not the done thing to knock.

Sir Timothy ffrench-Wilkins looked up at Blish with a welcoming smile. "Ah, Blish. Good of you to come." He remained seated, and did not ask Blish to sit down.

"Sir Tim." Blish stood respectfully at ease, legs slightly apart, hands loosely locked behind his back.

ffrench-Wilkins liked his underlings to address him in that manner, instead of the customary use of the initials of office favored by his predecessors.

"You're no doubt wondering why I asked for you," ffrench-Wilkins said. "I've been hearing some very good things," he went on, before Blish could say anything. "How long have you been with us now?"

"Five years, Sir Tim."

"Like it?"

"Very much."

ffrench-Wilkins had pale, watery eyes that, confusingly, looked as hard as steel.

Here were eyes, Blish thought, that could drill like lasers and leave nothing in their wake. To the mandarin gods he was mere cannon fodder. Which meant to the chief god he was . . . what? And what was the real meaning of this very personal summons?

Blish found it difficult to imagine it had anything to do with his lunchtime conversation with Allardyne. Or had Allardyne in fact been primed by the PUS? Had the lunch been a lead-in to this?

He kept the neutrally respectful expression upon his face as he waited for the Olympian to tell him more.

"You've done some traveling for us, I believe," ffrench-Wilkins was saying. "How would you like to do some more? Nothing fancy. Just a stroll through the EC. See how our . . . hah . . . friendly enemies are getting on."

Why was the PUS doing this personally? Blish wondered. Something as routine as this could have been done through normal channels. Were they shifting him out of the way for a few days? If so . . .

ffrench-Wilkins's next words appeared to supply an answer.

"Had lunch the other day with my old friend Durleigh," he said to Blish. "Quite an admirer of yours. Proud father-in-law you've got there, Blish."

Now it was becoming clearer. Sir Richard Elsin Durleigh, Baronet, member of Parliament, "Red" Durleigh to his most intimate of friends, was anything but. Durleigh was the bluest of a true blue Conservative, with a gigantic C. The only thing red about him was the mist that tended to blot out the world before his eyes when anything that did not fit his own brand of politics, or his personal attitudes, hove inconveniently into view.

The marriage of his priceless daughter to a man who was adopted was bad enough. The fact that such a man—irrespective of the untarnished reputation of the parents who had nurtured him into what he had become—was inescapably a brown child of the Caribbean had turned the mist crimson. There were times when Blish was certain it had taken up permanent residence in Durleigh's brain, forever destroying the possibility of rational thought where the marriage was concerned.

To Durleigh, the Blish family had committed an unpardonable sin. They had *connived*—as he saw it—in the whole awful business. He'd never gone as far as saying his daughter had been kidnapped and turned against him, but on occasion, he had come perilously close. Thus, for the permanent undersecretary to claim Durleigh admired his son-in-law was stretching the truth so far that it was howling from the pain of the experience.

Blish's suspicions crystallized. Durleigh was hoping for yet another go at trying to persuade Charlotte to end the marriage. Clearly, he wanted Blish out of the way long enough to enable him to make this latest attempt. It was an ongoing battle, and who better than his old school chum, the permanent undersecretary, to deliver the right conditions?

Blish wondered whether the PUS knew the whole story and was being smoothly duplicitous, or whether Durleigh was fooling him, too, with the outward display of family togetherness.

Durleigh had long given up trying to get Charlotte to visit her parents without the man she'd married. Since the last time she'd done so, she had decided to insist that Blish accompany her, or she would not go. On that occasion, Durleigh had subjected her to a terrible emotional onslaught. She had gone to spend the weekend, but had left within a few hours of arriving, after a constant barrage from her father about the inevitable doom that would be visited upon the marriage.

"*Think of the children!*" Durleigh had shouted at one stage.

At that time, Charlotte had not yet even given them the glad news that she was pregnant with the first, and had walked out without telling them.

Blish could still remember the heartbreaking manner in which she had cried that night. Even now, two children later, he was still angered by Durleigh's behavior toward Charlotte that day, and found it extremely difficult to understand how a man who professed to have such a great love for his daughter could be so poisoned that he was blind to the pain he was causing her.

Durleigh, and those like him, were readily able to hide beneath a cloak of spurious concern, instead of peering more intimately at their own motives. If everybody cared so much, who were the mysterious ones against whom the children had to be protected?

Blish had once asked Charlotte the question.

"You'll never get an answer," she'd replied in her forthright manner, "because they already know. Themselves."

As he stood there in ffrench-Wilkins's hallowed office, he reflected once again upon the measure of the luck that had brought him someone like Charlotte. The even greater wonder was that she had a father like Durleigh—or perhaps it was because of it.

"Ten days or so should do it," the PUS was saying. "Do the rounds. Strasbourg, Brussels, Bonn, so forth. No particular order. Set up your own itinerary. Can only enhance the old *curriculum vitae.*"

On the face of it, that was true enough. A personal interest by the PUS could not, should not be sneezed at. Such patronage was gold to a career, but Blish could not rid himself of the nagging doubt.

Then there was the very real problem of Branko. He did not like the idea of being away from Charlotte and the children at such a time. But what could he say to the PUS? He'd already told Allardyne he'd not seen Branko in years, and Allardyne would be only too pleased to point out the deliberate omission.

But Branko, by his own admission, was a Russian.

More to the point, had been a Russian *agent* since the Cambridge days. Allardyne would enjoy such an advantage and could do considerable damage if Blish did not watch his own back.

"You seem uncertain," ffrench-Wilkins remarked mildly. "Don't you want to go?"

Refusal. Gold turning to dust. A career killer, Blish knew, even if on the surface the choice was ostensibly his.

"No uncertainty," Blish said firmly. "I'll get on with it right away."

"Good man. Full details will be with you early next week."

"Thank you, Sir Tim."

"Thank you, Blish."

The audience was over.

On his way home, Blish continued to think about the meeting. It still did not make sense. ffrench-Wilkins taking the time out to personally authorize a European trip when there were so many other matters requiring his attention—Bosnia, for example, to mention just one nightmare—it simply did not sit comfortably.

"So what is *he* playing at?" Blish wondered aloud in the car as he negotiated the Sloane Square roundabout, or tried to. He'd been sucked into another traffic jam. No lorry this time, but two black cabs making for the same spot and, improbably, hitting each other.

Then the Rover swayed slightly. Blish turned sharply to check. Someone was trying to open the door of the car from the passenger side.

Branko. Wearing dark sunglasses.

He tripped the central locking system and Branko entered quickly, shutting the door with a firm pull.

"So you took my advice," he said cheerfully into Blish's astonished silence.

"Wh . . . what?"

"The doors. You keep them locked now."

"Er . . . well . . . where the devil did you spring from?"

Branko grinned. "Convenient, those two taxis hitting each other like that."

"You didn't—"

"No, no. I don't think even I could get two London cab drivers to hit each other just for my benefit. I was watching out for you. This little accident was a bonus. Can you get out of here?"

Blish looked about him, his mind full of questions. He was positioned on the outside of the ring of cars. Careful maneuvering should enable him to make his way into a side street, although this would be taking him away from the route home.

A silver Mercedes sports convertible had positioned itself on his left, waiting to filter into the traffic stream in an attempt to turn right into Sloane Street, effectively blocking his exit. It was driven by a dark-haired young woman. As yet, there was no other car to prevent her from reversing.

"I'll have a go," he said, "if the lady will let me through."

He indicated by sign language that he wanted to move out. She smiled at him and obliged by reversing far enough for him to work his way around the other cars and toward the street he'd selected. He gave her a brief wave of thanks as he went past.

"Very pretty," Branko commented, turning to check on what she was doing.

"Fancy her, do you?"

"No. Just making sure of something."

"Making sure—oh come on. You're surely not going to tell me *she* was 'conveniently' in place?"

"No, I'm not. But you can never be sure of anything in my line of business."

"Not even of you?" Blish suggested pointedly.

"Especially not me."

"That helps a lot."

But the Mercedes was still stuck in the traffic jam as Blish drove along the street and stopped. The kind young woman was going nowhere for a while.

He turned to look at Branko, studying the other's clothes keenly. Branko was expensively dressed. Soft blue jeans, pale blue shirt, linen jacket, and brown oxfords—and no ponytail.

"I saw you earlier today, didn't I?" Blish challenged. "Only then you looked like a down-and-out. You were on that bench, weren't you?"

Branko gave another of his grins. "Just letting you know I'm around."

"Talking of which . . . where have you been?"

"Around."

"That's it?"

"That's it."

"I see. And I suppose you've got a whole selection of disguises, to suit—"

"Not as many as you might think. It's just a matter of altering what people unconsciously expect to see: a change of walk, a slight stoop, cheek padding . . .

You'd be surprised what can be done with very little. Ask any makeup artist."

"Perhaps. But I did recognize you . . . well I thought I did."

"That's because I allowed you to notice something familiar. It was the way I sat on that bench. Your subconscious remembered the posture from years before. But you still weren't sure, were you?"

"No," Blish replied thoughtfully. "Which was the reason I turned to check."

"I've made my point."

There was a brief silence as Blish pondered the way things were appearing to drag him inexorably deeper into the alien world in which Branko seemed to move—a world the Czech/Russian had inhabited for all those years and which promised to be more frightening with each passing moment.

"Have you any idea," he began, "of the shock you gave me last time? I've been running scared for the safety of my family ever since."

"Prudent."

"Just 'prudent'?"

"It will keep you on your toes. This is a very dangerous game."

"Branko," Blish said with heavy patience, "I'm not in any game. I don't *want* to be in any game."

"You entered the game the day you joined the FO. Someone else was watching you today," Branko added.

"Watching *me?*" Blish remembered the feeling he'd had on his way to lunch with Allardyne. But if it wasn't Branko . . . Allardyne's "little bird" perhaps?

"And I was watching *him.* One of the Mad Major's

men. They're hoping to spot me making contact with you—"

Blish looked very alarmed. "But you have!"

"I said *hoping* to spot me. They've been trying since I walked out with their dirty money. They're still looking, all over the world—the Mad Major, his own people, others from Russia who are even more dangerous, and your own people. They haven't found me yet. They don't even know I'm in this country."

"Sooner or later, they will."

Branko shook his head. "Only if I choose to let them . . . or *you* let them."

"Don't be ridiculous. I haven't even told my superiors I've seen you. God knows how that's going to look when they do find out."

"When the time is right, you can tell them."

"And when will that be?"

"Soon enough."

"My family, Branko," Blish retorted sharply. "What about them?"

"If you listen to my advice and don't panic, they should be okay."

"*Should?* Damn it, Branko! We're talking about my wife and kids. I don't want 'should.' I want certainties!"

"Now *you* are being ridiculous. Uncertainty is the stuff of life."

Blish stared at him. "I'm not hearing this."

"Look," Branko said. "What do you want of me?"

"What do *I* want of you?" Blish continued to stare at him as if the Russian had suddenly gone mad. "You came to me! Or was that just some bad dream I was having? Am I going to wake up soon and find you're not here at all?"

Branko was silent for some moments, eyes fixed through the windscreen upon a far distance. "Perhaps I was wrong about you."

"What's that supposed to mean?"

"I thought I was coming to someone with guts, not just another career diplomat with his eye on the main chance."

Blish felt a sudden anger. "You've got a bloody cheek, Branko. You appear out of the blue after years of silence. You tell me you were not the poor Czech dissident running from oppression that we all gullibly thought you were, but in fact a bloody *Russian* spy. You tell me you're involved with the illegal movement of weapons-grade nuclear material, and you've double-crossed the people who planned it and not only took their money, but killed some of them in the process.

"Those same people, plus a few others, plus some of our lot are all looking for you. And I, with a toehold at the FO, have lied about seeing you to someone who would just love to see my career go up in flames. I've got a wife and two little kids that I worry about and who are going to have enough problems in life without my bringing them more—*and you're telling me not to panic?*"

Branko looked calmly at him. "Feel better now?"

"*Jesus!*"

"You shouldn't blaspheme—"

"Since when do bloody Russians care about—"

"Calm down. Besides, haven't you heard? Religion's making a comeback in the Motherland. A sure sign that shit's following."

"Don't tell me to calm down."

"Okay. Give those people a show if you want."

Blish looked around quickly. "What people?" No one was looking at them.

"I had to stop you somehow. Your litany might have built itself into a crescendo."

Blish glared silently at him.

"I'm beginning to wonder," Branko went on calmly, "if your parents have not done too good a job on you. You seem to have forgotten where you came from—"

"Don't you tell me about where I've come from. I know exactly where, and it's nothing to be ashamed of. I haven't forgotten, and I'll never forget."

"You've stifled it well then. They've bred the street kid out of you. You've done the route, the fast track. The public school, the university, the wife, the kids, the career." Branko reached across to briefly flip open Blish's jacket. "The fancy suits. What's this one . . . ah Dunhill. The last time I saw you, it was an Armani. But where's the six-year-old street kid who already knew the world was a very dangerous place?"

"He's still there."

"Tiger? Or house-trained, fat kitty cat?"

"Don't try to goad me, Branko. It won't work."

"Of course it will work. You're already angry. And you'll need your anger, if you're going to get through this. You may even have to kill to do it."

"That's it. That is *it!*" Blish looked furiously at Branko. "You've crossed the boundary. I was willing to give you the benefit of the doubt, perhaps help in some way by putting you in touch with people at the FO. Now you're telling me about *killing?* Have you gone out of your mind? What the hell do you think I am? I'm a civil servant, for God's sake. I talk to people. I negotiate. I don't kill them. That's what people like you do."

"And you employ us to do it for you. I have come here," Branko continued into Blish's awkward silence, "at considerable risk to my life. I decided to contact you because out of all the people I used to know over here, you are the only one whose integrity I still trust. I can only hope they have not yet taken it out of you. So don't prove me wrong."

"My parents gave me—"

"I'm not talking about your parents. I'm talking about becoming like those you work with; the Mackillens, the Allardynes . . . you are surprised that I know his name. Don't be. I know a lot of things that would startle you.

"As I said in the beginning," Branko went on, staring through the windscreen once more, "there's a nightmare coming down upon us. The theft of the nuclear material is only part of it. There are some people back home who call themselves the Four Horsemen. Forget the raving nationalists you see on your TV or the intelligence reports your own 'diplomat' colleagues may supply you with. Some of those are dangerous, of course, but the truly dangerous are the ones in the shadows. And the most dangerous of *those* are the Horsemen.

"Understand that they are not publicity-seeking bombasts. They are highly placed, highly intelligent and educated, and extremely motivated. They are well organized, and they seek nothing less than a new Soviet Union, smarter, tougher, and more efficient than the old monolith. Don't make the mistake of thinking these are disaffected apparatchiks yearning for the return of the discredited system.

"These people have as much contempt for the old Union as any Western hawk. The big difference is that they've learned from the mistakes of the past. The sort of Union they envisage would never have ended the Cold War. They want neither NATO, nor the EC, to continue as viable organizations and your national infighting is music to their ears. Every time you talk about a veto, or make noises about leaving, they raise a glass in your honor. Every time they watch your total lack of coordination in places like Bosnia, they fall about laughing. I actually saw two army generals with tears in their eyes from laughter the last time a UN statement of intent in Bosnia was broadcast."

Blish listened in troubled silence while Branko continued with his tale of nightmares to come.

"The problem is," Branko said, "before they can arrive at their goal, much will go very badly wrong. What I'm saying is that the cure will kill the patient. Whole countries are out of control on Russia's borders, and there is a lot of scope within the nation itself for a civil war that will make the Bolshevik revolution look like a blue-rinsed matrons' tea party. Old allies and political fiefdoms are screaming for independence. Most wouldn't know what to do with it when they did get it, but they're prepared to go to any lengths.

"Factions are also playing their own games against each other. The Horsemen intend to stop them all, as this conflicts with their own plans. Unfortunately, some of those movements are prepared to resort to extreme action, irrespective of the consequences. And, believe me, they are unhinged enough to try.

"You in the West must take your share of the blame for much of this. You tend to appease any lunatic nationalist in the quite insane belief that reason will prevail, or that they somehow follow a political line that is roughly in concert with yours. You have supported obscenely murderous regimes because you thought they were anticommunist. By the time you have woken up to the fact that you can't reason with them, you're facing a far bigger problem than the one you started with. One of the results of your procrastination is staring you in the face just across your borders. You could have spoiled our game many times, you know, if only you'd supported some of those people we armed in the bad old days.

"They would have come over to your side and would have made better governments. Many only came to us because we gave them the arms. We always knew we didn't have their hearts and minds. They took communist weaponry, but what they really wanted was Western-style living. Even today, you won't get many of our people admitting that. The West made some very serious errors of judgment."

"You didn't do so well in Afghanistan," Blish put in, feeling the need, to counter the catalog of Western disasters, to at least point out the former Soviet Union's own operational failures, and Russia's newer ones. "And just look at Chechnya."

"Granted," Branko agreed readily. "Afghanistan was a mistake of the old Union. The *new* Union, had it chosen to go into somewhere like Afghanistan, would have done so with a highly efficient, overwhelming force and would have totally ignored any Western protests. Chechnya would have been handled in the same way. Those in the circle of the Horsemen are all against the Chechnya fiasco—*not against* the mission itself, but against the way in which it has been conducted."

Branko paused, removed his dark glasses, stared hard at them before putting them back on.

"I believe one of those factions within one of the republics has the nuclear material and is in the process of making at least one weapon, maybe two."

"For *use?*" Blish asked in a disbelieving voice.

"Of course it's for use. Why else would they have gone to such trouble? You forget . . . these people do not have the sense of restraint of a big power. They are not thinking beyond their immediate desires and will chuck those things anywhere it suits them; at an Eastern target, *or* Western, and to hell with the consequences. It could be Moscow, London, or Washington, or any other population center across the globe.

"Some of the people chasing me are after the money. Others want to stop me permanently because of what I know, or what they *think* I know; and, of course, your own people would probably like to know all these things I've just told you and more. But even I do not have all the information. I am trying to find out, while making sure I continue to survive."

"Why have you decided, after all the years of doing the kind of work you did, to break with—let's call it—tradition? You must have known the risks."

"Perhaps I just liked having all that money so much, I wanted plenty of time to enjoy it."

"I know it's more than that."

"It comes to the same thing. Those idiots will

bring the world close to its end. No amount of money will be of much use to me then. Or to any of us, for that matter."

"I still say there's more to your reasons than that, but have it your way."

There was a stillness upon Branko's face. "The hounds are out there, Jordan, and on my heels. They will let nothing stand in their way. That includes you and your family, if they find out I've made contact. When they get close enough to them, believe me, you will be prepared to kill. It's either that, or see everything you love die. I believe when that time comes, the housebroken pussycat will take a backseat and in its place . . . "

He let his words fade as he opened the door and got out. He shut it, then knocked on the window.

Blish pressed one of the window lift switches on the right armrest. The glass sighed downward.

Branko leaned forward to peer in. "Watch out for blue Astras on your tail. I'm not saying they'll only be using those cars, but be a little more aware." He paused. "Oh yes—if you do decide to send your family away, don't send them anywhere that is obvious and familiar. It's what you'd be expected to do.

"Always do the unexpected, if you can. This means not sending them to stay with your parents, or Charlotte's. Other relatives, and friends, are out too. It is much safer to pick a place from a brochure. It's a random choice and that way, they can't second-guess you. Meanwhile, I'll divert them for as long as possible with false trails for them to tag. I'll make contact with Mackillen. It may fool them into believing I've decided not to come to you."

Branko grinned at the thought of Mackillen feeling the heat, gave the car a light double pat, and walked away.

Blish sat there for long moments as he watched Branko turn right, past a corner shop that sold groceries. He started the Rover, then eased it forward until he was positioned at the top of the narrow street and could see along its entire length.

But Branko had done his vanishing act again.

Blish turned the car round and headed home.

The silver Mercedes sports car was parked in Eaton Place. The dark-haired young woman sat at the wheel, peering critically at herself in the rearview mirror.

Then she saw the image of a man approaching. She kept looking into the mirror, watching as he drew closer, her expression neutral.

He stopped by the passenger door and she turned to face him.

"Did I do okay?" she asked.

"You were perfect."

"Do you want to drive?"

"No. You might as well continue." He climbed in.

"Where to now?"

"Let's find Mackillen," Branko said.

Blish arrived home to be greeted by a yogurt-faced Amanda, a soaking wet Mianna, and a pensive Charlotte.

"Daddy, Daddy, Daddy!" squealed Amanda, half-running, half-skipping up to him.

"Hi, princess." He stooped to plant a kiss on the

one clear patch on her cheek, then straightened to kiss Charlotte and Mianna.

The smell of something very tempting being prepared teased at his nostrils. Charlotte enjoyed cooking and was superb at it.

"Mmm," he said appreciatively. "That smells fantastic."

"Trout," she informed him, "but don't go and look. Here." She handed him the wet Mianna. "You hang on to this one while I try to get some of that stuff from Amanda's hair."

"What happened?"

"Sophia's lot came round and your daughters decided it was a good idea to feed everybody themselves, and got rather enthusiastic about it. Mianna thought it was also a great fun to pour mineral water over her head."

"They're *my* daughters are they, when they do that?"

Mianna giggled and tried to undo his tie as he followed Charlotte, with a happy-looking Amanda in tow, up to the bathroom. Amanda kept putting a finger to each cheek to wipe off more yogurt, then lick it clean.

He knew Charlotte's preoccupied expression was not because of Amanda's adventures with the yogurt. He decided it would be prudent to wait until after the children were bathed and put to bed before trying to find out.

Bedtime stories read and both kids tucked in, Blish stood by the door of their bedroom for some moments watching them. He felt the warmth of Charlotte's body as she stood close by, and he reached out to put an arm about her waist, a powerful sense of protectiveness coming over him. He'd had so little as a child before the Blishes had found him, and now he had so much. But his biological mother, before the sea had claimed her, had given him all she could: complete and unselfish love.

It had sustained the child left all alone in a hostile world. It had given him the strength to survive until his new parents had found him. No one was going to take these riches from him.

So was Branko right, after all? Would he really kill to protect his family? Unconsciously, his arm tightened about Charlotte's waist. To lose her and the children did not bear thinking about.

He felt Charlotte watching him closely as he quietly shut the door to the children's bedroom. She said nothing as they went down the stairs. Throughout the excellent dinner, they talked only about the children, friends, things to do. When they'd finished they cleared the table and loaded the dishwasher; then he made the coffee. Still nothing was said.

It was after the second cup that Charlotte finally touched upon the subject that was on her mind.

"Daddy called."

She was sitting in a corner of the Biedermeier sofa in the smaller of the two reception rooms, legs tucked beneath her. He was on the floor, leaning back against her.

He said nothing for a while, suppressing the annoyance he felt.

"Jordan? Did you hear what I just said?"

"I heard."

"He wants us to go over for a weekend."

"'Us'?"

"I said the usual. No visit without you. He keeps hoping for a different response, and keeps getting the same one. You'd think he'd have given up by now. You'll never guess what he said."

"Tell me."

"He said you were going on a short trip."

Blish remained perfectly still. How could Durleigh have known so quickly? Had the PUS told him it was in the bag *even* before Blish had been summoned into the Olympian presence? *Or had someone else told Durleigh?*

Would Allardyne have known?

"When were you going to tell me?" Charlotte asked in the reasonable voice that she tended to use when she was at her most lethal.

So that's what her mood was all about.

"I only found out this afternoon," he said. "And I was going to tell you at dinner, except I was worried about you because you seemed upset about something. I thought at first it was your father. If I'd known it was this . . . Charlie, there's something very odd going on. I can't believe your father already knows I'm going on a short trip to Europe. The PUS literally called me in this afternoon. It was the first I knew about it. I was a bit surprised he took the trouble to tell me himself. Then he mentioned your father, saying what good pals they were. He even said how proud your old man was of me."

"*Daddy?*"

"That's what I thought too," Blish commented drily.

"You're right. It stinks. And Daddy thought he'd

use the opportunity to have another try at getting me to leave you. The *bastard*."

"Hey, that's your father you're talking about . . . even if I do agree," he added with a smile as he turned to face her.

She was looking at him worriedly. "You don't believe I'd ever leave you, do you?"

"The thought never enters my mind."

"Good. Because I'd never forgive you if it did." She leaned down to kiss him, and nearly toppled off the sofa. "*Mmm!*" she squealed in mild panic as she lost her balance and, this time, tumbled down on top of him.

"Better down here, anyway," he said, rolling on top of her and reaching beneath the loose folds of her skirt.

"And what do you think you're doing?" she said softly, eyes big and round, pupils dilating as she looked up at him. Her legs seemed to have spread apart of their own volition.

"Something that would make your father livid."

She gave a slight gasp. "You . . . you doing this for him . . . or for me?"

"For you . . . and for . . . me . . . "

"Your . . . your fingers are so lovely and . . . and long. Did I ever tell you that?"

"Often."

"Oh God, Jordan. I love it . . . when you do this!" She was heaving gently beneath him. "Take those knickers off me . . . "

"Not yet."

"Please!"

"No."

"This is . . . ooohhh!" She shuddered and began to kiss him vigorously. "What, what are you doing?" she murmured against his mouth. She closed her eyes and mewling noises came out of her as she undulated slowly against him.

He took a long time before at last drawing off the knickers with calculated slowness. The sight of her long golden legs brought an involuntary intake of breath from him, the desire for her making his entire body feel as if someone had suddenly shot a bolt of fire through him. She did that to him every time.

When he at last entered her, it was with a continuing acceleration that brought a high squeal in response.

"It . . . it was mean . . . mean of you to make me wait," she moaned at him, her body now moving in an increased and perfect rhythm. "But I love it. Oh God, I love it! Don't leave me, don't leave me, don't ever leave me . . ."

She repeated the same words over and over as her movements grew in intensity, matching his own exactly.

"I won't, I won't, I won't . . ." he grunted in return.

They rolled over and she was on top of him now, riding him frantically. She raised her skirt and bunched it about her breasts as she rose and fell, impaling herself upon him. Then they shifted again and this time, she was on her stomach on the floor, the voluminous skirt up to her shoulders, buttocks high, hands outstretched. He was upon her, moving, penetrating deep within her, his own hands gripping hers, using the purchase as leverage.

He moved against her powerfully, drawing great

squealing cries from her as she clamped at him, pulsing with a great rising intensity deep in there. It was as if she was milking him and the feverish sensation that his entire body was about to burst seemed to fill every aspect of his being. Then she was shaking and lifting him, straining against him, her hands gripping so tightly it must have hurt; but he felt no pain.

Their long drawn-out sighs mingled as their bodies were held in a tension that seemed to go on forever. Then at last, with a pleasurable, gradual relaxation, they collapsed against each other.

Blish rolled off her and onto his side. He reached forward to draw her close.

"Oh God, Charlie," he said in a low, hoarse voice. "I love you."

She made a satisfied sound deep in her throat and nestled into his embrace.

"And I love you," she murmured. "For always."

Branko was right, he thought. He would kill to protect what he had.

The revelation both stunned and disturbed him.

Islington High Street, London. 2100.

Branko entered the crowded, noisy bistro and stood patiently, eyes searching for a table.

A pretty young "resting" actress in a black body stocking that left absolutely nothing to the imagination came up to him and glanced at his companion, the driver of the silver Mercedes. Black body stocking wore soft shiny boots with hard-looking toe caps. A name tag seemingly pinned directly to her left nipple identified her as Phoebe.

"Table for two?" Phoebe asked with a smile that was remarkably friendly, considering the gauntlet she regularly had to run every time she moved between some of the tables. The other waitresses didn't seem to have the same problem.

He nodded. "Is that one over there, in the corner, available?"

It was in a perfect position, with one of the chairs in the corner itself, giving a clear view of the entire place. It also meant the solid walls of the building would be at his back.

Phoebe gave him another of her well-practiced smiles. "You're lucky. Someone just canceled."

She led them to the table with a walk that drew loud comments of admiration from a group of men in city suits. Many had removed their jackets to reveal that some of them still favored brightly colored braces. One of these was the man Branko had hoped to find: Giles Mackillen. At the moment, Mackillen was too busy laughing loudly at a joke he'd just told to notice the newcomers.

The woman with Branko was wearing a skirt that was short enough to come perilously close to uncovering her bottom. Her bare legs were of a shape that invited a dangerous temptation to caress them. Some of the loud men were beginning to notice. Phoebe had competition. She probably felt relief.

Branko's ploy had been deliberatcly thought out. He had seen the bright yellow Porsche 911 cabriolet parked along the street. From the very beginning, part of his overall strategy—even before he had made contact with Blish for the first time—had been to discover which car Mackillen had chosen to buy himself. The eventual discovery had not been a surprise.

Giles Mackillen would not have been Giles Mackillen without a personalized number plate on his car. The specially bought registration of the yellow cabriolet parked outside was MAK 113N, but

Mackillen had bunched the letters and numbers together and, with strategically placed fastening bolts, had made it into MAKILЭN. Branko thought it ironic that the "3" now looked like a Byelorussian Э. He wondered if Mackillen even knew it.

As they took their seats, the young woman with him crossed her legs in such a way that it would not be long before Mackillen's other colleagues, and the man himself, began to notice.

"What can I get you to drink?" Phoebe inquired.

Branko glanced at his companion. "Eva?"

"A white wine, thanks," she said to Phoebe.

"Any particular choice? We've got an Australian Chardonnay, French—"

"I'll have the Australian."

Phoebe put some squiggles on her pad. "Australian Chard . . . and you, sir?"

"A whiskey, I think. Do you have the Macallan?"

"It's really your lucky day today. We do indeed. Ice?"

Branko looked horrified. "My God. No."

Phoebe smiled at him. "Thought not."

"And I'll have a double."

"A double it is. Thank you."

Phoebe went on her meandering way to the accompaniment of tracking heads and eyes from Mackillen's group.

Before long, their eyes began to wander toward Branko's table, or, more correctly, toward the legs of the woman Branko had called Eva. Soon, he knew, Mackillen's own eyes would make the discovery.

They did, just after Phoebe had brought the drinks. Branko gave a faultless performance of not being aware of scrutiny when Mackillen, first having checked out Eva's legs, glanced at Branko and frowned, as if trying to remember something.

"He'll be coming over anytime now," Branko said to Eva. "Go to the toilet as soon as it looks as if he's going to approach. If he's still with me when you come out, go to the car and take off. I'll meet you later."

"Okay," she said imperturbably.

"And make a production of it," he continued. "I want him to have an eyeful."

"Okay," she said again, happy to do his bidding. "It's quite fun, helping an international policeman."

"Er . . . try not to let everyone know about it, Eva. This is very sensitive."

"Oh, sorry. Of course. You did warn me before."

"Exactly."

To Eva, Branko was with an unnamable international police organization. He'd met her at a party given by some people he knew. During his years as an agent, and feeling that it might one day become necessary, he'd created his own private network of contacts that Moscow knew nothing about. These people had a special function. He liked to call them his artesians. Over the years, they'd known him as someone who dealt in import and export and had money. Now he was back on the scene, with even more.

Many were professionals—some already well moneyed in their own right—whose various talents he made use of from time to time. He paid handsomely for their services. None asked questions, knowing they would receive no answers. None knew of the Cambridge connection, nor that he was Russian. In any case, they preferred to know as little as possible.

Eva, who had a very strong attraction for Branko, was the daughter of a friend of a financial advisor in the network. She'd been invited to the party and was totally unaware of Branko's true activities. She did not know him as Branko.

Having very successfully impersonated various police officers from different nations on many previous occasions, he had no difficulty in bringing realism to his current role.

Mackillen had the physique of a rugby player and, indeed, was one. He'd played during his university days, and now played for the City conglomerate for which he worked. He did this expertly, cleverly, and brutally. His mean eyes and cropped black hair served to so accentuate the brutal image, it was sometimes hard to believe that he actually came from a background of privilege. When it suited him, he even spoke with the rough accents of a deprived neighborhood.

Many players from opposing teams, and even those he knew personally, had many reasons to regret meeting him on the field. One unfortunate actually said that Mackillen didn't go on the field to play rugby. He went to wage war. The victim, a merchant banker, had been hospitalized by a particularly nasty tackle from Mackillen. "Killer" Mackillen, his team called him. He loved the name, and did his best to live up to it—in business, on the playing field, and in his dealings with women.

"Women like it rough," he was fond of saying.

He now allowed his eyes to stray yet again, toward Eva's legs. "Christ," he moaned to his nearest drinking companion. "Can you imagine those wrapped round your neck?"

"What a fickle Killer you are," the other countered. "A while ago, it was Phoebe's knickers you wanted to get into."

"For how long have we been coming to this place, Gavin?"

"As long as I can remember."

"And have any of us had any luck with Phoebe?"

"Nope," Gavin Hastings replied with mellow cheerfulness, "but I live in hope."

"You've got as much chance as a snowball in hell, old son," someone else put in.

"Speak for yourself, Rupe."

"My chances are infinitely better," Rupert Trigg declared, and they all laughed skeptically.

Phoebe went undulating past.

"Isn't that right, Phoebe?" he called to her.

"Is what right?" she asked, not stopping. She knew exactly what they were discussing. They always did, at some stage of every evening that they came into the place on their way home, which was often. They tended to spend a lot of money and she didn't mind what they thought—as long as they didn't try to grope her.

"She knows, you know," Hastings said.

"Of course she knows," Mackillen said. "She's a witch. That's why she wears those lusty black things. I swear to God if you pulled her name tag the nipple would come too."

"Why don't you try?" someone dared.

"And get those boots right in your balls," another predicted.

There was more laughter, in which Mackillen himself joined, but for a fleeting moment his eyes glinted with a particular nastiness that was directed at the last speaker. This man played rugby for another company and, on occasion, played against Mackillen's team. It did not bode well for him, next time he came up against Mackillen on the playing field.

Mackillen again looked in Eva's direction.

"I can see the stalks growing on your eyeballs," Hastings said. "Her boyfriend looks as if he can handle himself, too."

Mackillen's brow furrowed. "I've got the strangest feeling I know him; but I can't seem to remember where from. I have a good memory for faces."

"Or for feces," Trigg said, laughing raucously.

"You're drunk, Rupert," Mackillen snapped coldly. "Perhaps it's time you were heading home to your wife."

"Don't remind me," Trigg retorted sourly. "Can't imagine why I married the bitch."

"Her father's money might have had something to do with it."

Another chorus of laughter rose above the general noise of the brasserie, Trigg laughing the loudest. "Some compensation, I suppose. And I do get to bonk sweet little Jenny from the PR department," he added in a low voice, chuckling at the thought.

"Not for long if Sara ever finds out."

"And who's going to tell her? Any of you?" Trigg looked at them all in turn. "We're each as bad as the other. Let's see. Gavin's made it with Pauline Henderson—"

"Oh no! Not Essex girl, Gavin. Shame!"

Hastings looked embarrassed. "Look. It was only a one-nighter—"

"I should hope so too—"

"And as for the Killer himself," Trigg plowed on, "there's a certain colleague's wife—"

"Shut it, Rupert!" Mackillen cut in. "The drink's beginning to talk." He stood up. "I'm certain I know that bloke. I'm going to have a word."

"Do try and keep your eyes off his girlfriend's thighs," Trigg said. "He might not like it."

"When I need your advice, Rupert, I won't ask for it."

"He's made up his mind," Branko said urgently. "Off you go."

She stood up slowly, making certain Mackillen noticed her. His eyes darted to her legs even though he halfheartedly tried not to be too obvious.

She gave him a quick smile as she went past.

Branko could see by his stance, as he paused between two tables to allow her some room, that he desperately wanted to turn round to have another look at her, but he resisted it and continued to approach.

He stopped by the table and said, awkwardly, "I do hope you won't think me rude, but I'm certain I—*Good Lord! Branko!* I don't believe it! Where—How—"

Branko stood up. "Hello, Giles. I wondered if you had recognized me. I didn't want to interrupt you and your friends." They shook hands, and Branko grinned. "Especially if you didn't remember."

"I don't bloody believe it!" Mackillen was saying. "How many years?"

"Too many. Getting old."

"Rubbish. You don't look much older than the last time I saw you. So what have you been up to?"

Branko waved a hand at Eva's chair. "Please sit down."

"But what about—"

"Oh, she will be in there for ages. You know women."

"Don't I just." Ignorant of Branko's ulterior motives, it was the kind of attitude Mackillen could relate to.

"Plenty of time for us to catch up on old times before she gets back," Branko added.

"Yes. All right." Mackillen sat down, enjoying the residual warmth left by Eva on the chair. "So tell me. What have you been doing all these past years? Did you go back home?"

"After the Wall went down, yes. It's all different in the Czech Republic now."

"But your country's split. Czechs and Slovaks going their separate ways."

"It was a shotgun marriage. Now, we've got the divorce. Perhaps it will be for the better. Time will tell. And—this will astonish you—I work for the state."

"What? You?" Mackillen stared at Branko with a strange respect. "Don't tell me the poacher has become gamekeeper. You're not in the *secret* police!" he added in hushed tones.

"Those have gone too—"

"Come on. There are always secret police. Only the names change from time to time."

"But I am a policeman—"

"Ah!"

"Not 'ah.' I am on the staff of our international police."

Mackillen was looking closely at him. "Doing what?"

Branko smiled thinly. "It is all right, Giles. I am not financial. But there is plenty of criminality in other things, all across the newly liberated borders."

"Criminality," Mackillen repeated thoughtfully. "There was a time when that term was used by the state to describe dissidents, people like you . . . or the way you used to be."

"Perhaps. But these are different—very real criminals who do terrible things—and they're spreading all over Europe. They kill people, too."

"And they're here in London?"

"Oh yes," Branko said truthfully, but with a meaning that was very different from Mackillen's. "They are here."

"I wish you luck. I suppose you know what you're doing."

"I do. I know these people's methods. I can handle them."

"No gunfights in this town, Branko. Our police would take a very dim view indeed."

"Do not worry. I shall have cooperation."

"I expect so," Mackillen said uncertainly. "Who would have thought it? Dissident Branko a tough copper. How life changes."

"It certainly does," Branko said with a smile that held its own secret meanings.

"And your . . . companion? Is she also police?"

"No. She's just a friend."

"I see. Some friend, you lucky devil!"

"You think she is nice?" Branko asked with a straight face. He could see Mackillen's friends giving them surreptitious glances and thought he might as well play to the gallery.

Mackillen swallowed the bait like an avaricious pike. "Nice? She's gorgeous! Tell you what. Have you anything planned for later? Why don't you two come with us—"

"I'm so sorry, Giles. Not for tonight, but certainly we must do something together."

"And bring your friend."

"Of course."

"Great! I'll look forward to that. I promise you a hell of an evening."

"And I'll be looking forward to that, too."

"So tell me," Mackillen continued. "Have you seen any of the others? Jordan, for instance?"

Branko shook his head and began to lie shamelessly. "I only arrived yesterday. There's plenty of official work for me to do. You are the first of the old Cambridge friends that I have seen and was very surprised to find you in here. This is obviously one of your favorite places."

"Oh yeah. Our sort of watering hole on the way home. I don't live very far, but some of the others go up to Hampstead and Finchley." Mackillen glanced back at his friends. "To judge by their state, they may all have to stay at my place for the night. Rupert Trigg's had it, for a start. If he got into that BMW of his right now, he'd be stopped before he'd moved two feet, for car being in charge of a drunk." He laughed at the joke.

Branko smiled politely.

"As you haven't seen the others," Mackillen went on, "you won't have heard about Jordan."

"Something's happened to him?"

"You could put it like that, but nothing bad." Mackillen sounded disappointed. "He's married, you know."

"*Married?* To whom? Anyone I know?"

"You certainly do," Mackillen replied grimly, his naturally mean eyes looking even meaner for the briefest of instants.

But Branko had caught it. "Not to Charlotte," he said with blatant innocence.

Mackillen nodded. "The very same," he replied bitterly.

"Incredible. But you don't sound very happy about it. He is your friend, isn't he? He's one of the circle. Charlotte's a very good catch. A lucky man."

It might have been the drink, or Branko's words, or even Mackillen's own dissatisfaction with himself. Whatever the reason, it brought a sudden outburst from him, an outpouring of years of resentment and envy, poisoned by a very real sense of thwarted superiority. Perhaps he'd found it easier to bare his true feelings to Branko, who was, after all, a foreigner he did not see every day.

"Think about it, Branko," he began. "I mean someone like Charlotte, for God's sake! She could have had anyone she wanted. *Anyone.* We'd have groveled at her feet, licked her toes if she'd asked. She's also got a brilliant intellect. She could have had any job in the City. But what does she do? She becomes a *housewife.* She turns her back on all of us and marries the street orphan, from the *Caribbean* for Heaven's sake! That's carrying missionary zeal a bit far! She must have felt sorry for him. As if that wasn't enough, he's with the Foreign Office. Got there through his parents, of course.

"Don't . . . don't get me wrong. I'm not prejudiced. Jordan's a great guy. He deserves all the breaks. But does he deserve someone like Charlotte? When I think of them . . . When I think of him climbing aboard that beautiful white . . . No . . . that's not what I really meant to say. I mean, he's not sort of *black* black, is he? Damn it, Branko! They've got kids now! Two of the little bastards!" Mackillen stopped suddenly. "I need a fucking drink."

He turned round and spotted Phoebe. "Phoebe, my little ray of sunshine," he called loudly. "We need a refill."

She looked at him impassively and came up to the table. When she was close enough, Mackillen put his hand on her inner thigh as though he had the right to do so.

"Lovely Phoebe," he said. "This is Branko. An old, old friend. He'd like a fresh drink, and so would I." Believing her initial lack of complaint about his hand meant acquiescence, he began to move it higher.

"If that hand does not let go of my thigh right away, Giles," she began sweetly, "I'll boot you out of that chair."

He let go of her quickly, but did not appear to take offense. "You're mean to me, Phoebe."

"Someone has to be. Now. What would you like? The usual?"

"Yes. And whatever my friend's having."

She looked at Branko with an apologetic smile. "The Macallan?"

"Yes, please," Branko said, his eyes telling her he sympathized.

"Thank you, gentlemen."

As she went away, Mackillen said, "Bloody gorgeous woman. Won't touch us though. I suppose if the Sunshine Kid were here—"

"The Sunshine Kid?"

"Bloody Jordan! Who else? I suppose if he were here, she'd go for him, too. Christ. What is it with these women? They must have something exotic. You know . . . forbidden fruit, and all that."

Listening to the mean-spirited tirade, Branko lost all reservations he'd had about the hell he was going to drop Mackillen into. The real envy of Jordan Blish, and the suppressed hate, was all there in the mean eyes. Mackillen was the kind of man who would have an affair with Charlotte, if he possibly could, out of sheer malice.

"Her family never went to the wedding you know," Mackillen continued with barely hidden glee. "I was there, of course. It was still a good day. His parents—that is his adopted parents—had pushed the boat out for him. Sort of reversal of the custom. After all, it's the bride's father who usually pays. Almost no expense spared. But they couldn't hide the fact that old Durleigh and his wife were conspicuous by their absence. Charlotte looked—God, Branko—she was absolutely gorgeous. Radiant, beautiful and far too good for him."

"If she is the Charlotte I remember," Branko began quietly, "she knew what she was doing. It takes a lot of love to go against your family like that."

"What the hell does *she* know about love? She was just getting back at her father!"

Branko realized that Mackillen's remark almost mirrored the one he'd made to Blish about the marriage.

"Do you truly believe that?" he asked.

"Not to do so is to accept that she really loves him. I can't stand that thought."

Phoebe returned with their drinks and quickly undulated out of range of Mackillen's groping hand.

He picked up his drink. "Here's to old friends, and to those who steal the woman you love."

"To old friends," Branko stressed, leaving out the remainder of Mackillen's bitter toast.

"What's happened to your friend?" Mackillen inquired after a while. "What's she doing? Building the loo?"

"Probably needed some air. It's very crowded in here now. I should go and see if she's all right."

Mackillen stood up. "Let's both go."

Branko raised a hand to stop him. "No need. I'll find her. But let us get together. I will call you." He smiled. "And I will bring Eva."

Mackillen gave a smile that did not quite reach the eyes. "I'll hold you to that." He held out his hand. "Good to see you, Branko, after all this time. And what I just said about Charlotte and Jordan . . . Drink talking."

They shook hands.

"I've forgotten it."

"Knew you'd understand."

"I certainly do."

"And do call."

"I will."

"Ah. You'd better have my card."

"Of course," Branko said, accepting the one Mackillen had taken from a jacket pocket.

"My office direct number's on this one, and my private home number. Really good to see you, Branko. And forget the bill. I'll settle up with Phoebe."

Branko hesitated. "Well . . . "

"I won't take no for an answer. Now go and find that tasty woman. See you soon."

"You will," Branko promised. "Good-bye, Phoebe," he added to her with a quick smile as she came up.

"I'm paying," Mackillen informed her.

"Right," she said. To Branko, she added, "Do come again."

"I'll do that."

He worked his way through the crowd, then turned to give them a brief wave before going out into the cool night air. He felt relieved. He'd never realized how much hate and resentment had festered within Mackillen for all those years, and wondered if Jordan Blish was aware of it. Mackillen was definitely not a man to trust, and the perfect sacrificial goat to be left tethered, waiting for the tigers . . .

There was still plenty of traffic about. The theater rush hour had not yet started, but several cars were looking for parking places—people arriving for late dinners at the many restaurants in the area.

A quick look to where the Mercedes had been parked confirmed what he already knew. Eva had returned to see Mackillen still at the table, and had driven away as arranged.

As soon as he was a short distance from the brasserie, he put on the earphone and waited in shadows in a quiet lane that was close by.

There were the usual snatches of conversation before the familiar screech came on, followed by the burbling noise of the descrambler, then clear speech, in Russian.

" . . . with Mackillen."

"Did this person approach Mackillen?"

"No. Mackillen went to him. They greeted each other like people who hadn't met for some time."

"Diryov?"

"Hard to tell. The place is packed. I have to say whoever he is, he doesn't look like any picture we've got of Diryov."

"That doesn't surprise me. Where is this man now?"

"He's gone."

"What? Haven't you followed him?"

There was an almost-audible sigh in the pause that followed. "I thought we were supposed to be watching Mackillen. That man could have been anybody."

"And the woman with him?"

"Just someone he must have picked up. She left long ago."

"Could you recognize her again?"

There was a longer pause this time. "Have you any idea how many good-looking women there are in that place?"

"*I am not interested in your sexual desires! I want Diryov! Find him!*"

"Yes, sir."

"*There was insubordination in your voice. I will not have insubordination!*"

The transmission ended.

■ ■ ■

Branko had seen the surveillance car the moment he'd left. It was a white Volkswagen Golf with one man in it, behind the wheel. His companion was standing near a small overspill of customers from the crowded brasserie, nursing a drink. Coming up from the shadows, he was at the driver's side before the man knew what was happening.

The man jerked slightly as the metallic snout of the gun touched his right temple.

"Don't move!" Branko commanded softly in Russian, "and don't make a sound. There's a silencer on this. You won't hear when you die, and neither will your friend."

"Di . . . Diryov?" It was hoarse whisper, tinged with a very real fear.

"Who's that? And I said no sound!"

"Wait! Wait!" came the urgent whisper. "Just listen! Return the money and—"

"Everything will be all right? What do you people think? I was born yesterday?"

"You don't understand!"

"I do. I do. We've talked long enough. Sweet dreams."

"Wait!"

Something sharp had gone into the man's neck. He collapsed almost immediately.

Branko walked quietly away.

The other man was still nursing his drink, and still keeping an eye on Mackillen's crowd.

■ ■ ■

The man moved away from the door and crossed the narrow lane to where the Golf was parked.

"They're still drinking in there," he began in Russian as he bent down to peer into the car. "And I thought we Russians—" He gave a soft exclamation. "Andrej? Are you sleeping? *Andrej!*"

He yanked open the door, and the driver fell out.

He swore comprehensively under his breath, quickly put the drink down on the pavement, and, looking round to make sure no one had noticed, shoved his companion back in and, with some difficulty, maneuvered him into the passenger seat.

A couple strolled by and glanced at him curiously.

"Drunk," he explained in English.

They smiled at him sympathetically and walked on.

He got in behind the wheel, started the car, and drove off.

"It must have been Diryov!" he was saying into the radio. "Although it doesn't look like him. He's decided to contact Mackillen. Perhaps Mackillen can help him make the money disappear. As for Andrej, he's very still. I think he's dead, but I'm not sure."

"Meet us at the rendezvous point. We'll take care of Andrej. Another team will cover Mackillen. You're compromised now."

"I want to stay on it. I want the bastard."

"You'll do as you're told!"

Branko had heard it all before the Golf went out of range. He smiled to himself. It was working out as planned.

He hailed a black cab and gave a theater address in the West End. Once the cab had dropped him off, he waited until it had turned a corner before walking on. He then caught a bus that took him close to where Eva had her flat. It took him just five minutes to walk the rest of the way.

She was there, waiting for him.

"All okay?" she asked.

"All very okay."

"Oh good. Now what do we do with the rest of the evening?"

"I feel like getting undressed."

"So do I."

"Whoever gets to the bed first goes on top."

She beat him to it.

Durleigh was walking upon a well-tended lawn, the grass a rich, luxuriant green. Amanda and Mianna walked with him, one on each side, holding on to his hands. From time to time, he turned to smile at them. They smiled back happily. The three of them walked on.

Suddenly, the lawn ended in a cliff. Durleigh stopped, let go of Amanda, picked Mianna up in both hands, and held her high. She thought it was a game and giggled.

Durleigh's face, no longer benign, now had a dark red countenance. His eyes seemed to blaze with a fierce malevolence as he threw the still-giggling Mianna over the cliff.

Amanda rapidly understood what was going on and tried to run away, but Durleigh was far too quick for her. He seized her and tossed her, screaming now in terror and fighting him, over the same cliff.

He paused to survey his handiwork. From beyond the cliff, a great mushroom cloud boiled upward, held in a huge chalice of fire, and from within the fire and the cloud came the cries of Amanda and Mianna.

"Daddy, Daddy, Daddy!"

Then Durleigh turned, his face once more benign and smiling as he walked back up the lawn.

The cliff, the mushroom cloud, and the fire disappeared.

And the children's voices were silent.

London, 0400 hours.

"No!"

Blish sat up in bed, his face damp. He checked the bedside clock. Through the slightly opened curtains, the early dawn bathed the bedroom in a surreal light. Both he and Charlotte liked having the dawn light in the room. There was a primeval feel to it that always aroused them. It was something that had astonished and pleased them when they'd each first confessed to each other this almost-unearthly affinity they felt for the new day. It was another factor that bound them close. Both the children had been conceived at dawn.

He looked at Charlotte, who was still fast asleep, and passed a hand over his eyes. The world was still in one piece. The children were still alive.

Christ, he thought. *That was a hell of a nightmare.*

He was certain he'd shouted loud enough to wake the entire neighborhood.

He put a gentle hand upon Charlotte's cheek. She moved against his touch and smiled in her sleep; then her eyes slowly fluttered open. She rolled onto her back and spread her arms wide. He could see by the movements beneath the bedclothes that her legs had done the same.

She reached over and pulled him on top of her, shifting to accommodate him in a way that sent him into a fast arousal.

"Mmm!" she said drowsily. "That's . . . nice . . . nice . . . "

"You're hot in there," he said. "A furnace."

"I'm always hot in there."

He said nothing to her about the dream.

JUNE

1

Moscow. Friday, 1500.

General Kurinin was not a happy man.

The reports he'd so far received during the course of the day had given him no cause for cheer. In Bosnia, the West seemed as confused as ever and appeared hell-bent on digging its own hole even deeper. The more they dithered, the more likely was the chance of an all-out conflagration that would not only suck in all the parties within Bosnia itself, but many beyond its borders.

Of the former Soviet Republics—from the Baltics to the Far East—no one remotely in his right mind could hold out much hope for their future stability in the current climate. Kurinin did not mind the idea of conflict. That would come inevitably, and had already been taken into account. Put bluntly, he wanted none of the predicted conflicts to occur before the Horsemen were fully prepared. There was a process that first had to be worked through.

All round the globe demented, unstable people were presenting a serious threat to the grand strategy itself, forcing continuing modifications to it. He was well aware that all good plans should always be flexible; but the irrational activities of such individuals, driven as they usually were by zealotry of one kind or another, made the world the increasingly unstable place it had become. If ever there was a need for a powerful force on the world stage to curb these idiocies, now was the time. The West had long since abdicated that role, and the resulting vacuum was being filled by benighted people.

Without doubt, one such group had recently benefited from the purchase of the stolen weapons-grade nuclear material that everyone was still trying to trace. Now news had come that a minisubmarine had, months before, been purchased by an unknown buyer, or buyers.

Months before.

Kurinin was furious. Why hadn't someone picked up on this earlier? Why no satellite sightings? Even clandestine trawlings of the West's communications had divulged no information on the missing sub. For such a transaction to have escaped detection for so long could only mean help at the very highest levels. Some small country somewhere had made a lot of money selling one of the submarines it had originally purchased legally. So far, inquiries had failed to identify the country, the type of submarine, and the eventual purchaser. No country ever gave the absolutely true state of its forces. Some augmented them, while others conveniently managed to "forget" a unit here, another there.

"We do it all the time," he muttered to himself.

Kurinin felt in his bones that the nuclear material and the submarine were at some stage destined to be put together. It was one of the more nightmarish scenarios the Horsemen had taken into consideration, but the manner of its manifestation had taken them completely by surprise. The problem was to discover where the submarine was being prepared, and to terminate the activity as swiftly as possible. It also meant a whole team of operatives would have to be diverted from other tasks to concentrate on this, just when they were needed elsewhere.

And what if they could not find the submarine in time? This left a truly fearsome question unanswered.

What was the designated target?

So far, he had decided to pass nothing on to the West, even through "unofficial" channels.

They would probably bungle it, he thought sourly.

This serious threat to the Horsemen's plans had been caused by *Russians*, with the theft of the nuclear material. The problem had thus to be solved "in house," without endangering their cover.

At all costs, the identity and objectives of the Horsemen had to remain a closely guarded secret until the time was right. There were those, even in the West, who would attempt to thwart a move to unseat the present regime. By the time the West got to know what was happening, it would be facing a *fait accompli*.

It was the only way.

But Diryov was still at large, and that was very bad news indeed. It was time for some serious pressure to be applied on all sorts of people.

London the same day, 1800 hours.

"Mr. Mackillen? Giles Mackillen?"

Mackillen paused uncertainly, half-in, half-out of the yellow Porsche, and looked round to face the tall, erect man, who reminded him of a retired army officer. The hood of the car was up and he braced himself against it. He noticed that the stranger's right foot appeared to be stiffly turned outward and wondered idly whether it was because of an artificial leg.

"I'm Mackillen," he said without warmth. "Can I help you?" His tone of voice was really saying I'm busy, don't take up too much of my time.

The man gave a particularly chilling smile. "Some people call me the Mad Major. Behind my back, of course; but I know they do. I'm going to ask you to come with me. I think you should. It would be a smart move. At strategic points, my people are covering you with guns. If you fail to do as I say, you will not live to regret it."

Still braced against the car, Mackillen gaped at the man who had called himself the Mad Major. A part of him thought there was something elusively familiar about the accented English. The other part was almost in a state of blind panic, completely unable to come to terms with the suddenness of the danger that had just dropped into his life.

"Who . . . who are you? How did you get in here?"

"Don't move, Mr. Mackillen! Stay exactly as you are."

"This is a *secure*, private car park! How did you get in here?"

Mackillen had summoned up a last vestige of arrogance, but his repeated question brought only a cold silence in reply. "What . . . do you want with me?" he went on hesitantly, eyes shifting frantically, trying to spot the other guns. "Money? You're *stealing* my car?"

"Don't be so trite, Mr. Mackillen. Why would I want your car? Such a vulgar color, too. But I suppose you need to shout your presence. Please get in. You're taking me somewhere."

Mackillen could not help his next words. "I am?" His tongue appeared to have a mind of its own.

"Please continue to get in. You must be feeling uncomfortable, and I will not repeat myself again. How convenient of your firm to provide an underground car park that operates itself. And not very secure, I am afraid. At least, not to us."

The Mad Major went round to the passenger side, opened the door, and got in. As he'd walked, Mackillen had detected the slightest dragging of the right foot.

After the slightest of hesitations, Mackillen got in behind the wheel. The initial shock wearing off, he felt a little bolder. "Are there really more of you?"

"Take a look."

Mackillen stared through the windscreen. Three very mean-looking men were standing a short distance away. Even if the silenced machine pistols dangling from hands held at their sides had not been so evident, they would still have looked very mean. Mackillen did not feel bold anymore.

"All right," he said. "No trouble. Where to?"

"First drive out of here, then I shall direct you. And don't try to outrun my men, who will be following closely. Your car may be fast, but, again, you will not live to regret the mistake."

But the three men appeared to have vanished.

Then Mackillen felt a slight prod in his side, and looked down. Since he had never suffered this kind of experience before, the gun that now seemed to be attached to his body was the most evil thing he had ever seen.

He couldn't know that the silenced weapon was the Dragunov-designed Klin machine pistol with a thirty-round magazine, a muzzle velocity of 430 meters per second, and a muzzle energy that would punch a crater in his body at contact range. He didn't need to know. He was sufficiently scared and respectful of it.

"No mistakes," he said shakily. "Just tell me what you want."

"I require many things," the Mad Major said mysteriously, with unnerving calm. "But for now, just drive."

Mackillen started the Porsche and drove out of the car park. Emerging into daylight, he followed the narrow exit lane toward the security barrier. There was one guard at the gate.

"Give no warning!" the Mad Major hissed. "Unless you want him to die."

They arrived at the barrier and stopped. The guard, recognizing the car, raised the red-and-white-striped pole, and waved them through.

As he unhurriedly drove past, Mackillen felt a stab of bitter irony. There was once an officious guard who used to stop everyone, irrespective of position, despite the fact that he'd known every car that came in daily. Eventually, his overzealousness caused such a high degree of irritation, his firm was asked to replace him with someone less fanatically obsessed. The guard had been an ex-serviceman who loved bossing people around.

Mackillen now found himself wishing the ex-sergeant had been in place in the guard booth.

It was a doomed wish. The Mad Major would have shot the control freak of a sergeant without compunction.

The down-and-out man watched as the yellow Porsche, with the two men in it, accelerated away. He watched as the dark Jaguar XJR saloon, which had been parked a short distance from the car park barrier, followed a short while later. There were four other men in it.

No one took any notice of him as he shuffled on his way. People walked past him as if he wasn't there, and so they didn't see the tiny smile upon his face.

Within the bowels of the mountain the two small, vertical launch tubes for the mini nuclear missiles were nearing completion. There was still a long way to go, for the weapons were themselves not yet ready. There were also many inert trials to be carried out before they would be positioned in the tubes in preparation for the eventual launch. There could be no test firings, which meant the first and only launches had to be successful.

Though the material in the Diryov/Branko-supplied briefcase had already been in an advanced stage of construction, inserting it into one of the missiles still required careful work. The missiles were themselves only slightly longer, at 4.4 meters, than the X-35 air-launched antiship missile meant to be carried by the Su-27M, among others. With a diameter of .75 meters, including retractable, stabilizing, and directional fins and vanes, there was just enough space within the vessel for the added launch tubes. The second weapon would be armed by another batch of material, obtained from a separate source. The buyers had not entirely trusted the Mad Major to deliver twice.

The minisubmarine gleamed darkly in the artificial lighting of the cavern as the engineers, scientists, and crew worked with urgent dedication. Its partially submerged hull gave the impression of some primeval creature waiting balefully and patiently to go out on the hunt, while its small army of drones groomed it.

"If the weapons don't leave these things cleanly," one of the crew said, "we'll fry the damned boat."

"Then you'll have nothing to worry about," an engineer who was working on one of the launch tubes told him. "Whoosh! Boom!" The engineer laughed.

"Very funny."

A stern-faced man approached, stooping low as he made his way through the cramped hatch, before straightening slightly to stand near the first tube. Space being at a premium, he had to stand with curved back to clear a bulkhead. He was the captain.

Before his country had decided to go indepen-

dent, he'd been the commander of a far bigger, fast attack Soviet submarine that had spent most of its patrol missions shadowing Western submarines. The recent political changes had left him disillusioned and angry. He had watched his career vanish. It was for this reason—one of many—he'd agreed to skipper this boat. None was political. For the job, he'd accepted a large sum of money. He felt no guilt about what he would be doing. As far as he was concerned he, and many like him, had been betrayed by those who'd only be getting what they deserved.

Once the attack was launched, he and his crew would scuttle the boat and make their escape underwater while the missiles were in flight. They would then be picked up at a prearranged point and dropped off near the cavern, which by then would have been completely evacuated.

They would enter it via the submerged entrance, collect replenished air supplies that would be left for them, and continue through a subterranean channel for another kilometer. At that point, the channel became a shallow underground lake. They would leave the water, dump their diving gear, put on dry clothes, and work their way through a natural, rising tunnel for another two kilometers, before emerging above ground. There, they would be met by people on horseback for the final stage of their escape route. Each had already chosen a different country in which to enjoy his reward.

That was the plan. The escape route had been tested, and it worked.

"What's the joke?" the captain now asked.

"I was just wondering," the crewman started to

explain, "what would happen if the weapons didn't clear the tubes."

"You'll be toast," the captain said bluntly.

The engineer laughed again. "That's what I told him."

"How much longer?" the captain demanded of the engineer.

"A month, six weeks maybe—"

"A month!"

"What do you expect? You're not at a fully equipped, fully manned base, you know. We're working under very difficult conditions, and there's just a few of us, for better security. If you don't want to fry yourselves when those things go off, you're just going to have to be patient."

There were thirty people in all, including the highly skilled, specialist soldiers—some of them women—who guarded the cavern.

"I've been in this place for so long," the captain remarked, "I'm beginning to feel like a troglodyte."

"It's not so bad," the engineer said cheerfully. "We've got filtered air, filtered water, sunbeds, women, plenty of food for at least a year—"

"I'm not staying down this hole for a year," the crewman said. "And as for women, you can forget those amazons."

"I don't mind. I don't have a wife to go back to."

"I don't have a wife either. That doesn't mean I'll take anything. Anyway, nobody in here has a wife or husband outside, to worry about."

This was not strictly true. The captain had a wife and three children; but no one within the cavern knew that.

"Look at it this way, this place makes a good nuclear shelter," the engineer said with ghoulish humor.

London, 1930 hours.

Blish walked out of the children's bedroom softly and pulled the door to, without clicking it shut. He had still made no mention to Charlotte of the vivid nightmare that had invaded his sleep, but it had not left his mind.

He made his way downstairs and found her curled up on her favorite Biedermeier. Two martinis were waiting on a small, low table, close to hand.

"Are they down?" she asked.

"Well into the land of nod. They were pretty tired today."

"*I* was pretty tired today," she said. "It was that dawn workout, I think. Martini, sir?" She handed him the drink, her eyes telegraphing her meaning as he sat down next to her. "What about you? Hard day at the office?" She raised her glass, bringing it close to his, to clink softly against it. "Cheers."

"To us," he said.

"And the children."

"And the children. Rather a quiet day for me," he went on. "I spent most of the time preparing my itinerary. I'm making the trip very low-key. Strictly an observation job."

"You mean they want you to spy on those nasty Europeans to make sure they're not wasting our money on things like specially curved bananas, or whatever." Charlotte liked to make fun of the wilder fantasies of those who hated the EC.

"Something like that," he said, smiling vaguely at her.

The radar was not fooled. "What are you hiding from me?"

"What do you mean?"

"Is there something else you're meant to do over there?"

He hid the relief he felt. For a moment, he'd thought she'd heard him shout his way out of the dream during the night, and had been about to ask him to tell her about it.

"If there is, I've no idea."

"In that case." She shifted one of her legs and prodded him with an arched, bare foot. "There's time before dinner."

"The kids—"

"Are all the way upstairs, and we'll hear them on the intercom, as well you know."

He put down his drink as she slowly uncoiled her body until she was stretched out on the sofa, her legs rubbing against his back with slow deliberation. She put her own drink down.

He leaned over, one hand braced on the back of the sofa, the other on the edge of the seat, near her right shoulder. Her eyes sparkled at him as her tongue reached out slowly, in its familiar way, to lick at her upper lip.

"What are you, madam?"

"A good wife, a good mother, a good hostess . . . and a harlot in the bedroom, on the floor, in the kitchen, on the stairs, in the garden . . . "

He kissed her fully on the mouth, silencing her.

"Mmm!" she said in anticipation.

"What are you going to do to me?" Mackillen asked. "Where am I?"

He tried to make his voice sound firm, but it was difficult to do so, considering he was bound to an upright chair, with a bright light directly above his head. Beyond the circle of light, all was in shadow, although he could just see beyond its perimeter, if he peered hard enough. Sometimes, he could sense movement behind him. That made him shiver.

The Mad Major had ordered him to drive about twenty miles from where he'd been taken, and into a disused suburban garage. But it had not ended there. They'd made him get out of the car and had bundled him into another after shutting the Porsche in the garage. He had then been gagged and blindfolded but, strangely, not bound. That had only occurred after he'd arrived where he now was and the blindfold removed, to leave him blinking in the bright light until his eyes had become accustomed to it. He'd lost track of time and had no way of gauging the length of the second part of his journey.

These people were crazy. They'd kidnapped him for no reason. They'd not taken his money or credit cards; nor, it seemed, were they interested in his car. So what was this all about?

"*What do you want of me?*" he asked again. His head turned frantically as he desperately tried to see a face, any face.

Though he was frightened, he was still sufficiently

consumed by anger and humiliation not to feel the terror he should. That would come soon enough.

There was a long period of silence, broken only by whisperings in the dark beyond the light, and the barely perceptible fall of footsteps.

Then he heard something being wheeled toward him. A hospital trolley came into the circle of light, pushed by the Mad Major. On the top shelf was a rack with six big needles, each filled with a substance he dared not speculate upon. Next to the rack were surgical instruments. On the bottom shelf was a single, large bowl.

The Mad Major stopped, drew to full height, and approached Mackillen slowly, his ominous gait making him seem like a creature from the hidden recesses of the mind. His eyes glowed darkly at Mackillen. He stopped once more, and pointed to the bowl.

"That is for the blood."

Mackillen paled. "*What?*" he said weakly. It was almost a stifled scream.

"I am certain you understand."

"*But what do you want of me?*"

"It is no use yelling. No one will hear you—except our good selves, of course."

"Just . . . just tell me what it is you want!"

The Mad Major stared at him. "Remarkable. In such a short time, you've lost all your arrogance. Just a minute ago, you were still angry. You felt humiliated. How dare we invade your life like this. I could almost hear you thinking those thoughts. But now . . ." He let his words die, and walked away.

"No, no!" Mackillen shouted, dreading who would come next to use the things on the trolley. "Wait! Just tell me! Please! What do you want?"

"Tell us about Diryov," came the Mad Major's voice out of the darkness.

Mackillen's astonishment was plain. For some moments, he even forgot his fear.

"Who the hell's Diryov? What are you people? *Russians?* I thought the accent sounded familiar. We've had one or two of your lot coming to us about trade and finance. Was this Diryov one of them?"

"No."

"Well I don't understand. And anyway, haven't you heard? The Cold War's over. We're all friends now." Mackillen, relieved that he had no idea who this Diryov was, strained briefly against his bonds. "You're not supposed to do this kind of thing anymore. Now you know I haven't a clue what you're talking about, you can let me go."

A strangely inhuman laugh came from the man in the shadows. "Such naive misconceptions," the Mad Major said. "The war goes on, Mr. Mackillen . . . only in a different guise. Diryov is the man you know as Branko."

"*What?* You're mad!"

"I did tell you that's what they call me."

"*Branko?* Branko's not Russian. You've really got the wrong end of the stick, old son. Branko's an old student friend. He's Czech. He used to fight your lot and your stooges in the days when they called his country Czechoslovakia."

The crazy laugh came again. A sudden, silenced shot coughed out and a tiny splintering crater appeared in the bare, planked floor, next to Mackillen's right foot. A shrapneling splinter pierced his trousers above the bound foot to enter, searingly, the flesh just below his calf.

He screamed with both the shock and the suddenness of it and leapt so sharply in the chair, he lifted himself clean off the floor. When the chair slammed back down, it nearly toppled.

"*Jesus!*" His breathing had become loud, rapid, and shallow.

"Do calm yourself, Mr. Mackillen. You've only been pricked by a splinter of wood, I suspect. You can pull it out later. But you can save yourself all the terrors I am certain you are now imagining. All you must do is tell us about Diryov. Let us call him that. It is his true name, whatever else you have known him by."

"Are you . . . are you saying . . . saying that . . . that Branko is . . . a *Russian?*"

"I am saying nothing to you, Mr. Mackillen. *You* are about to give *me* information. While I am certain we could have a very stimulating conversation on the finer points of espionage, this is not the time for it. I want to know why he came to see you, and what information he passed on."

"He didn't come to see me," Mackillen answered rapidly. "Not exactly. He was in a wine bar I use a lot. I hadn't seen him in . . . oh years. He said nothing to me."

"You talked. He must have said something. Just a moment ago you gave us the perfect reason. You said Russians had visited your firm about finance—"

"Yes, but not Branko . . . er . . . "

"Don't interrupt me again," the Mad Major said coldly.

Mackillen felt his blood congeal. "No! No I won't!"

"Remember it. We were talking about finance. My interest is in finance; a great deal of it. Diryov would need a means of disposal. An old friend in the business would exactly suit his purposes. I know of your firm's activities, Mr. Mackillen. You have interests worldwide. Perfect for someone who needs to spread large amounts of cash invisibly."

"I don't understand. Are you telling me he has a lot of money?"

"He has a fortune, Mr. Mackillen, and it isn't his."

"But . . . but I still don't understand. He told me he was a Czech policeman on the trail of criminals . . ."

The maniacal laugh pealed out once more. "He is inventive. I will allow that." The laughter died abruptly. "On the top shelf of that trolley, Mr. Mackillen, are six horrific biological and chemical ways of death. Injecting you with just one would give you a long, excruciating experience before you stopped breathing. Injecting you gradually with all six would cost you your mind before the inevitable happened. Then, while you were still alive, we could use the surgical instruments. You were quite right. Things have changed. Some of us don't beat people up anymore. You are quite fortunate."

Mackillen had listened to the Mad Major's calm recital of the horrendous properties of his wares with mounting terror. His face now looked sickly in the harsh light. His lips sagged and trembled uncontrollably.

"Why did he come to you?" his tormentor demanded.

"I don't know!" he replied miserably. The sweat of fear seemed to be popping out of his skin in tiny bubbles that joined each other in glistening chains, to stream down his face.

"Diryov is a ruthless man," the Mad Major said.

"He has already killed one of my men by injecting him with something as lethal as those here with us. My man died quickly. You will not.

"He chose you, over his other old 'student' friends like Tamblin, or Blish. I want to know why."

Blish! Mackillen's mind focused upon the name of the man that he hated. Why hadn't Branko chosen Jordan Blish instead? Then Blish would be here, tied to this chair, facing these mad people. But where was Blish? Probably screwing Charlotte again, and again, and again.

"*Bloody Blish!*" he screamed suddenly. "*Bloody fucking Blish!*"

The Mad Major listened to this outburst calmly. "Why Blish?"

"*Branko should have gone to him instead!*" Mackillen yelled, barely under control now. "*Then you'd be torturing that bastard instead of me!*"

"You do not like Blish? Your own friend?"

"*I hate him! I hate him! I hate him for screwing Charlotte!*"

"Remarkable what insights you can gain from observing someone under severe stress," the Mad Major said conversationally in Russian to his unseen companions. "This poor excuse for a man has channeled his fear into the hate and envy he has for Blish, and wishes this situation upon him. Who would have thought it? A woman. It never ceases to amaze me how foolish some men–even highly intelligent ones–can allow themselves to become, over a woman. Quite remarkable. It will not be difficult to get him to betray Diryov, even if he knows little.

"Mr. Mackillen," he continued, switching back to

English, "there is a way out for you. And good profit, too. Enough to enable you to buy at least four more cars like the one you've got."

"What . . . what do you mean?" Mackillen said slowly, visibly trembling and not daring to believe the Mad Major.

"Exactly what I've just said. I shall give you a contact number which you will divulge to no one, or I will have you killed. I may do it myself. Is that understood?"

"Yes." Mackillen did not allow himself to hope too quickly.

"You are to call that number the next time Diryov gets in touch. If you please me with your efforts, a very large sum of money will be deposited to any account you wish. Will you do it?"

"*Yes.*" There was no hesitation.

"What a shit," someone remarked in Russian. "What do we do with him when he gives us Diryov?"

"What do you think?" the Mad Major replied in the same language.

The other person grinned in the darkness.

Blish rolled off Charlotte and onto his back.

"We're on the floor again," he said as he stared up at the ceiling.

She made a soft sound deep in her throat and rolled across to lie half-on and half-off him.

"Perhaps we should start there."

"You always say that," he said, holding her close, loving the softness and the smell of her, especially after sex. "I think your corner of that Biedermeier must be sprayed with something. It always starts you off."

She nuzzled his neck. "*You* start me off." She began feeling between his legs. "Mmm!"

"What's got into you tonight?" He enjoyed the wandering, playful hand as it continued its explorations.

"You have," she said and began moving until she was completely on top of him. "And you're going back in." She raised herself slightly, then descended with a long sigh of pleasure. "You . . . ooohh . . . *are* back in! You're in! You're *in!*"

She covered him with her warmth and her softness.

"*Mr. Mackillen!*"

"Wha . . . what?" The dazed Mackillen jerked into startled awareness in the back of the car. It had stopped.

The blindfold was removed. "We are back where we left your car, Mr. Mackillen," the Mad Major said. "You may go home."

The driver got out and opened the door for him.

The Mad Major climbed out, favoring his right leg, then reached in for Mackillen.

"Come on, Mr. Mackillen. We haven't got all night."

Mackillen stumbled out, limping slightly. He had eventually pulled out the sliver of wood from his leg. It had been a good six inches long and had gone in deep. He had gasped as he'd extracted it, but, surprisingly, there'd been very little bleeding. The tiny wound appeared to have sealed itself with coagulated blood. He would clean it when he got home.

Someone had opened the garage door. The car was still there.

"Your keys." The Mad Major handed them over. "There will be little point in bringing any police to this place. We won't be using it again. But if you do, you will be killed. Remember. Good night, Mr. Mackillen. I look forward to hearing from you. Don't disappoint me."

The Mad Major got back into the XJR. Doors slammed shut. The powerful car rushed away with a muted roar.

Mackillen stood uncertainly, scarcely daring to believe he was still alive. As he stood there on unsteady feet, his body shook uncontrollably. Then he felt a sudden dampness in his upper trousers and realized what was happening. His total humiliation was now complete.

He had not even seen the Jaguar's number plate.

He got into the car and drove to his home in St. John's Wood, traveling at the most cautious pace he could ever remember. Even the most slightly erratically driven Porsche, he knew, would, at this time of night, attract police attention like flies on a cowpat. He would have been mortified to have been stopped, for the officers would, inevitably, have caught the stench of urine.

He would not have been able to explain, and, even if he could, would they have believed him? Drunk in charge of a urinated car. He could just see their faces. Is this *your* car, sir? Trying hard not to laugh as they booked him.

He was very careful. The Mad Major's threat—more accurately a promise—was impossible to ignore.

As soon as he'd made it to his large, expensive flat, he immediately removed all his clothes and ran a very hot bath. Eschewing chilled lager from the fridge, he poured himself a very stiff gin laced with cold tonic. Then he went into the bathroom, climbed into the water, and took a drink before lowering himself into it.

The heat in the bath and the cold of the drink made him shiver involuntarily. His hand shook violently and he dropped the glass. It shattered explosively on hitting the hot water.

Miraculously, no sliver hit him; but that put paid to his having an immediate bath.

"*Oh sod it!*" he yelled.

His fear of the Mad Major, as well as the frustrated helplessness he felt, was channeled into that yell. He climbed gingerly out of the bath and lowered his dripping body slowly to the floor. He drew up his knees and clasped his arms about them, leaning against the bath.

He sat like that for a long time, staring into space.

Chelsea, the next morning. Breakfast.

"I saw that, Amanda," Charlotte said.

Amanda had been surgically removing the yolk from a hard-boiled egg. "But I don't like the yellow bit, Mummy."

"You've liked it before. Why not today? See how Mianna's doing."

Mianna had decided she could feed herself and was sharing her own with various parts of her face, but white and yolk were getting the same treatment.

"*She'll* eat anything," Amanda said scornfully. She looked to Blish for support.

"Don't look at me," he said. "Mummy's running this show." To Charlotte, he said in a whisper, "Smart. She's cutting down on cholesterol."

"Don't you dare encourage her!" Charlotte whispered back.

Sharp as well as smart, Amanda said, "What are you whispering about?"

"She's got your radar," Blish murmured. Aloud, he said, "Just a little joke with Mummy."

"Why aren't you laughing?"

Charlotte put a hand quickly to her mouth to hide a smile.

"We're not going to have the why questions this morning, are we?" Blish said. "We're going to eat our egg."

Amanda stared hard at the disemboweled egg. Blish waited.

"I suppose so," she said at last.

"Thank you."

"That's all right, Daddy."

She began to eat the whole egg, rules of engagement for the breakfast table established.

Charlotte was still trying not to smile.

"What are your plans for the day?" Blish asked her.

"Sophia's having them while I pop out to find new ways of spending your money—"

"*Our* money," he corrected. "We're in this together." He'd always wondered whether sometimes she wished her father hadn't cut her off. She'd have had her own money then.

"No," she said.

"No?" He looked at her, puzzled. "We're not in this together?"

"No, I don't wish Daddy hadn't cut me off."

His eyes widened in surprise. He was certain he hadn't voiced his thoughts.

"Don't look so astonished," she said. "I know you well enough, Jordan. I know how you feel." She reached out a hand to touch him gently. "*Our* money. I'm going to spend our money."

"Don't you sometimes wish you'd taken a job in the City, like some of your other women friends?"

"And have a nanny push my kids around in a park, or poke around in our house? Forget it. I want to be with them at this age. They need me. Later, when they've grown some more, we'll see."

She always saw, in her mind's eye, the child with no parents wandering the streets of Trinidad. Any time you can spend with your children, she thought, was precious. She couldn't bear to think of anything happening to them, and Sophia and her mother—when her father wasn't around—were the only two people she fully trusted to look after them in her absence.

She leaned across suddenly, and kissed him.

"What was that for?" he asked.

"Do I need a reason?"

"No."

Amanda had seen it. "Yeeuchh!" she said.

"Eat your egg," they told her together.

"I have," Amanda said loftily.

"I'm not happy about it, Jordan."

"This has been a long time coming," he said. "I can't keep putting it off. Might as well be now."

"I won't go shopping," she said, looking at him anxiously. "Let's all go down together. I'll get the kids." The children had gone to Sophia's.

Blish shook his head. "He'd only try to upset you, in order to use that as some kind of weapon against me. This is something I've got to handle alone."

They were outside the house, standing next to their cars, which were parked nose to tail. Blish had decided to go down to Surrey to confront her father. He was going to tell Durleigh to stop trying to wreck his marriage to Charlotte. It had to be done.

"He'll be very nasty," she warned, her eyes tense with worry.

"I know," he acknowledged, remembering the nightmare. He still hadn't told her about it.

"Jordan—"

"I'll be fine. Off you go and do your shopping. I'll be back by late afternoon. I doubt if I'll be asked to stay for tea," he added drily.

"Be kind to Mother. You know she'd help if she could."

"I know."

Charlotte bowed her head to stare at the ground. "Despite everything, she continues to love him. I just can't understand that."

Blish knew she was not talking about their own problems with Durleigh.

"Whatever I've got to say to your father," he told her gently, "I'll do so privately. I'll get him to follow me into the garden."

Charlotte looked up at him once more, the brown eyes searching his face. "She'll probably be at an upstairs window watching. Whatever he does, don't let it get physically violent. He'll goad you. He'll probably strike you too, for good measure. Don't hit back."

"That depends on how hard he hits me, or tries to."

"Please! For Mother's sake. For my sake . . . for the children. You must promise me. You're much stronger than he is—"

"Your father's no weakling, Charlie. He's an ex–rugby Blue—"

"That was a long time ago—"

"And he's a big sod—"

"You know what I mean, Jordan. You can still knock him down. I don't want Mother to see that, and, knowing Father, he'd use it against you, even though he will have started it deliberately. He'll say you came to the house to make trouble. In fact, I wouldn't put it past him to have planned exactly such a scenario. Just be careful."

"I will."

She put a hand to his cheek and gently placed her lips on his. "I love you."

She went to her car, got in, and, with a brief wave, drove off. He stood watching until the white Volvo 480SE had turned the corner.

He got into the Rover. "All right, Durleigh," he said as he started the car. "It's you and me."

Remembering Branko's warning, he checked his mirrors; but there was no strange car lurking in the street behind him. All the others parked the entire length of the short road were on residential permits, and were familiar to him.

As he drove away and turned the same corner as Charlotte, he saw nothing that he could clearly identify as a tail. He eventually turned into the Kings Road, heading toward Putney Bridge, still confident there was no one behind him to worry about.

But there *was* another car following him.

■ ■ ■

"I wondered whether I would see you here today. Old habits die hard."

She was startled to hear the familiar, but unexpected voice behind her in the Knightsbridge store, and turned quickly round.

"Giles! What on earth are you doing here?" She stared at him, completely taken aback.

The mean eyes were doing their best to look warm. "Looking for you, actually. I remembered how you liked shopping here on Saturdays. Found anything yet?"

"But why?" She continued to stare at him, trying to work out what he could want with her, in this store of all places. "Why were you looking for me?" She turned, moved toward a dress she'd found interesting, and did not now look back at him.

He followed. "Strange way to greet an old friend, Charlotte."

"It's not as if you've been away on the moon, Giles."

"I might as well be."

"And whose fault is that?"

Charlotte began to resign herself to the fact that her hope of having a few self-indulgent hours on her own to browse and buy, if she felt like it, had now disappeared. Over the years, from the times at Cambridge and even *after* she had married Jordan Blish, Mackillen had continued to try his luck. He'd bombarded her with invitations to dinner, to lunch, for a drink, for coffee . . . using every excuse he could think of.

"You went out with me once," he now reminded her.

"*Once*, Giles. We went to that restaurant in Cambridge. We went as friends. Nothing more. Because of that, it was an enjoyable evening."

"Then came the Sunshine Kid, and everything changed."

She had been casually inspecting the dress as she spoke. Now she stopped and turned to face him once more, eyes freezing over.

"What was that?"

"Things changed."

"What you just called Jordan. I've never heard you say that before."

Under her steady gaze, he tried to pass it off lightly. "Oh come on, Charlotte. I meant that in the nicest possible way."

She wasn't smiling. "You could have fooled me."

"You're being oversensitive—"

"*Over*sensitive?"

He looked around anxiously. "Okay, okay," he said quickly, keeping his voice low. "I apologize. I shouldn't have said it."

The cold eyes were still upon him. "It's because Jordan considers you a friend that I have never told him you call me with invitations to lunches and coffees, and even dinners."

"My God. Would he prevent you from seeing me for lunch?"

She moved on to another dress. "No. That's just the point. He wouldn't dream of it, although he'd probably have second thoughts about dinner. *I'd* have something to say about it if he told me he was taking some female out to dinner, as a social thing. But then, I'm not as tolerant.

"I'm not a prisoner, Giles, whatever you'd like to think. I haven't accepted any of your many invitations because I don't want to. Besides, what are you doing here on a weekend? I'd have thought you could find many women to get into that Porsche of yours and scoot off to Paris, or wherever."

"There's only one woman for me."

"Oh yes?"

"You."

"There's only one man for me, Giles. I married him."

All things considered, he took the unequivocal rejection very well though, for a fleeting moment, something quite nasty lived briefly in his eyes. His self-control was perhaps due to the very public nature of the store and to the fact that she had moved on again, this time to study a wildly expensive scarf.

He found himself wishing even more that Branko—or Diryov, as that Russian lunatic had insisted on calling him—had gone to Blish instead. The horrors of the night before should have been visited upon Blish; and perhaps Blish would not have been fortunate to survive, as he had done. Then Charlotte would be free—

His fantasizing came to a sudden halt. She would not be totally free. There were those wretched kids. They would be a constant reminder of Blish; but they would not be part of *his* life. What would he want with a couple of mongrels? If there could be a way in which Blish got entangled, the mad Russian would do the rest. He would see to Blish and the kids. Then

Charlotte would be free without those two shit-faced brats, and clean again.

Mackillen was so absorbed by his desires for Charlotte's body that, as he stared at her legs, he failed to realize that his obsession with her was beginning to drive him mad. It never occurred to him to consider what would happen if Charlotte were to lose her family, and he had actually persuaded himself that she would rush into his arms for comfort. He was going out of control and didn't know it.

"So where's the man of the house?" he asked her casually.

"Gone to see Daddy," she replied; then, to make sure he didn't think she'd be on her own all day and possibly the evening, added, "I expect him back during the afternoon."

"You're joking. Jordan's actually gone to see your father?"

"Yes."

"By invitation?"

"No."

"Oh, I'd love to be a fly on the wall when they meet." Mackillen could barely contain his glee.

"I'm sure you would." Charlotte stopped again. "Giles, I'd really like to just wander around. You know, take my time looking at things. I love doing that. I might not even buy anything. I'm sure you've got much better things to do than tag along looking at women's clothes with me."

"I'd be happy to, but point taken," he said with unexpected equanimity. "By the way, have you seen Branko?"

For a reason she would never be able to explain, Charlotte heard herself say, "Branko? Do you mean *the* Branko from our Cambridge days?" She gave him an uncomprehending stare.

"The very same."

"Good heavens! It's been years. What made you think of him so suddenly?"

"Dunno, really." Mackillen did some of his own lying, hiding his disappointment. If only Branko had been to see Blish! "I suppose it must have been because we were talking about Cambridge earlier."

"That's probably it."

"Yes. I'd better leave you to your shopping," he added, sounding regretful.

Now that he was leaving, she relented slightly. "Why don't you come round to dinner with us one evening? Bring one of your girlfriends."

"Why not? I'll think about it."

"All right. Give us a call when you've made up your mind."

"I will."

They both knew he wouldn't.

"'Bye, Giles."

"'Bye, Charlotte. Take care."

"And you."

He leaned forward to kiss her on the corner of her mouth but she moved slightly, so that it landed on her cheek instead.

He appeared not to mind but beyond her vision, the unpleasant spark lived briefly once more in the mean eyes.

The metallic gray Saab 9000CDE Turbo had been following the Rover all the way from the Kings Road, and once on the A3 trunk road out of London, had kept at a distance of about half a mile. The blond man at the wheel had always ensured that there were at least three cars in between.

It had been very easy to keep tabs on the Rover and he drove at an easy, unobtrusive pace. The last thing he wanted was to be stopped for speeding. Twice, he had seen patrol cars lurking in the traffic, hoping for a sucker with whom to enliven the day.

He drove on, listening to Beethoven's Ninth. Every now and then, he would mouth a silent *pom, p-pom pom pom* to the music. The Rover was nicely in his sights.

Blish saw the Saab coming up in his mirrors just after he had passed Milford, and was approaching the wooded expanse of Witley Common. He intended to leave the A3 to turn left for Witley and the A283. Then it would be on to just outside Chiddingfold, where the Durleighs had their splendid Elizabethan manor house.

The Saab followed him into the turn, and he thought nothing of it. It was still there when he eventually reached the A283 and turned right to continue southward.

He frowned. Was this one of those people Branko had warned about? He felt a slight increase in his pulse rate. He slowed down. The Saab made no move to pass. This went on for half a mile, then the gray car flashed its lights.

"Pass then!" Blish muttered with relief. "How much more room do you want?" It was only one of those drivers who seemed unhappy unless they had the entire road before they could overtake.

Blish slowed right down. He was close now to his destination, and it didn't matter.

But the Saab didn't pass. Instead it matched speeds and flashed again.

"Bloody hell!" Blish snapped impatiently, pulled as far off the road as he could, and stopped. "Now you've got the whole road." He took his left hand off the wheel and waved for the man to pass.

But the Saab had stopped too, directly behind him.

"What the devil—?" he said, and put the car into gear ready to scorch off.

The driver's door of the Saab opened quickly and the blond man was shouting.

"*Jordan!* Wait. *Wait!*"

The blond man was *Branko.*

Blish slipped the Rover out of gear, switched off, and got out.

"God, Branko," he said as he walked toward the other. "Will you stop scaring the wits out of me? And what's this? You've got blond hair now?"

Branko grinned and leaned against the Saab. He patted his hair. "Nice wig, eh? Very realistic. As for my little charade with the car, I had to make absolutely sure no one else was following. That's why I stayed on your tail for so long."

"I was just about to take off like a bat out of hell."

"I know. And you're still not checking for tails often enough."

"I haven't got your expertise, Branko. So what's wrong? Why have you followed me all this way?"

"Nothing's wrong as such—yet. But things are

moving. Some people picked up Giles last night. My ploy worked."

"My God. They were that quick?"

Branko's eyes stared directly into Blish's. "These people are tough and nasty, as I've told you. The stakes are very high for them—for all of us, too. They now believe he's my contact. They grabbed him at gunpoint, took him to a place I already knew of, and put him through a grilling. They didn't torture him, but they could have if they'd wanted to. He was certainly scared enough when they released him. I'm certain he bought his release by promising to betray me."

Blish, thinking of Charlotte and the children, was looking extremely worried. If these people Branko was talking about had moved so ruthlessly, what chance had he if they even harbored the slightest suspicion that he'd seen Branko?

"Charlie and the kids—" he began.

"Are quite safe as long as we are not tied together. You can't send them away yet. That will alert everyone because it will make them wonder why. The moment will have to be just right—when it is obvious they are about to find out. *Then* you move them. And you'll have to be quick about it. Those people are very fast, as Giles Mackillen found out last night."

"And if they'd thought they'd made a mistake with him?" Blish now asked.

"They would have killed him," Branko replied calmly. He didn't say he expected the Mad Major to kill Mackillen anyway, whatever remuneration had been promised. "I've told you," he went on, "that these people play a very hard game. By giving them Mackillen, I'm keeping them away from you. We need to buy the time until I can find out who's got the weapons material, and what's going to be done with it.

"It's a tough race against all this, but I must find out so I can tell you, before they can get to me. Then you prime your people, and let them do the rest. We can only hope we can persuade your bosses and colleagues of the immediate certainty of the danger so that they'll move quickly enough to stop whatever is being planned. As a real bonus, that will also stop the Horsemen."

"Those—Horsemen you've talked about—they're not going to like that."

"No they're not. But their choices will be limited. They will want to stop those insane people with the material as much as anyone else. In fact, I am quite certain they're trying right now. If they can find those idiots before us—and by that I mean the West—they can stop the threat *and* still retain their anonymity. They can stay in the shadows until they are ready. This is most important to them."

"And if they don't?"

"I never said this was going to be easy."

"Christ," Blish said quietly. "Christ," he repeated, thinking of the implications and remembering his own personal nightmare. "Oh by the way," he continued, forcing the vision of Durleigh and the mushroom cloud beyond the cliff from his mind. "I've got to take a little trip to Europe. I can't postpone, or decline. Orders from above."

"When?"

"Next week."

"Good."

"*Good?*"

"Yes. Perfect, in fact. It takes you out of the firing

line and I'm going there myself. Another piece of the puzzle is falling into place. There is a contact who can help me. Someone who has been in deep cover since the bad old days."

"Like you?"

"Like me," Branko admitted shamelessly. "Although mine was only in short . . . detachments."

"And where is he?"

"*She.* She'll be in Germany, but is mainly based in Brussels. I suggest, since you're going to be away, that you tell Charlotte as much as you feel is necessary to put her on her guard. Make plans for the getaway, and give her a code word that you can tell her on the phone, so that she can get moving at a moment's notice. And don't worry. She's no weakling—"

"I know."

"There you are. She'll move fast if she needs to. It is important that she get away before the people who grabbed Mackillen can reach her. If they do, you will be in very serious trouble."

"I'm in serious trouble already."

"Not yet," Branko said. "Not by a long way. You will know it when it happens. Now tell me . . . why are you down here?"

"A reluctant confrontation that can't be put off any longer," Blish replied. "Charlie's parents live just south of here, not far from the county border. Her father's been trying to break up the marriage from the very beginning. He tried to break us up before we got married, and still hasn't given up. For Charlotte's sake, I've left well alone. But with someone like that it's a form of appeasement, and it doesn't work. I've decided it's time I put him straight about a few things."

Remembering his recent conversation with Mackillen, Branko said, “I wish you luck.”

“I’ll need it. The trouble with Durleigh is that he’s never taken time off to understand Charlotte’s feelings toward him, after all the things he’s done. His abuse of—”

“He’s abused Charlotte?” Branko inquired sharply.

Blish looked at him curiously. “Not that I know of. I was about to say his abuse of his own marriage. He’s betrayed her mother so often, it’s become routine. He’s got someone on the go right now, and sees her whenever he goes up to London. Charlotte’s mother wanted to come to our wedding, but of course the bastard stopped her. She still loves him, despite all that’s happened.”

“I think Charlotte loves you in a similar way.”

“I could never cause her such pain.”

“She already knows it. She always did. I was never supposed to say this to you, but what the hell, it’s years now since I made the promise, and you were not even together at the time. She told me she intended to marry you, and have your children.”

Blish stared at him. “She *said* that to you?”

“She certainly did, and all those years ago. Sometimes, it is easier to pass confidences on to relative strangers than to close friends. It’s like someone who goes abroad and behaves outrageously, totally unlike how he or she would behave in his or her own country. She found it easier to say something like that to me. Her secret, she felt, was safer. And it was.”

“Until now.”

“Yes. But I think it is time you knew about the very special woman you’ve got as a wife. She is a gem among the glass beads.”

"I know that. Charlie is my best of best friends, which is what I believe a wife should be. Right or wrong, that's my personal opinion. I trust her implicitly, even though I do realize how vulnerable that makes me. Things can change. But I've bet my shirt on her. You could say I've gone belly-up. She has my unprotected stomach at her mercy, and can do considerable damage if she has a mind to."

"And now that you know a little more about her?"

"I appreciate her all the more."

"Then you must be prepared to protect her."

"I am, as best as I am able to. But what was all that in the car about her reasons for marrying me?"

Branko grinned. "Just keeping you on your toes. Time to go and slay your dragon, while I make myself scarce. See you in Europe."

"How will I find you?"

"How are you traveling?"

"I'm flying over, but I've got autonomy. I think I'll pick up a car over there and drive myself around. I can give you a rough itinerary."

"Good. I'll find you when I need to."

Blish told him the itinerary, and they returned to their cars. He watched as the Saab pulled out to clear the Rover, then accelerated down the road.

Branko did not wave.

Moscow, the same moment in time.

Kurinin did not take weekends off. With the future of the Motherland at risk, he did not intend to take any time off until certain pressingly immediate problems were resolved. Diryov had to be found—so did the missing submarine, and the weapons-grade material. In any order.

He tapped an entry code and walked into a small office in the Personnel Section. It was a highly restricted area and in the days of the old KGB, it held a comprehensive database on all members of the armed forces of the then Soviet Union. The main database computer had been considerably updated, but its function, like that of the office itself, had not changed.

As he entered, the only person in the room, at the computer keyboard, began to get to her feet.

Kurinin waved at her. "Please retain your seat, Captain. Have you got everything ready? And are our channels of access secure?"

"Yes, Comrade General, on both counts." She was a fully cleared member of the Horsemen's forces.

"Excellent." He drew up a swivel chair. "All right. Let us begin. Find me the list of every seagoing naval command held, prior to the removal of our forces from the republics. I want *everything*, even a tug, and every rank."

Her fingers tapped rapidly at the keyboard. "There'll be plenty, General. We had a navy then."

He nodded. She had spoken the truth.

On the seventeen-inch full color screen, a string of names by rank, full details of their ships, fleets, and locations began to stream. At last the streaming stopped and the total figure appeared. It was an impressive number.

"You're quite right," he said grimly. "We once had a navy."

"We will again, Comrade General."

He smiled at her. "We shall, Captain Lirionova. We shall."

"Yes, sir."

"Now give me all the submarine commanders of that time. All ranks, and every type of subsurface vessel."

Again the fingers flew. Although this new total was much smaller, it was still an impressive number. The submarines were listed first by group: ballistic missile—nuclear; ballistic missile—conventional; cruise missile—nuclear and conventional; hunter-killers; fleet submarines—nuclear; patrol submarines—diesel-electric; training submarines, and on the list went, including reserves. Then there was each class of boat, and its designation.

"No wonder the West was scared of us," he said, looking at the total. "We were impressive. Now hold that list and compare it with the year Gorbachev was removed."

When the new list came on-screen, there was a sharp decline.

"The rot's started," he said grimly. "Bring us up to date."

The very latest list, though it far surpassed that of many a Western nation, still made depressing reading when compared to the original.

"So are the mighty fallen," he murmured softly. "All right, Lirionova. Give me the names of every sub commander who is no longer serving, irrespective of where he originally came from."

There were plenty, several of whom came from the former republics. There were many Russians, too.

"Look at this," he said, staring at the screen. "In

addition to the Russians, there are Ukrainians, Georgians, Chechens—ha! we know about *those*—Latvians, Estonians, even a few Czechs, Azeris, Armenians, Byelorussians . . . Every single state in the old Soviet is represented, and any one of those names could be our man, every one perhaps filled with resentment over the way things have gone. I can't say I entirely blame them."

Kurinin raised his arms, locked his hands behind his head, and stretched.

"Now we've got to do some whittling down," he said, bringing his hands back down. "List all those commended for bravery, originality, or for exceptional captaincy."

The list shortened again, but was still extensive.

"Mmm-hm. Remove all those with families. We're looking for a lone wolf."

Lirionova did so, but still came up with a list that exceeded a hundred.

"I never realized just how many good men we've lost," he remarked softly. "The price we're paying is not just in ships lying rotting at their berths, but also in men who have lost their dignity. Some of those will bite back, to our cost, unless we can channel their resentment positively. Let's see this new list in groups, by republics."

"If I may make a suggestion, Comrade General."

"Go on."

"The person we're looking for may not necessarily come from one of the former republics, even those with grudges—"

"Which, given the current state of affairs, is all of them."

"Yes, sir," she agreed drily. "Our lone wolf," she continued, "may well be Russian."

"You're quite right, and I've considered the possibility. At the risk of sounding chauvinistic, I believe only a Russian would be bold enough to carry out whatever is being planned, with *precision.* The plot itself would be hatched in fevered brains. The conspirators would be mad enough to do anything, irrespective of the outcome. But a Russian of the right caliber—*he* would ensure the precision of whatever the action is supposed to be."

"Meaning they've bought him?"

Kurinin nodded. "Financially, or politically. He would have to be reasonably young, and fit. Remove all those with medical problems, and all those above fifty years of age."

She did so. The list of names was now down to forty-five.

"Another thought, General," she said.

"Go ahead."

"Some of the names we've just removed are those with terminal cancer, brought on by service aboard nuclear-powered boats. All have been exposed to leakage of some sort. It is just possible that one of them might have felt he had nothing more to lose. Some have only recently lost their families, through conflict in the republics. They would be very bitter and may feel justified—"

"I grant you that is a possibility. But my instincts tell me he's a fit man. His anger will be more powerful, especially if he has all his faculties. He feels betrayed by what has befallen the old Union. You see, I *can* understand what he's going through. It's a good point you've made, but let's keep looking."

"Yes, sir."

"Bring up the psychological profile of each, plus the citations for any decorations received, and a picture to go with the profile."

He began reading as each name came up. "Kedlov, Russian, forty-six. A lot of decorations. Personally rescued his second-in-command from a blazing diesel-electric submarine, after ordering everyone to abandon ship. Suffered superficial burns . . . but traumatized by hearing the dying screams of a trapped crewman whom everyone had apparently forgotten, and whom he could not reach in time. He blames himself, though the evidence shows that two cowardly sailors had secured the hatch in panic, leaving their colleague to fry in a compartment that had turned into a furnace. We can discard him. He's in no fit state to command a dinghy."

By the time they had worked through the profiles, twenty likely candidates remained. Ten Russians, two Ukrainians, one Byelorussian, one Chechen, one Kazakh, one Azeri, one Lithuanian, two Georgians, and one Armenian. All heroes of one kind or another, all highly skilled submariners.

"We have one more elimination process to go through," he said. "Then we should have the core element of this group. Check to see which of these twenty have hired their services out to any foreign country, or the republics."

Ten of that number were currently employed in supervisory and training roles abroad. One, the Lithuanian, was serving with his republic's fledgling forces as a patrol boat commander.

"So," Kurinin began, "with the exception of our

lieutenant commander from Lithuania, we've got three in various Middle Eastern countries, two in Africa, one in South America, two in Southeast Asia. One in—*Australia—?*"

"He's become a stockman—"

"How on earth—oh well, he's young enough. And our last one—"

"Is a drunk. He's been regularly picked up by the Moscow police for brawling."

"This is a tragedy," Kurinin said, a hard, grim edge to his voice. "The man's heavily decorated, and once commanded a ballistic missile submarine. Can you believe it? This is a man who used to play hide-and-seek with some of the best American submarine commanders around. Yet what is he now? A drunk on the streets of Moscow. What are we *doing* to our people?"

"We'll be putting things right again, Comrade General."

Kurinin gave her a brief, tight smile of appreciation. "It's good to know we'll have people of your caliber with us, Comrade Lirionova."

"We'll be there when the time comes, sir."

"I'm certain of it, and the support of like-minded comrades like you among the junior officers gives us the courage we need to carry it through. And now," he went on, "let's check on our other nine prodigals. Give me a full printout on all of them. The search will begin immediately."

"Yes, General."

The remaining nine were five Russians, one Ukrainian, the Azeri, one Georgian, and the Chechen. There was no current information on their whereabouts.

But Kurinin had made a fundamental error in his scan of the database. The person he wanted had already been eliminated. He had assumed that the rogue submariner would not be a family man.

This mistake would bring a very high price.

By the time that Captain Lirionova—working weeks later on a private hunch—would highlight the name, it would already be far too late.

The Surrey/Sussex borders, England.

The Elizabethan manor was an imposing structure with a superb, panoramic view of the South Downs and just about everything necessary for gracious living. With six bedrooms and six en suite bathrooms, four reception rooms, a music room, a conservatory, plus assorted ancillary buildings and secluded grounds of at least twenty acres, it was no shack.

There was also a vast, beautifully kept lawn bordering a wide lake with an attendant, decorative pond. An indoor swimming pool at the back of the house, leading on from the conservatory, would not float an ocean liner, but it would safely accommodate a small motorboat. During summer months the pool, housed by what seemed to be an extension of the conservatory itself, could be opened up to become an outdoor pool. This, then, was the opulent home of Sir Richard Elsin Durleigh, Bart., M.P., and his long-suffering wife—and Charlotte's birthplace.

Charlotte had once said that the only reason Durleigh would not divorce her mother was the thought that she would get everything and pass it on to her daughter, who in turn would share it with Blish, who, as her husband, would thus have rights to the property. This would equally mean that Amanda and Mianna would be the subsequent inheritors. To Durleigh, this was a true nightmare. Cutting off Charlotte had appeared to solve that problem.

But that was only temporary, as Charlotte's mother had already indicated that her own share would be her daughter's. As a consistently wronged wife, her position was very strong indeed. A divorce would most certainly cost him the property and, with equal certainty, his seat in Parliament, despite his comfortable majority. Emily Durleigh was well loved in the community. Durleigh's only recourse, therefore, was to attempt the destruction of Charlotte's marriage to Blish, by any means possible.

These thoughts were very much in Blish's mind as he drove up the gravel drive and stopped before the vine-covered porch of the big three-storied building. Durleigh, he knew, would have seen him arrive, but there was no one at the solid, wooden double doors.

He climbed out of the car and waited, checking the leaded windows of the central section of the house and its two wings, to see if anyone was peering out. After a while, he went up to the porch and pressed the white button on the prominent bell push. No answering sound came back, but that was normal. The sprung bell would ring deep within the recesses of the building.

After about five minutes, Durleigh himself appeared at the door.

"What do you want?" he snapped. The anger was already beginning to show.

Durleigh still looked like a rugby player. He also looked fit for his age, and still had a full head of white-blond hair that was only slightly receding. He was casually dressed in cavalry twill trousers, and a sports jacket that came from Savile Row. His open-necked shirt was stuffed with a regimental cravat. His eyes, glaring at Blish, were colder than gravestones on a winter's night.

"Not the welcome I expected," Blish said calmly, "considering the PUS said how proud you were of me."

"Did you come here to bandy words?"

"No. I came here for a serious talk. But I am curious to know what kind of facade you showed Sir Tim. He clearly believes we get on marvelously."

"What goes on in my family is my affair. I see no reason to wave it about in public."

That was rich, Blish thought, considering everyone knew of the affairs that were very much outside the family.

"Before you get upon your high horse and look smugly down upon me," Durleigh was saying, "remember this: your appointment is window dressing. A sop to all those dreadful, politically correct people. Do you believe you're only there on merit? Good God man! Have a dose of reality. Being married to my daughter has done you no harm either, even though your adopted parents may be well thought of in some quarters."

In some quarters. Durleigh was virtually saying he was not in that group.

Blish kept his anger in check, remembering what Charlotte had said; that Durleigh would deliberately set out to goad him. "I think we should take a walk in the garden," Blish said, ignoring Durleigh's insults.

"Why should I walk anywhere with you?"

"I want to talk about Charlotte. I believe that, despite yourself, you'll want to hear. I don't guarantee you'll like it."

Blish walked away, not waiting for Durleigh's reaction. As he strolled toward the garden at the back of the house, he heard Durleigh's furious footsteps stomping after him.

He walked the length of the wide, gently sloping lawn until he reached the thick, neatly trimmed hedge, directly behind which was a two-foot-thick solid, ancient wall. The ground fell quite steeply beyond the wall, to open fields below. The drop reminded him of the cliffs in his dream. Perhaps his own memory of the place had triggered the symbolism. Beyond the fields was the spectacular view of the Downs. He waited there, savoring the view, until the angry strides finally caught up with him.

"Say what you've come all the way here for, then leave!"

"Strange," Blish said mildly, not looking round. "Such an exquisite view. The grounds, and the house, are beautiful. There's a seeming aura of peace about this place. A wonderful location to be born."

"It will stay wonderful, Blish, because you won't get your hands on it! Not ever!"

Blish turned to look at him, his own eyes totally devoid of any warmth. Durleigh actually took an involuntary step back, not expecting such coldness from someone he'd always considered well beneath his class, especially when it came to ruthlessness.

"Don't judge me by your standards," he told Durleigh. "I'd have Charlotte if she'd come from a hovel, as long as she wanted me. That's what you can't understand about your own daughter. She has qualities she couldn't possibly have got from a raving hypocrite like you.

"I came all this way to tell you something simple enough for you to grasp. Charlotte and I are married for as long as we want to stay that way, and, if I understand her correctly, that's going to be for a very long time indeed. So don't even try any of your tricks on her while I am away. She despises you for what you have done to her mother. I despise you for what you're trying to do to her. If you keep this up, she'll not take your calls anymore, nor will she return them. If you do not change your attitude to her and our marriage, the next time you come to our house will be considered trespass.

"I don't care what you say to me, or about me, but from now on, you leave Charlotte alone. She's not your baby daughter anymore. She's my *wife*, and the mother of our two children. And *that* is a dose of reality for you. Good-bye, Durleigh."

"*Sir Richard* to you, you insolent black—"

But Blish was already making his way toward the front of the mansion.

Throughout, Durleigh had been growing more and more apoplectic with rage as Blish had spoken. Now Blish's calm dismissal of him forced the anger into the open. He ran after Blish.

"*Stop, damn you!*" Durleigh yelled furiously. "How *dare* you turn your back on me! You defiled my daughter! You took her without my consent! There was a time when you'd have been whipped within an inch of your life for this!"

Blish kept on walking, hurrying to reach the car before Durleigh got to him.

But Durleigh was running faster, moving remarkably quickly. He reached Blish, and grabbed a shoulder to wrench him round. As Blish began to turn, Durleigh swung a big fist toward his face.

Blish ducked the blow easily, pulled himself free, but did not strike back. He kept walking.

Durleigh ran up and again grabbed him. Blish again freed himself just as Durleigh swung wildly. Missing his target yet again, Durleigh staggered and nearly fell. He lost ground as Blish walked on.

"Stop, you blackguard!" Durleigh shouted. "Stop and fight like a man!"

Blish walked on, thinking ruefully about what the tabloids would make of it, if one of their hounds were lurking in the bushes. He could see the screaming headline. BONKING MP TAKES SWING AT FOREIGN OFFICE SON-IN-LAW! They would also make a meal of the fact that he was black.

But there would be no headlines. Durleigh had long since taken out an injunction that would have made the presence of any reporter within half a mile of the grounds, without consent, ferociously expensive for the newspaper involved. It wouldn't necessarily stop them if they smelled a juicy story, however.

But on this day, there were no long-range lenses peering at them.

But there was a pair of binoculars.

■ ■ ■

Blish had reached the car by the time Durleigh had again caught up with him. The hand did not reach for a shoulder this time. Instead, the fist came powering at him.

He caught sight of the movement on the periphery of his vision and, once more, ducked successfully out of the way. Durleigh stumbled and fell heavily on the gravel, bruising his hands as he put them out to cushion the fall. He yelled in pain as a sharp pebble raked one palm.

He got to his feet, seemingly out of control now. "Damn you!" he roared, and began to rush at Blish.

Blish had moved away from the car so that Durleigh would not slam into it. This forced the charging baronet to change direction, causing him to miss his footing slightly.

"Stop it! Stop it!"

Emily Durleigh, who'd clearly been watching, had rushed out of the house and was hurrying toward them.

Oh no, Blish thought.

It was the last thing he'd wanted, especially knowing how Charlotte had felt about his coming here. Then he saw, with horror, *that she* was *running toward her husband to stop him.*

Charlotte's mother was the kind of woman who had been born into the wrong decade, perhaps even the wrong century. She was far too delicate in attitude for the robust nineties, and though she had a strong will whose power she could display when she wanted to, she seemed to lose all control over it where her husband was concerned. The fact that her belief in loyalty and faithfulness to the man she had married frequently fell upon stony ground did not seem to deter her.

Blish had always wondered why, for he could find no rational reason for her continuing support of a man who was so ill-deserving. So many women, he thought, at times seeming like a majority, appeared to give their love and loyalty to men who abused them and treated them with scant regard. This bizarre phenomenon appeared to cut across all boundaries: class, ethnic, intelligence.

He thanked God for Charlotte.

His own mother had succumbed, blindly following a man who had left her to rot in the back streets of Trinidad. Thinking of that unknown man brought a long-simmering anger to the surface, and it focused upon Durleigh.

As if in slow motion, Blish began to move toward his mother-in-law in an attempt to pull her out of the way. It was clear that Durleigh had no intention of stopping, nor of reining in his punch. The fist was swinging again, intending to connect heavily on Blish.

It was hopeless. Blish saw he was going to be too late and felt despair as Emily Durleigh got between her husband and her son-in-law. Durleigh's fist connected solidly with the side of her head. Blish watched in horror as, with the force of the blow, her gray-streaked blonde hair seemed to rise in a swirling cloud about her face. Then she was falling, a leaf tumbling in autumn.

Durleigh had come to a shocked halt, staring disbelievingly at his fallen wife, who lay frighteningly still. Blish reached her and began to pick her up.

This seemed to jerk Durleigh out of his stasis.

"See what you have done?" he snarled. *"If you hadn't come here—"*

"Typical," Blish said without looking up, the anger boiling now, but forcing himself to speak calmly. "Blame everyone but yourself. You've got long experience of that."

"Take your hands off her you—!"

Blish gently let go of his mother-in-law and stood up, facing the man who had done this to her. It was as if the years had fallen away, the upbringing of his parents stripped from him, to leave the street kid staring out of his eyes—a street kid with a burning hatred for a father who had let his frightened young mother die alone and heartbroken, far from home. For a fused moment in time, Emily Durleigh personified that woman.

She lay there between them, like a catch to be fought over by two wild animals. Branko, he thought, would have understood.

"If *you* touch her," Blish said quietly, "I swear to God I'll tear your head off your shoulders."

He lowered himself once more to pick her up, and gently carried her over to the house.

Durleigh made no move to stop him, clearly believing Blish had not only meant what he'd said, but could have done it. A subtle shifting of power had taken place.

A man who looked as old as the house itself hurried anxiously out, stared at Blish's burden, then at Durleigh, who'd remained where he was, rooted to the spot. The old man's eyes held a suppressed fury as he looked at Durleigh.

"What happened, Mr. Blish?"

"Brandon, are you ever going to call me Jordan?"

"No, sir. What happened?" the old man repeated as he stood back for Blish to enter. He turned to glare once more at Durleigh. "Did he hit her again?"

Blish was stunned. He'd never known of this. "He's *hit* her before?"

"Not for many years. He used to, quite regularly, when your wife was a child, sir."

"My God. I never knew. Charlie never told me."

"She wouldn't, sir. Not something like this."

"She took the blow that was meant for me," Blish said.

They entered one of the reception rooms and Blish laid her gently down upon a large sofa.

"I'll do something about the swelling," Brandon said. "I've done it before." He went out quickly.

As far as Blish knew, Brandon had been with Emily Durleigh's own family seemingly forever.

"Jordan." Her eyes were open and glistening with tears. "I'm sorry you had to see this."

He took her hand in both his own. "Why did you run out like that? You could see he was not going to stop."

"I had to try."

"I could have handled it."

"I know you could, but I just could not have allowed it. Don't you see?"

He nodded. "I do see. Before I came down, I promised Charlie I would not strike back."

"I knew that must have been it. I was watching, of course. I saw you dodging him, saw him get more and more furious—When he gets in a rage, he's quite uncontrollable. Who knows how it might have ended?"

"Shh. That's it for now. Brandon's gone to get something for your head. How do you feel?"

"A little woozy, but I'm all right." She paused. "Brandon, you said. Has he—?"

"Yes. He has."

"Oh dear. I never wanted you to know that. What will you think of us?"

"It won't change what I think of you. Charlotte has a wonderful mother."

She patted his hand. "Thank you, dear boy. And her father?"

"It won't change what I think of him either," Blish said in a hard voice.

"He wasn't always like this, you know," she said.

"Why do you defend him, Emily? He's *always* been like that."

"Oh . . . you should have seen him as a younger man. Handsome and strong, and quite a catch. I know, I know. You think I'm a foolish woman."

There it was again, Blish thought. The defense of the male as right bastard. Did such men hold the secret, after all? Without doubt, Durleigh was highly successful with women.

But he didn't want to be like that, Blish decided. Better to risk having your stomach emotionally slit open.

I have Charlotte, he told himself.

A gem among the glass beads, Branko had said. Branko was right.

"I don't think you're foolish," he said truthfully to Emily Durleigh. "I think you're a very brave woman."

He let go of her hand as Brandon came in just then and began to attend to her with practiced and familiar ease.

"Ah, Brandon," she said softly, her eyes now closed. "Always there when I need you."

"Shall I call Dr. Casham?"

"No, no. I'll be all right. Don't drag the poor man out. Jordan?"

"I'm here."

"You will take good care of our Charlie, won't you?"

"Always."

"Thank you, Jordan. I know I can count on you. You're very good for her, no matter what anyone else says. I know she's very happy with you. Don't let anyone spoil it."

"I won't. You can count on that too."

"Thank you, Jordan," she said once more.

He leaned down and kissed her on the forehead. She gave a little smile, but did not open her eyes. Her breathing had relaxed. She looked beautiful and strangely childlike as she rested, he thought. The swelling on her temple was not as bad as he'd at first feared.

Looking at Brandon, he signaled he was about to leave. The old man stood up, and followed him into the vast hall.

"Where's the rest of the staff?" he asked Brandon.

"Keeping out of the way, sir. They tend to, when Sir Richard has one of his moments."

"I see," Blish said, appreciating Brandon's massive understatement. He glanced toward the room where Emily Durleigh was dozing. "Will she be all right?"

"Yes, sir. He won't touch her again. I'll make certain."

"What happened the last time he did?"

"I'd rather not say, sir."

Blish had a feeling that Brandon had taken appropriate action in some way or another. As it had been years before, Brandon must have been quite a strong man. Even now, his stance was still erect.

"It's okay," Blish said. "I won't pry further."

"There's something you ought to know, sir," Brandon began. "I am doing this with Lady Durleigh's permission. This house . . . belongs to her family."

Blish stared. "*What?* Charlie never said."

"She does not know, sir."

"But I don't understand."

"Lady Durleigh wanted it that way. On her marriage to Sir Richard, she gave him joint ownership. A wise caution prevented her from giving him total ownership. Sir Richard was . . . not a man of property, you see. Lady Durleigh wanted you to know. She said you would understand."

Blish, aware that his mouth was open, closed it slowly. "Yes. I do understand."

Emily Durleigh wanted her daughter and son-in-law to inherit, whatever Durleigh tried to do.

"That is all I am allowed to say, sir."

"It's more than enough. Thank you. Tell me something, Brandon."

"I shall try."

Blish looked at him for long moments. "No. I won't ask. I think I know."

For the first time, a particular emotion appeared in Brandon's eyes. "I . . . I appreciate that, sir."

"Take care of yourself and . . . take care of her."

"I will," Brandon said firmly.

As he went out, Blish knew that for all those years, Brandon had been in love with Emily Durleigh.

Durleigh was still standing where they'd left him. His head jerked round as Blish came out.

Blish gave him a hard stare. "Don't say a bloody word!" He climbed into the Rover and started back down the drive.

Durleigh turned to follow his progress and was still there, long after the Rover had disappeared.

So were the binoculars.

The man with the binoculars drew a small personal radio from a pouch in his camouflage jacket.

He did not identify himself as he spokc into it, nor did he address the recipient of his message.

"He's on his way back," he announced. "Out."

There was no reply. He had not expected one.

He returned the binoculars to his eyes. Durleigh was still standing there.

"Bloody politicians," the man said. "The things they get up to."

He'd been watching the Elizabethan mansion for days.

Blish entered the Chelsea house.

"I'm back!" he called from the hallway.

She came down the stairs in a white T-shirt and nothing else, her bare legs a temptation that was very difficult to ignore.

"The children are still with Sophia," she said. "We've got time before I pick them up."

She came close, pressed herself against him as she put her arms about his neck, and kissed him for long moments.

"This is a nice friendly way to be welcomed home," he said.

"I heard you arrive." She took his hand. "Shall we?"

"Don't you want to know how I got on?"

"Afterward. I just want to remind you of something." Her tongue flicked out to reach for the upper lip in the way he knew so well, and could never resist.

"A gem," he murmured as he allowed her to lead him up the stairs to their bedroom.

"What?"

"Just doing a little reminding of my own."

Afterward, she lay with weary satisfaction upon him. "Oohh! When did we last do it that way?"

"Who's keeping score?"

"Rruff!" she said, pretended to bite at his nipple, then ran her mouth in a series of kisses down his body. "Oh," she continued, as if surprised. "There's a sausage down there! I think I will have a bite."

"Don't you dare!"

"All right. How about this?"

"This" soon had him squirming with pleasure. Then she stopped.

"Hey!" he said. "Don't stop now!"

She worked her way back up and grinned at him. "Wicked tease, aren't I?"

"You can say that again."

"Now you can tell me what went on at the house."

"*Now?*"

"Now."

"Mental cruelty," he said.

"Sexual cruelty, more like." She kissed him quickly. "Now tell."

So he did.

She stiffened, went pale, and, almost before he had finished, started rolling over to grab at the bedside phone.

Brandon answered the call and assured her that her mother was well, and was resting.

"I must come down!" she said into the phone.

Blish ran his eyes along her naked back as she lay on her side speaking to Brandon, and felt the pull of arousal. He left her alone, watching her body shake as she listened to what Brandon had to say, and knew she was crying softly.

It was quite obvious the old retainer was trying hard to persuade her not to rush down to Surrey, as a row with her father would be inevitable, which would in turn only serve to upset her mother further.

"All right, Brandon," she said, giving in reluctantly to his counsel. "But you will call if there's any problem?" She listened further, then, "All right. I'll wait to hear. But don't hesitate. All right, Brandon," she repeated. "Thank you."

She hung up slowly, but did not turn round immediately. The tremors of her body grew and Blish moved across the bed to put his arms about her. She turned round then, and the sobs at last broke through, her tears spilling onto his chest.

He held her close, saying nothing, and letting her get the whole thing out of her system.

"Why does he do it?" she said through the sobs. She bunched her fists. "Why, why, *why?*"

He had no reply for her. He simply lay there, giving her the comfort she needed.

When her crying had subsided, she wiped away the tears with the back of her hand and looked up at him.

"Thank you for carrying Mother inside. Brandon told me what you did. Would you really have hit Father?"

"Yes," he said. There was no doubt in his mind. "I'm sorry, but I would have broken my promise to you."

"You would have had every right to," she said. Her

lips trembled slightly. "Oh, Jordan," she went on softly in a small voice. "I'm a strong person. I had to be when I was growing up. But I don't know what I would do without you. I would be so alone."

He kissed the lid of each tearful eye, then brought her head into the crook of his neck.

"And I," he said, "do not want to be without you."

Moscow, two days later.

General Kurinin's worldwide intelligence network had done a swift and thorough trawl to find the remaining sub captains. They got results, but not the ones he'd hoped for.

Of the five Russians, one was serving on a cruise liner as a barman; another had managed to buy a share in a small trawler of which he shared the captaincy; two others ran a shady bar in Leningrad/St. Petersburg. The bar's activities were suspect, to say the least, but had nothing whatsoever to do with smuggling nuclear material, or with submarines. The last of the five Russians was in a hospital, suffering from a sexual disease.

The Ukrainian had gone to America and was now running a used car business in one of the dangerous parts of Florida. The Azeri, who'd also qualified as a helicopter pilot during his service, now flew civilian choppers in the Caspian Sea oil fields. The Georgian now lived in a mountain village, retired from the world, he'd said when asked. The Chechen had died in the fighting with Russian troops.

Kurinin studied the reports disbelievingly. It was not possible. *Someone* was going to captain that sub. Surely, not a *Western* mercenary? It seemed, on the face of it, inconceivable. Nothing was impossible in life, as he well knew; but the idea of a Westerner doing this for . . . He paused. Even if that were the case, from which nation?

He discarded the thought, positive he was going up a blind alley. He was certain he'd been on the right track. But just where had he gone wrong?

Another journey through the files with Captain Lirionova was called for.

He returned to the room in the documents section.

"From the very beginning, sir?" she asked.

"I'm afraid so. This may have to be done several times until we find the anomaly."

"I'm happy to do it."

"Comrade Lirionova, your dedication will not go unnoticed."

"It is for the Motherland, Comrade General. Nothing is too much."

"You have the spirit we need," he told her approvingly.

In the cavern beneath the mountain, the sub captain climbed out of the conning tower to meet a surprise visitor.

He stared uncomprehendingly at the man in the wet suit.

"General?" *he queried uncertainly.*

The general's was a well-known face, and he'd commanded one of the best army units of the old Union. He still commanded it, but during the upheavals of the last years had kept himself, and his unit, well out of the limelight.

What, wondered the submariner, was such a man doing here among the bunch of fanatics planning this madness?

"Hell of a way to get here," the general began conversationally. "First by fishing boat, then by a chariot attached to its bottom. First I needed to complete a sub-aqua course to enable me to do this."

The chariot, a small torpedo-like submersible with two seats cut into it for its frogman crew was, in time of war, a disposable weapon with a charge in its removable nose. It destroyed itself and its target. The one in the cavern was used only rarely, to bring important people in.

"You are clearly very surprised to see me," the general was saying. "Although I do realize your sympathies are not with us, you are the best man for the job. So we are pleased to have you carry out the mission. I have studied your operational records thoroughly. Very enviable."

"Thank you."

"May I inspect your boat?"

"Of course."

They went aboard, and the captain took the general to where the launch tubes were being worked on.

"Very impressive," the general said. "Very impressive indeed."

He watched the work for a while, then indicated they should move on.

As they crawled through a hatch that took them away from immediate earshot, the general said, "Is there somewhere we could possibly talk privately?"

The captain looked neutrally at him. "Nowhere is

totally private, but my quarters are the best under the circumstances."

"That will do."

The cabin was not as cramped as the general expected, though it was no open space. The captain closed the watertight door.

"This should do, General."

The general leaned against a bulkhead and said, "You're a very intelligent man, Captain. It will not take you long to work out that with my involvement in this venture, it takes on a more complex profile than just a revenge action by political, or religious, extremists. It will, of course, look *that way. I am telling you this because, sooner or later, you will come to that conclusion."*

The captain said nothing and waited.

"What is planned," the general went on, "is a shot across the bows of the Motherland, and the world. It will galvanize people into action."

If the captain thought that was a sure way to start a limited nuclear war, he said nothing. He would be well away from the area by the time, after the initial shock, they started chucking the things around in response to the two weapons from the submarine.

The general was looking at him. "You do not agree?"

"Whether I agree or not is immaterial, General. I am engaged to carry out the mission, and I shall."

The general nodded slowly. "A true professional. I like that. I wish you would join us."

"I think not, General. But you can depend on me to carry out the mission."

"I know I can. Pity you won't join us though."

The captain decided not to comment.

Then he said to the general, "General, when will I get the target information, so that we can start programming the rest of the launch sequence?"

"When the time is right," the general replied, smiling to soften the bluntness of his response.

The captain looked at him and said nothing further.

London, evening of the same day.

Charlotte sat on the Biedermeier sofa, legs tucked beneath her, face very grave.

Blish was in his usual position on the floor, head resting against her. She passed a hand through his hair, as was her custom. The part-Carib genes had given him the gleaming head of hair that had been mildly countered by those of his father and, as a result, had put a hint of curling in its rich darkness. Most evenings, with the children put to bed and dinner over, she liked to relax, with one hand moving gently through the softness of his locks.

But on this occasion, she was doing so absently.

Blish had at last told her all about Branko. Completely attentive, she had remained totally silent throughout. There had been no exclamations, no display of panic. She had simply listened, taking it all in.

"We'll have to get the children somewhere safe," she at last remarked in an unexpectedly steady voice.

The calm manner in which she had spoken made him feel a great warmth for her. Two days before, fearful that her mother was at risk from her father, she could think only of rushing down to the family home. And previously, when Branko had first appeared on the scene, she'd been frightened of the unknown dangers his presence might unleash. But now, knowing more and faced with the reality of the nightmare that could descend upon them at any time, she was behaving entirely differently. She was battening down the hatches and preparing for siege.

The blood of her maternal ancestors, the blood of generations who wouldn't lie down and surrender, was in her veins. Inside, he knew, she was probably panicking, but was determined to control it. Her children were at risk. Like mothers everywhere, like his own mother, who'd fought until she no longer could, Charlotte was placing herself between them and whatever the danger might be.

"Have you told anyone else?" she now asked.

He shook his head. "Not yet. Branko thinks it's not a good idea. Speaking now could make things a lot worse. We've first got to find out where that nuclear material's gone."

"So you're all on your own."

"I'm not really the one doing anything. Branko's got the ball. I'm just a sort of messenger."

"You know what happens to messengers."

He turned his head to look up at her. The brown eyes seemed to have gone darker as they looked down upon him, glowing in stark contrast to the bright sheen of her blond tresses.

"This messenger will make sure he stays as safe as possible."

The eyes looked deep into him, conveying many things that remained unspoken. "I ought to be furious with you," she said, "for keeping all this to yourself. But

I do understand why you did it." The hand kept stroking his hair. "You're a very junior diplomat, Jordan," she added. "Not some . . . well . . . spy. That's Branko's stuff. Perhaps you should talk to someone who could—"

"And who would that be?"

"The PUS, for one. He knows everybody, and everything . . . or should. You've said yourself that Monty Allardyne was asking about Branko. Perhaps you could talk to him, if you feel reluctant to involve the PUS."

"*Monty?* You know what he's like."

"Unfortunately, yes. On second thoughts, perhaps not—"

"And anyway, I don't know enough to tell the PUS at this stage. There's nothing worse than having incomplete information when you request an audience. Besides, I could be virtually signing Branko's death warrant by talking too soon. He's lived this long because he knows what he's doing and he's had all this planned a long, long time. I've already blundered into something I barely understand as it is, and could easily cause more damage, instead of making a helpful difference.

"Those are very, very nasty people out there, Charlie. They don't take prisoners unless it's to do very unpleasant things to them. They don't as yet know Branko's contacted me. That's why we're not receiving their attention, and I intend to keep it that way. One word from me to anyone, and we'd be in the line of fire before we took another breath. Branko says so, and I believe him. But . . . we take precautions, just in case."

She remained silent for a while. The hand had paused now, just resting upon his head.

"Part of me hates Branko for bringing this to us,"

she said quietly after long moments. "But I suppose," she went on grudgingly, "I ought to give him some brownie points for at least having the common sense to come to you, because he felt you're the only one he could trust. But he's put our children in danger—"

"I'm certain it's not what he intended. I yelled at him a bit about that. He's right about one thing. Whoever's got the nuclear material has already put our kids and kids all over the world potentially in very grave danger. If they do succeed in using those things, God only knows how it will end."

Another silence descended between them.

Then Blish said, "Incidentally, he also thinks I've got the best woman in the world."

Despite her worries, she gave him a tiny smile. "At least he's got some perception."

"Such modesty." He reached up for her. "Come down here so that I can inspect you more closely."

"Still need to? After all these years?" But she came down off the sofa to tuck herself into his embrace.

"What years?" he asked, as he brought his lips to one of her favorite spots just beneath the left ear. "I love the scent of your body. Do you know that?"

"It's something else you love," she murmured against the crook of his neck.

"That too." He began to stroke her leg and upper thigh gently.

She gave him a playful smack. "And you can stop that wandering hand. We've got serious things to discuss. Like where do we take the kids if the man Branko calls the Mad Major comes looking for us."

"Branko suggests it must be nowhere that can be linked, even remotely, to friends or family. If things get dodgy while I'm away, I'll call. Just get out fast. No questions, no conversation in case anyone's listening. We really ought to pick a place at random from a brochure so we both know where it is. If you've got to leave, make a booking when you're away from the house. Use a public phone. Not your mobile. Mobiles are about as secure as sieves."

She gave it some thought, then said, "Too uncertain. I've got a better idea. There's a place Mother and I went to when I was about six—"

"No family links."

"That's just it. There isn't one."

"But you said you and your mother—"

"There's a story behind that." An edge had come into her voice, leading Blish to believe the occasion had not been a happy one for her. "Mother's tried to leave my father before, you know."

When Charlotte was really angry with Durleigh, she tended to describe him as Father, or "my father," instead of Daddy. But when she used the word Mother, it was always with a great warmth in her voice.

"It was after the first time she'd discovered one of his affairs," she went on. "It hurt her so much, I couldn't stand it. I used to hear her crying softly, when she thought I wasn't close enough to listen. She'd think I was out in the garden or something. She cried a lot, sometimes for days, it seemed. I hated him for what he was doing to her."

Charlotte spoke in a voice that was devoid of emotion. Blish knew it was a protective device, stifling the pain of the memory. He listened while she told him about a part of her childhood she'd rather not have been forced to talk about.

"One day, about mid-morning," Charlotte went on, "she appeared at my school and said we were going away for a while. She said it was a holiday. She'd packed my things. I thought it was a strange time for a holiday, especially as it was during the school term. Her eyes were swollen, so I could see she'd been crying again. She bundled me away and we drove off. She told no one—"

"Not even Brandon?"

"Not even Brandon. I think she was trying to make us vanish from a life she'd come to hate. We drove for hours. At least, that's what it seemed like to a child who was at once scared and excited by this unexpected adventure. Finally, we ended up in a village . . . Not really a village, I suppose. More like a small group of houses along a single road that ended in some woods.

"But it was in a beautiful location, in a wooded valley. There was a stream on the opposite side of the road and, hidden among the trees, on the slope away from the stream, a few detached cottages. I remember thinking how absolutely quiet it was, even quieter than where we lived. There, you could still sometimes hear the faint sounds of traffic; but in that little village, our car seemed to make enough noise to wake the whole world. When Mother turned off the engine, the place seemed to be asleep.

"Mother decided we'd stay. She'd seen a sign about a cottage for rent. It belonged to a very nice old couple who lived in the village and was very clean and quite beautiful, with a wonderful view of the valley and the houses below. A steep drive with hard-packed gravel went up from the road to the door. There was a lovely little sloping garden, with space to one side to leave a car. There was no phone.

"Mother paid in cash to cover a month. She had no idea for how long we were going to stay there. There was a small shop along the road, where we could buy the basics for living. If we needed bigger shopping, the nearest really big grocery was five miles away by the narrow road through the valley, and across one of the hills. Many of the houses in the village were second homes for people who normally lived either here in town, or in places as far apart as York, or Birmingham, and in one case, Newcastle."

"And where is this little bolt-hole?"

"Shropshire. It's near Wenlock Edge. No one will ever find us there if they don't know where to go. The old couple are gone, of course, but they had a daughter. *She* had a little girl about my age at the time, although I didn't see her much. Mother kept us very private. I was very lonely."

She fell silent once more, remembering.

Blish gave her a comforting squeeze. "Won't the family have sold it by now?"

She shook her head. "Just before I went up to Cambridge, I went back on my own—the first time since Mother and I had been—to see if it was as I remembered it. I suppose I was revisiting something that had a great impact upon me in my past, before I really entered the world as a young adult. It was as if I'd only been there the day before. Even the garden looked the same, except it seemed smaller because I had grown up. The family were very good to me and treated me like a long-lost relative.

"They never forgot us. I think Mother wrote to them, but I'm not sure. They're never going to sell the cottage. They'd made the promise before the old people died. The only risk is that they may have tenants occupying it. I'll have to check—"

"Remember not to do so from here. Best not to take chances. I never really trust even ordinary domestic phones these days."

"What an admission from someone who's with the FO."

He smiled at her. "Someone with the FO would know. Besides, you don't trust them either. So we've got the bolt-hole," he continued. "Now we need a signal that no one could possibly understand, if I do need to alert you by phone."

"Lothar," she said immediately.

"*Lothar?*"

She nodded. It was a private joke between them and was her nickname for the Biedermeier sofa. She'd always felt that political repression in many parts of early nineteenth century Europe had been personified by Metternich's own political repression of Austria, which in her eyes had served to bestow a subversive aura upon the Biedermeier movement. Despite the fact that she valued the sofa highly, using it as a love-making prop was her way of showing late twentieth-century solidarity with the people of that designing movement. The 1820 Scandinavian-built sofa had been put to the sort of use its makers had never dreamed of. Then again, perhaps they had.

"Who could ever guess what we meant?" she said to Blish. "And if by some incredible chance they discovered it was our name for our bonking Biedermeier, they'd still not be able to work out its true meaning."

"All right," he said, giving in. "Lothar it is. The uptight prince would turn in his grave."

She freed herself from his embrace, went back to the sofa to recline upon it. With her right foot on the floor, she raised her left leg and perched it by the ankle upon an arm of the sofa.

"Perhaps if the good prince had done some rigorous bonking himself, he wouldn't have been so uptight."

He looked at her, feeling a stirring within him. "You know what happens to me when you do that," he warned in anticipation. "I thought you were frightened."

"I am. But fear's also exciting. And I'm very excited. There's nothing underneath for you to remove."

"So I see," he said, and quickly began to remove his trousers.

His entry into her, slow and smooth, was facilitated by the fact that she was moistly eager to receive him.

"Mmm," she murmured at him. "See? I told you . . . I was excited. If only sofas could talk . . . what stories this one would . . . tell . . . *Ooh!* Every . . . every time you do that, it . . . feels like the first time all . . . all over again . . . and . . . again . . . *and again!*"

The Biedermeier took a pounding.

Later in bed, she showed him a small photo album she'd kept hidden with some very personal memorabilia. There were fading monochrome pictures that had been taken by the daughter of the owners of the cottage, and the more recent ones in color, taken by Charlotte herself on that pre-university visit. She'd also got out a map to show him how to get there.

The cottage was neatly white, overlooking its pristine garden.

"It's very pretty," he said, glancing at her. "A good bolt-hole."

A thought briefly entered his mind. Would she, like her mother, have used it, he wondered, had there been any trouble between them? Until that evening, he'd known nothing of its existence and would not have known where she'd gone. He did not voice the thought.

But she instinctively knew he'd considered it. "No. I wouldn't have." Her eyes did not turn from his as she said that.

"I should have remembered to be careful about what I think around you," he said. "You read minds in your spare time."

But she did not smile at the lightheartedness of his remarks. "All you've got to remember is that I love you. You're not going to get rid of me easily."

He put an arm about her. "I've no intention of doing so. Remember *that*." He then pointed to the album, and the map. "If things get hot and you do have to go to the cottage, take these with you. It wouldn't do for the Mad Major to find them—"

"He'd come *here?*"

"Branko expects him to, if he thinks there has been a contact between us."

"But the alarm system—"

"Will not be much of a problem to people like that. I'm willing to bet that Branko's probably got some high-tech equipment himself that would allow him to get through. In this electronic world, every system has a counter—or someone, somewhere, is working on one."

"I'll take every map I've got of the area," Charlotte said, needing no further convincing, "and anything that links with it. Okay?"

He nodded. "With a bit of luck, we might not have to use the cottage at all."

But life had a habit of not keeping to plan, nor of paying much attention to luck.

A Thames-side restaurant near Tower Bridge, two days later.

The lunchtime crowd had not yet reached full capacity. Giles Mackillen was sitting by himself at a window table, with a panoramic view of the river. Between him and the next occupied table was another with a "reserved" card upon it, giving his position a temporary privacy.

"Mr. Mackillen." The terrifyingly familiar and unwelcome voice spoke softly behind him.

The Mad Major moved into view and sat down uninvited.

"I'm . . . I'm expecting someone," Mackillen began lamely.

"I will not be very long. I shall be finished before she gets here."

"How do you—?"

"Mr. Mackillen, Mr. Mackillen. You should give me more credit. We do know your habits. But your sexual desires, with one notable exception, are of no interest whatsoever to my colleagues, or myself. If you choose to impress a gullible young secretary with an expensive lunch in order to get into her pants, that is your business. I am more interested in the progress of our little . . . venture."

"I haven't seen him."

"I am aware of that. I think you should try harder."

"But—"

"This should help you." The Mad Major had put something upon the table. It was a thirty-five-millimeter film cassette, with a well-known brand name. The film had obviously been used up, for there was no telltale tongue of celluloid peeping out of the slot.

"A roll of film?" Mackillen said, puzzled.

"This *looks* like a roll of film. It is, in fact, a very powerful, transmitting microphone."

Mackillen stared. "What . . . what do you want me to do with it?" His eyes gave darting glances at the cassette, as if expecting it to jump up and take a bite out of his nose.

"This type of film cassette is innocuous. Everybody uses it. Take this to Blish's house and leave it anywhere. It's powerful enough to pick up conversations in any part of the house, wherever it may be positioned . . . even in a bathroom."

"Blish! But Branko's never been near him."

"Perhaps. But in my line of business, Mr. Mackillen, it pays to consider *every* possibility. He may not contact Blish at all. In which case, we'll hear nothing more interesting than Blish's domestic . . . activities." The Mad Major watched Mackillen's expression keenly as he went on. "Of course, this also means bedroom activities . . . "

Mackillen's countenance had begun to darken, as expected.

"Just think," Branko's nemesis continued, enjoying the sexual torment that showed nakedly upon Mackillen's face. "We'll hear what he gets up to with his charming wife, and how far up he goes; she with the quite glorious legs—"

"Shut up!" Mackillen hissed.

"Mr. Mackillen," the Mad Major said coldly, "don't ever tell me to shut up again."

Mackillen caved in immediately, vividly remembering his recent experience. "Um . . . sorry. I . . . I . . . it . . . won't happen a—"

"For your sake, let us hope not. Console yourself with thinking of what will happen to Blish if Diryov . . . or Branko, if you prefer, does make contact." The Mad Major stood up. "The cassette is also magnetic. You can attach it to any suitably unobtrusive surface. Once you have positioned it, it will activate itself. That is all you need to do. Call the number I gave you when you've done it. Don't take too long." The warning, and all it promised, was as cold as it was implicit.

"But how do I get in?" Mackillen inquired worriedly.

"I'm certain you'll find a way. Please look more cheerful for your guest. Good day, Mr. Mackillen."

As he left Mackillen's table, the Mad Major saw a young woman with bouncy, full breasts and an excited, bright smile, making her way toward the panoramic window. She wore a smart outfit of high-necked white blouse and a short, pale blue skirt that ran out of length more than halfway up her thighs. The smile was clearly directed at Mackillen.

"What a wonderful smile," the Mad Major said to her.

She was startled by this unexpected compliment from a total stranger, but also quite pleased. "Thank you," she said, eyes flashing at him.

"You are most welcome." He continued on his way.

"What a nice man," she said to Mackillen as she sat down.

"Yes. Nice."

Then Mackillen remembered the invitation from Charlotte Blish. Charlotte had probably expected, and had also hoped, that he would never take it up. She had judged the situation quite accurately, until now. And had she not said to bring a girlfriend?

He looked at his companion as he poured her a glass of the expensive wine that had cost a small fortune. "How would you like to come to dinner at the home of a very good friend of mine in Chelsea? I have a standing invitation and I'd like to take you. His wife's a splendid cook. She could open a restaurant and be up there among the best. And he's with the Foreign Office. We'll have a great time. Say yes, and I'll arrange it."

Her eyes widened. They were baby blue, pupils fully dilated. She was clearly impressed, and very pleased he'd asked her to accompany him. She was also very eager to see him later that evening, knowing they would eventually end up in bed.

"I'd love to," she said.

Mackillen had found his entry, in more ways than one.

Moscow, the same day.

While Giles Mackillen was looking forward to relieving some of his frustrated, sexual longings for Charlotte Blish on the ripe young body of his dining companion, Kurinin was experiencing a few frustrations of his own; but these had very little to do with sex.

He stood behind Captain Lirionova, watching as her fingers seemed to fly across the computer keyboard. Before coming to the high-security office, he'd scanned through the various intelligence reports on the world situation over the last twenty-four hours. They'd made depressing reading.

"How much sleep have you had in the last few days, Captain?" he now asked her solicitously.

"Enough, sir."

"That could mean anything," said. "You seem never to have left this machine. I greatly appreciate your dedication, but I need you fit and well, and alert. For reasons of security which I am certain you understand, I cannot allow you a helper to continue the search while you rest. Is there not a way in which you could instruct the computer to continue searching when you are not in attendance, and still keep it secure?"

"I can get it to do the basic searches, while remaining hidden," she replied without turning to look at him. "It can download the information into hidden files which it will only display when I call them up; and I can protect them with a code which will require too much time to break, for any practical purposes."

"Then do so at the end of this session. Get yourself some proper rest. Go away for a day. Think of the problem from another angle."

"I'm sorry we've not had much success so far, Comrade General," she said apologetically as she tapped a command into the computer. Then she swiveled her chair round to look at him. "I've taken the search from just before the war with the *Afghanski*," she continued, "to the present time. I have tracked all movements of all military personnel: resignations, promotions, desertions—both in the home districts and abroad—discharges—honorable and dishonorable—transfers to forces of the republics, deployments to United Nations commands, attaché posts worldwide, special forces assignments, special deployments to research units . . . and so on.

"I've run the sequence through several times, introducing variables with each run. The computer has instructions to highlight all anomalies. Each time, it brings up different ones, but so far, none of its suggestions appears to be what we're looking for."

Kurinin placed his hands in his pockets, turned from her to walk a few paces, while her eyes followed him. He stopped, turned to face her once more, legs slightly apart. His hands remained in his pockets.

"Do you believe in God, Captain?"

She stared at him, not certain whether this was a trick question.

He smiled thinly. "It's all right. I am not trying to trap you into admitting anything. For my part, if I did believe in God, or *a* god, I would be forced to think that if he did indeed create this world, he must have been so horrified by what he had done, he immediately went on a permanent holiday to recuperate. It's the only theory that explains the insanity in the world today."

"Yes, sir."

The thin smile lived briefly once more upon the edges of Kurinin's mouth.

"Safely spoken." He came back toward her to peer at the computer screen. "Something is nagging at me," he continued. "I've had an insistent feeling that the answer's been staring us in the face, that it's there for us to find but, somehow, we appear to be looking in the wrong direction."

"Or perhaps we are looking in the right direction, but picking up the wrong signals."

He nodded in agreement. "Time, for the moment, is not on our side; but keep at it. I have every faith in you."

"Thank you, sir."

"And take that day off."

"Yes, sir."

"But *find* me that sub commander."

"Yes, sir."

London, that evening.

Mackillen withdrew with deliberate slowness from the plump roundness of the girl's body.

She sighed with regret at this and brought her legs together, in an instinctive but somehow incongruous gesture of modesty. A short while ago, those same legs had been intermittently flailing, her heels pummeling at his buttocks as she'd shouted in wild abandon.

"I was good, wasn't I?" she now asked coyly.

Christ. Why did she have to say that?

"You were fantastic."

"*Really?*"

Jesus, he thought sourly. "Really."

"I was worried."

"Why? You've got a great body. I enjoyed being in there."

"Do you really mean that?"

"I really mean that. Excuse me for a moment." He rolled away to reach for the bedside phone and began to punch in some numbers. The connection was made and the phone at the other end picked up almost immediately.

"Four-oh, four-oh," the voice answered.

"It's me," he said.

"*Giles!*" Charlotte exclaimed in recognition and with much surprise. "What can I do for you?" she went on coolly. "I'm off to the bath."

In other words, hurry up.

He forced himself to remain pleasant. "Remember your invitation to dinner?"

There was a brief pause, and he knew she'd long ago wished she hadn't made the offer.

"Of course," she replied. "When would you like to come?"

The ever-polite Charlotte, he thought grimly.

"How about next week?"

"Ah. That could be awkward. Jordan's very busy at the FO at the moment. We'd need a month to five weeks."

Five weeks! He didn't have five weeks. He'd have to think of another way to get the cassette microphone into the house.

"Why don't I call you with a date when I've checked my diary?" he suggested with false calm.

"That's a good idea."

Thinking of her in a bathrobe had given him a growing arousal. He reached across to his conquest for the evening and felt for one of the bouncy breasts, cupping it. Misunderstanding the reason, she gave a barely audible sigh of pleasure.

"Fine," he said into the phone. "I'll be in touch."

"Do that," came the detached response, annoying him further.

"Fine," he repeated with the same pretended calm. "'Bye."

"Good-bye, Giles."

He grimaced at the phone as he put it down.

Bitch, he thought.

But imagining her without the bathrobe had by now aroused him fully, and as he turned over the young woman noted it, again mistakenly believing she was the object of his resurgent desire.

She smiled widely at him. "Come here, big boy!" she said eagerly, once more opening her legs in welcome as her fleeting modesty vanished without a trace.

He plunged cruelly into her, causing her to give a long, gasping scream even as she raised her pelvis, offering herself up to him to facilitate his entry.

"*Bitch, bitch, bitch!*" he grunted as he pounded at her.

"*Oh yes, yes, yes!*" she wailed in response, enjoying his savagery.

As he grunted and drove his way into his surrogate, he held in his mind's eye a sharp vision of Charlotte Blish writhing beneath him. The woman who was actually there no longer had an identity. The heaving body, the whimpering gasps and screams, the frantic opening and closing of moist thighs, all were Charlotte's.

He groaned his way to a long, shuddering climax. "*Charlotte!*" The name was drawn hoarsely, lingeringly out of him.

The body beneath him froze. "*Who the fucking hell is Charlotte?*" she screamed in outrage, her fists thumping at him. "Who is she? Have you been screwing me and thinking of her, you *shit?* Tell me. *Tell me!*"

He said nothing.

Suddenly, she began to sob and pushed him roughly off her. "You bastard!" she screamed again, humiliation reddening her face. "You fucking *bastard!* How could you *do* this to me? How *could* you?"

She got out of bed and began to pick up the clothes she had previously discarded with such cheerful abandon, sobbing loudly as she did so.

"I feel so . . . *used,*" she said between the sobs as she got dressed. "You're a prize shit, Giles Mackillen. Do you know that? A real bastard of a shithead. I hope someone breaks your balls one day!"

Still lying on the bed, he was staring at her almost clinically. "Where are you going? In half an hour, it will be midnight."

She looked at him with open contempt. "You're not going to tell me you're worried about me, are you? God. I was *such* a bloody fool!"

"I'll drive you home."

The tear-filled eyes glared at him. "I'm not getting into your fucking car, thank you very much! I'll take a taxi. Fuck you! Fuck your car! And fuck this Charlotte, whoever she is! You're never going to get into me again. I'm going home for a good scrub, inside and out. *Bastard!*"

She slammed the door as she left the bedroom. A short while later, he heard something crash in an expensive and explosive tinkling of glass, before the door to the flat slammed shut.

He didn't move.

"There goes something," he muttered.

He knew how he'd get into the Blish household. He'd simply turn up at the door. A polite Charlotte would find it difficult not to invite him in. Then he'd simply plant the microphone and, after a suitable interval, leave.

He wouldn't have to manufacture an excuse for his unexpected visit. Charlotte would think he was making a nuisance of himself, yet again. Neither she nor Blish would possibly suspect his true motives on that occasion.

He smiled ferally. It was so easy, and would at least go some way toward getting the Mad Major off his back. Better still, it would hopefully bring some serious grief into Blish's life. That made the whole thing worthwhile.

Mackillen's smile widened. He liked that thought.

"Who was that on the phone?" Blish asked as Charlotte climbed into bed after her bath.

She hesitated only slightly. "Giles."

"Mackillen? What did he want at this time of night?"

"Oh I ran into him when I went shopping the other day, and gave him a loose invitation to dinner. I also said he could bring whoever he was seeing at the time. It was really quite open. He rang to confirm."

"*Now?*"

"You know Giles."

"Yes," Blish said unenthusiastically.

She snuggled down close. "I feel a bit mean, actually."

"Why?"

"I'd been hoping he'd either forget, or wouldn't take up the invitation."

"Well we can't see him for a while. Not as long as this thing with Branko's going on."

"I did tell him you'd be busy for at least a month."

"Good."

"And—" She stopped suddenly.

He looked at her. "What?"

"Branko."

"What about him?"

"I forgot to tell you. Giles asked me if we'd seen Branko."

Blish said quietly, "And what did you say?"

"That we hadn't. I don't know why I did. I just felt instinctively that I shouldn't tell him."

He gave her a squeeze. "Good thinking. If you should run into him again while I'm away, we still haven't seen Branko."

She nodded. "Jordan?"

"Mmm."

"You know that Giles—"

"Still has the hots for you? So what's new?"

"You're not upset about it, are you?"

"Why should I be? I know you. That's what matters."

She inched herself upward until she could kiss him fully on the lips.

"I know why I love you so much," she said.

"Just keep stroking my ego and I'm yours forever."

"I'll stroke this," she said, an active hand moving beneath the bedclothes.

"Come here you," he said, grabbing for her.

"I've just had a bath," she protested weakly, her eyes already betraying her surrender.

"Have another . . . afterward."

"Ooh," she said softly. "Ooh yes. Mmmm!"

JULY

I

The British Airways Boeing 757 was climbing out of Heathrow to cruising altitude, on its way to Cologne/Bonn airport.

Blish was the only occupant of the twenty seats in Club class, in the front cabin. He had a window seat, and, as he watched the tufts of cloud flitting by, he wondered whether Branko would make contact in Bonn.

A short while later, the aircraft reached cruising altitude and the flight attendants wheeled out their trolley, to begin serving the in-flight meals and drinks.

He settled down to his meal in solitary splendor and was halfway into it when someone took the aisle seat next to him. He looked round in surprise to see a man in a smart, expensive city suit smiling at him. The newcomer was slim, with neatly trimmed blond hair and looked extremely fit. The hair was something special. It had not been simply cut but was *tailored* so that at the top of each ear it curved into a tiny, neatly symmetrical wing.

"I'm Charles Buntline, Mr. Blish," the smiling man introduced himself. "I do hope you don't mind me joining you like this." He held out a hand.

Blish stared at him, astonished. Then with a slight hesitation, he shook Buntline's hand. He noted Buntline's immaculate, double-cuffed white shirt and subtle, blue tie. Buntline's handshake was firm and brisk.

"You're of course wondering how is it that I know who you are," Buntline continued. "No mystery, really. My department sometimes . . . er liaises with yours."

"You're with the FO?"

"Not . . . exactly."

Blish wondered where the man who called himself Buntline had sprung from. He didn't look like the sort of person who ever traveled in Economy.

"You're also wondering," Buntline was saying, "how I got aboard. Actually, I was having a few words with the captain."

Having words with the captain. Blish had also noticed that since the time Buntline had arrived, no flight attendant had appeared. Did Buntline, who seemed able "to have words with the captain," as he'd put it, also have the sort of clout that could demand privacy for the entire Club class cabin? It was beginning to seem like it.

"I'll come straight to the point," Buntline said. "We're interested in your friend . . ." He paused. "Branko."

"Who?"

"Come now, Mr. Blish. That might fool Her Majesty's very average subjects in the street, but not me. I'll grant you have no idea who I am, and you've every right to be cautious. So let me help you out of your dilemma. You are going on a fairly autonomous wander through various EC countries, at the behest of the PUS. Monty Allardyne recently invited you to lunch and asked you about the ubiquitous Branko. How am I doing?"

"*You* are Monty's 'little bird'?"

Buntline looked amused. "Not the way I'd put it myself. But yes . . . I did prime him."

"And this trip is a setup? And the PUS is involved?"

"The PUS . . . er . . . gave us some cooperation."

"'Us'?"

"Need to know, I'm afraid."

Blish was furious. "I'm with the Foreign Office—"

"And I'm not." Buntline smiled. "Difficult, I know. I cannot order you, of course, but the PUS might be rather upset. I'm assuming that an upset PUS is not a very pleasant sight to behold. Probably has a terrible effect on careers, too."

Blish stared at him. "Are you blackmailing me, Mr. Buntline . . . ?"

"Heaven forbid. And it's Charles, please. Not Charlie, though. Never Charlie. Hated that at school. Almost went to your school, you know," Buntline carried on conversationally. "Mother's choice. But Father insisted on his old school. Eton, I'm afraid. You're Oundle, aren't you?"

"Yes," Blish answered before he'd realized it.

"Good school." Buntline almost made it sound like a

condemnation. "I'm on your side, Jordan. May I? Hate all this formal mister stuff. This is the situation. Your friend Branko is being chased by some very dangerous individuals, as you already know. What you may not know is that there's more than one bunch. He's in very, very deep indeed. We also think he's playing an elaborate game. We already know he's come to you for help."

"He hasn't. And what help could I give?"

"You underestimate yourself. And please, Jordan. No more pointless denials. I am on your side, though you appear not to think so at the moment. You've been dragged into something which without some—let us say—professional assistance, would swiftly turn into a very real nightmare. Not only for yourself, but for your family, too. You are all at great risk.

"You've got a very beautiful wife, and two exceedingly beautiful little girls. I will be blunt, in order to impress the seriousness of this upon you. Those people I've just mentioned would think nothing of killing them. They've already killed so many individuals—children included—three or four more will be of scant consequence. All in a day's work."

Charles Buntline was virtually echoing Branko's own words. It was uncanny.

"And you, Mr . . . er . . . and you, Charles. What is your score?"

"Of kills?" Buntline was singularly unperturbed by the question. "A few. No children, though. One has to have some standards."

"Standards." Blish repeated the word as if recoiling from it. "What precisely is 'a few'?"

"I don't keep a tally, old man. But do let me go on.

Here's a little tale. A man who's an extremely able operative, and who over the years has been at various times a sergeant, a captain, a major—not necessarily in that order—has seen combat in various parts of the world including Afghanistan, belongs to a unit that even the old KGB never suspected, and the same old KGB in its new clothes certainly doesn't . . . Are you still with me?"

"I'm going nowhere," Blish replied, looking pointedly round the cabin.

Buntline smiled minutely. "Very droll. Now this multitalented agent, on an intercept mission, not only delivers stolen nuclear material but absconds with the money he collected in return, to the homicidal fury of the moonlighting smugglers. It did not improve their sense of humor when the assassins they had sent to terminate him ended up being terminated themselves. Assuming that is what actually happened."

Blish looked interested. "What do you mean?"

"Ah! A spark. Oh he did kill those two incompetents. No doubt about that. But what I mean, my dear Jordan, is that there might not have been any nuclear material—or at least not all of the amount—inside the case he exchanged in St. Petersburg."

"*What?*"

"Yes. I had the same reaction, meself. It was a sting, old son. An attempt to trap not only the smugglers, but to trace where the material was going. The briefcase was tagged. Unfortunately, the Mad Major—"

"You know of him?" Blish had spoken before he realized what he'd done.

Buntline smiled wolfishly. "Good thing I'm on the side of the angels. You've just betrayed yourself and your family. If you know of the Mad Major, there's only one way you could have received the information."

Blish was shocked at how easily he'd made the mistake.

"Don't be hard on yourself," Buntline said kindly. "This is not your line of work, after all. Now we've got that out of the way, I shall continue. Unfortunately for the Mad Major, his little scheme had been rumbled and the nuclear material substituted for mostly worthless junk."

"Mostly?"

"They had to leave some in there so the bait would be taken."

"My God. They actually allowed weapons-grade material to go through?"

"If you want the fish, you've got to have good bait."

"My God," Blish repeated softly.

"It's a dangerous world, old son. Risks need to be taken to prevent the big disasters."

"But this one didn't work, did it? According to Branko . . ." Blish paused. Little point in continuing his denials. "According to Branko, enough material got through to make at least two weapons. So the operation must have failed."

"Partially."

"How can there be a partial failure with something like that? The material got through, or it didn't."

"'Partially' because not all of the material came from the one source. The operation came unstuck," Buntline went on, without going into further detail, "because I believe there was someone *on the inside* who wanted it to do so. The tagged briefcase was neutralized and the trail lost . . . "

"Which, I suppose, is why Branko's been trying find it. He came to me with other information, too."

"Which is?"

Blish remained silent.

Buntline's eyes grew very hard. "You are in a very precarious position, Jordan. There are those, as I'm certain you're well aware, who would like to see you fall spectacularly on your face and your career ruined. Some of those—let's be charitable—even number among your friends. There are none so venal as those who would wish to see a friend come unstuck. Look no further than the government's recent leadership elections.

"As for your misguided loyalty to Branko, or Diryov, or any of the other identities he's given himself in the past, let me paraphrase Forster. Faced with the choice of betraying your friend or your country, I'd strongly advise against betraying your country. Forster prays for the guts to betray his country. Yours would be used for garters. A very damaging case could be made against you, because of your association with Branko since your days at Cambridge. There are, after all, precedents."

Blish stared at him, horrified. "I'm not the only one who knew him. Are you accusing *me* of treason?"

"Good Lord, no. Wouldn't dream of it. I'm simply warning you against misguided altruism, and pointing out the many pitfalls. Of course you're not the only one who knew him; but you are the one currently involved, and Branko is an *active* Russian agent."

"But he came here to warn us! He put himself in danger to do that. He could simply have kept all the money and disappeared somewhere. I believe he's sincere. I know him—"

"You *think* you know him. An agent of his caliber should be able to gain the confidence of anyone he chooses. It's his job."

"Yours too?"

"I detect a certain bitterness," Buntline said calmly. "But yes. Mine too. The major difference is, I have your interests *and* your safety, at heart."

"So does Branko. I believe he has valuable information which he's so far held back, but which he—"

"Probably intends to use as a bargaining chip for something," Buntline put in, finishing the sentence. "We suspect as much," he continued. "Which is also why, contrary to what you may be persuading yourself to believe, we do not intend to reel him in. We want you to go on as before. Continue your itinerary. There are some changes, of course. A car has been arranged for you, replacing the one previously chosen by you. While this business is going on, I'd suggest you keep away from all our consulates and embassies. You never know who may be watching. You'll be pleased to know the PUS is in full agreement."

Blish kept his expression neutral and said nothing. He felt no overt hostility toward Buntline; but neither was he in the mood to give any great display of friendliness. Despite intimate knowledge of the situation, Buntline could still be anybody. Branko could fake identities. So could Buntline.

Fully aware of the doubts in Blish's mind, Buntline took it all in his stride and handed over a small envelope. "In there, is a list of hotels. Very innocuous, if someone decides to have a peek. Looks like stops on an ordinary motoring tour. Meet him at any of those."

"You want me to spy on him, or lead him into a trap."

Buntline put on one of his amused expressions. "I've just said, my dear chap, that we have no intention of reeling him in. You're with the Foreign Office. Follow custom. Be the diplomat and bend the truth for your country's sake, if you need to. But keep his trust."

"He came to help and you want me to spy on him." Blish insisted.

Buntline sighed. "My dear, dear chap. Transparent honesty in a diplomat, even a junior one, while very commendable, is a rather bad quality to be lumbered with. Do you believe for one moment he's been totally honest with you?"

Blish did not reply.

"Quite," Buntline said. "Now I must leave you to continue the rest of your flight in peace. A man will hand you the keys to your car at the airport. He'll be waiting in the café near Arrivals. Not the coffee bar behind the Foreign Exchange kiosk, but the café proper a little further on.

"The car's a metallic blue Mercedes E320. A rather nice motor, I've been told, and virtually brand-new, with BOT registration letters. This means Bottrop Stadt is the registering authority. That's just north of Essen. It's not a hired vehicle, so it won't seem obviously foreign-driven; and of course, CD plates would have given the game away. Are you good with left-hand-drive cars?"

"Yes."

"Splendid."

"I suppose you've tagged it?"

"You're catching on," Buntline said cheerfully. "Yes. Of course we have. This might amuse you. *Bothrops*, or more correctly *bothrops atrox*, is the zoological nomenclature for a rather large and venomous snake from the part of the world where you were born, the fer-de-lance. Strictly speaking, it's South American, but let's have a little poetic license. Perhaps you'll be . . . a somewhat poisonous feast to those who may see you as prey." Buntline managed to sound hopeful while apparently enjoying his little joke.

Blish did not look amused. "That's the poison frog's party piece."

"I prefer the *bothrops*. More aggressive. It carries out preemptive strikes." Buntline eased himself out of the seat. "Now I really must be going. We shouldn't meet again, unless things get sticky. In which case, they'll be very sticky indeed."

With that unsettling thought rippling its way into Blish's mind, Buntline left the cabin.

As if by magic, a flight attendant appeared.

Blish left the rest of the meal untouched.

Moscow, the same time.

Captain Lirionova stared at the anomaly that had been highlighted on the screen. It was not one she'd been looking for, but its presence was as explosive as any she'd hoped to find. She was so astonished, she at first refused to believe the information displayed upon her much-loved machine was correct and almost convinced herself it was an error.

To make quite certain before she called the general, she ran a comprehensive series of checks. The results were startling. More associated anomalies began to appear. There was no choice. She would have to alert the general.

She picked up a secure phone.

Kurinin hurried into the room. "You've found him!"

"I'm afraid not, General. But I've found something else." Lirionova moved slightly to allow him a better look at the screen.

He could only stare.

"This is not possible," he said at last, in a hushed voice. "Show me the others."

She brought the other related anomalies on-screen. There were several.

Kurinin mouthed a particularly obscene oath. Though no words were spoken out loud, Lirionova understood what he'd meant. It told her more clearly than anything else could just how agitated the information had made him.

"This is impossible!" he said tightly. "How could he have stayed hidden for all those years?"

The highlighted name on the screen was Diryov. There were many other aliases associated with him, above and below the highlight. There were different ranks, too.

"So he's really been quite a senior officer for all this time?" Kurinin asked.

"According to the information we've got so far . . . yes, sir. There may be other ranks he's used, hidden in there somewhere. His true rank may be even higher."

"How did you get access to this?" Kurinin demanded after a while.

She hesitated.

"Don't worry," he assured her. "You have my authority to go into any system. As far as this operation is concerned, no files are inviolate."

"I broke some entry codes, General."

He looked at her with respect. "Your talents are impressive. There'll be accelerated promotion for you after this."

"Thank you, sir." She hoped it would all end successfully. Promotion would be the last thing on his mind if she did not track down the submarine commander.

"You deserve it. Now tell me. Is it your opinion that Diryov worked, and is still working, for an intelligence directorate of whose existence we . . . *I* . . . am totally ignorant?"

"The truth, Comrade General?"

"I expect nothing else."

"Yes, sir."

There was a heavy silence as Kurinin stared at the offending information on the computer screen.

"I see," he said at last. "Can you find out to which unit this mysterious directorate happens to be attached, or whether it is fully autonomous?"

She shook her head. "No, sir. This is a defense in depth. I've managed to break this far through the outer levels of the security system they've installed, but now I'm getting a total blackout. The core is heavily protected."

"Show me."

Using the name Diryov, she requested access. She

was not even given an access-denied warning. The screen simply went blank. The same thing happened with all Branko's aliases.

"There must be a personnel list," Kurinin said frustratedly. "Ask for a personnel structure of this unit, chain of command and so on."

Her request was met with another blanked-out screen.

"Try asking for a list of Diryov's colleagues," he said, the exasperation clearly in his voice.

She got the same results.

Kurinin looked on, his expression growing harder by the second as the computer went into its now-familiar routine of shutting down the screen.

"I made an attempt to break through earlier," she said tentatively, "using a high-security bypass. But it's very risky, General."

"In what way?"

"The defense becomes an assault, leading to a total shutdown of the system *making* the inquiry. To ignore the warning is to trigger a destruct command that attacks the intruder at the source. In our case, this would mean the release of the destruct command into all our own files. I've already received one warning."

Kurinin stared at her. "How many warnings do you think are in place?"

"It depends entirely on who set up the defense program, and how idiosyncratic that person happens to be. All sorts of nasty surprises can be lying in wait. I've left a few of those myself in our own files. In this defense system, there may be as many as three and, sometimes, even more warnings, each arming one of those nasty surprises. Or, you may get the sudden death kind. I may already have received the only warning we're likely to get."

"So there exists, in the Motherland, this apparently autonomous intelligence organization which has been operating for years, and about which we have no accessible information?" Kurinin fumed.

"Yes, sir."

"This . . . this is . . ." Kurinin paused, reining in the anger he could now feel boiling within him. "This could mean that our country is being run by people who may not even be Russian—"

"Surely not, General!"

"I said 'could.' But how can we tell differently?" he demanded, the suppressed anger tightening his voice further. "How can we know who they may be? I appear to have been under the illusion that *we* of state security had control over all aspects of the nation. Now I discover there is one more tier, so secret, that even our own systems cannot penetrate its security. This is intolerable! It threatens everything! Try again."

"General!" Lirionova was alarmed. "We could lose our entire information system. Whole decades of information, both national and international—"

"*Try it!*" he barked. "There is too much at stake. The very soul of the Motherland is at risk."

With great reluctance and trepidation, she had one more go at trying to penetrate the secret organization's cover.

The letters came on, large and bright red on a black background.

ФИНАЛ

"That's it, General," she said. "Final. Interestingly, the translation is English. They clearly expect Westerners to try a hack as well. Understandable, after the incidents with the penetration of the American defense computers. They've installed two warnings. We've just had the last one. Any further attempt will mean an immediate attack upon our systems and we'll lose *everything*. *All* our stored information, without exception. There's nothing I'd be able to do to stop it.

"We'd be crippled as an effective intelligence organization, for an unacceptable period of time, perhaps fatally so. All our field agents would be at risk, despite our hardcopy archives. All our operatives in the Motherland and the Republics would be, to all intents and purposes, ineffective. While we were reduced to plowing through mountains of paper, we could be picked off by any other intelligence group, national and international. And as for the Movement itself . . . "

She left any further reference to the Horsemen unsaid. There was little need to add more.

Kurinin was only too aware of her warning, and its implications. He tightened his lips until they hurt. Who was running this secret unit? And did the president himself even know?

Kurinin doubted it. Something that had been in existence so invisibly for so long would not be encumbered by presidents, or even the party secretaries of the old regime. Unless, of course, one of them had set it up himself. If that were the case, which of those past functionaries was responsible?

Reluctantly, he accepted the reality of the situation—for the time being.

"All right," he told her heavily. "Leave it. There will be other ways of finding out. Their best security was that they were unknown. But they're no longer invisible. You did excellently to stumble upon them, Captain. Keep up the good work, and keep after that submariner. Apply any manner of lateral thinking that might take your fancy. You never know what else might turn up on that magic machine of yours."

"Yes, sir. General . . . do you think Diryov could be a double agent? Perhaps working for the West?"

"As the Americans would say, the jury's out on this one . . . for the time being. Until we know more, that has to be our position."

"Yes, Comrade General."

Southeast of Cologne and northeast of Bonn, Cologne/Bonn airport was roughly equidistant between the two cities.

Blish, his overnighter slung from a shoulder, walked through the low barrier of the Arrivals gate and into the single crescent-shaped concourse. The Foreign Exchange kiosk was straight ahead, and he moved over to his left to walk past it. Directly behind was the circular coffee bar with a few tables between it and the rear of the kiosk.

Blish glanced over at the customers, some of whom were at the bar itself, to check whether anyone was interested in him as he walked past. Over to his left, a high and wide window looked out upon the airfield. Some people were sitting by the window but no one there, or at the coffee bar, seemed to be on the lookout for him.

He continued a short distance past some shops and there, on his right, was the open plan café. He entered, bought a mug of coffee, and walked over to an empty quartet of seats and sat down to wait. His position gave him a good view of the raised ramp of the curving approach road to the terminal with its short-stop parking bays, and of the main car park below. There was the constant movement of cars and taxis, and sometimes a small coach, on the terminal approach.

Then he saw it. Beyond the wide, tall window, the snout of a metallic blue Mercedes was almost directly in front of him. The license plate was the correct one, unless there were more E320s of that color, all licensed in Bottrop.

"Mr. Blish?"

He looked to his left. A solidly built man with a blond crew cut and dark glasses, and dressed in jeans, white polo shirt, and a grayish sports jacket, was looking down at him.

"I am Kurt," the blond man continued. "I have your keys. As you can see, the car is right there."

"Yes. Thank you. Please sit—"

"There is no need. I must go." The man who'd introduced himself as Kurt placed the keys on the table. "You know Bonn and Köln?"

"I can find my way around."

"Okay. Good. Enjoy your stay. *Aufwiedersehen*, Mr. Blish."

"*Aufwiedersehen*," Blish said.

He watched as Kurt, moving with the economy of movement of someone who'd undergone a particular type of training, made his exit and merged, it seemed, into the scenery. It had been done so swiftly and unobtrusively that Blish could almost believe the keys had appeared by themselves. Buntline had clearly enlisted the aid of some branch of the German security services. Whatever he was, Charles Buntline certainly had clout.

Blish took his time finishing his coffee, then went out to the car. He put his bag into the boot, removed his jacket and laid that on the backseat, then went round to the front and climbed into the left-hand seat.

Buntline had certainly been correct about the Mercedes. It was sumptuous and smelled of new leather. The day was warm and Blish was glad to see there was air-conditioning.

He hesitated as he was about the start the engine.

What if Buntline was in fact not what he'd professed himself to be? What if the car had been wired not with a tracking device, *but with explosives?*

Christ, Blish thought as he sat there, the ignition key hovering by the slot. He realized he was shaking slightly.

He couldn't sit there all day.

He shut his eyes briefly, slid the key in, thought of Charlie and the children, and turned. The 220 bhp six-cylinder engine burst into smooth, powerful life. And that was it.

With great relief, he drove carefully away as he reacclimated himself to driving on the right-hand side of the road. Out of the airport he took the A59 autobahn, heading south toward Bonn. He took the Sankt Augustin turn off onto the 565, later crossing the Rhine on the Friedrich Ebert bridge into Bonn proper.

The first of the hotels on Buntline's list was on the outskirts of the city. His route on the 565 bypassed the center, eventually taking him toward the hotel, which was sited on high ground, and which gave a perfect view of the town and the surrounding countryside.

At the hotel, he was expected. He registered and made his way up to his room.

He was not aware that a silver Porsche 911 Turbo had trailed some distance in his wake.

It had followed him from the airport.

Having confirmed the location of Blish's hotel, the driver of the Porsche went back into the center of town and parked in the multistory underground car park on Oxfordstrasse. He then went in search of a public phone and made a call.

"Okay," he said when the phone at the other end was picked up. That was all he needed to do. The person at the other end already knew what came next.

He hung up and found himself a bistro close by. He entered, bought an ice-cold lager, then took a seat that gave him a clear view of the street. Five minutes later, a white Volkswagen Corrado VR6 with a dark-haired woman at the wheel pulled up outside.

He left his half-finished lager and went quickly, but without haste, to the car. He got into the passenger seat. The Golf moved swiftly away. Some time later, it pulled into the car park of Blish's hotel.

The man, carrying a rolled magazine, got out and entered the hotel. Next to the reception desk was a small, in-house coffee shop. The man walked toward it with the familiarity of a guest and took a seat that enabled him to observe the mail and key slots behind the desk. He ordered coffee and Black Forest cake.

He began to read the magazine while he waited for his order to be brought to his table.

He was just about to eat his first piece of the cake when the woman who'd driven the Golf entered with a white envelope. She went to the reception desk, spoke briefly to the receptionist, then handed the envelope over. The receptionist put it in a slot. The man noted the position. It would be easy enough to check the room number when he walked past.

The woman who'd brought the envelope went out again without looking in his direction.

This time, he finished both his coffee and his cake before moving. He paid, then casually got up and walked past the reception desk. He glanced without interest at the mail slots.

He now knew Blish's room number.

Chelsea, London.

Charlotte was in the kitchen, trying to persuade Mianna to eat lunch without drawing up strategic battle lines on the tray of her high chair with bits of food off her plate, when the doorbell rang.

"Oh . . ." she paused, realizing just in time, what she'd been about to say.

Amanda, who'd been quietly eating her own lunch, was now looking at her solemnly.

"Shit," Amanda said.

"Amanda!" Charlotte exclaimed in a horrified voice. "I don't want you to use that word! Where did you hear it?"

"You said it," Amanda replied calmly.

"I did?" Charlotte countered weakly, wondering at which unguarded moment Amanda had caught her out. Children were tape recorders. "Tell you what. Let's make a bargain. I won't say it, and you won't say it. How about that?"

"Okay," Amanda said reasonably.

"And besides," Charlotte went on, warming to the theme, "as we're big people, we wouldn't want Mianna to start saying things like that, would we?"

"No we wouldn't," Amanda agreed seriously.

My God, she thought. *I'm already haggling with my child.*

The doorbell rang again.

"Better see who it is, Mummy," Amanda suggested.

"Yes." Charlotte checked that Mianna's harness was secure on the high chair. "If you see Mianna even trying to climb out of the chair while I go to the door—yell."

"All right, Mummy."

"I won't be long."

Charlotte hurried to answer the door. She stared, astonished, when she opened it.

"*Giles!*"

"Hullo," Mackillen greeted. "I happened to be in the area and thought I'd stop by."

"Bit far from the City for lunch. This is very unexpected. You really should have rung first, Giles. It's a rather awkward time. I'm giving the children their lunch . . . or trying to."

"Oh don't mind me," Mackillen said cheerfully, making no attempt to leave.

To her annoyance, Charlotte discovered she was not sufficiently rude to shut the door in his face.

"You'd better come in," she said.

It was either that or stand at the door until he'd finally got the message. Distracted by thoughts of what Mianna might be getting up to, she had no intention of hanging around waiting to find out.

"Thank you," he said, trying hard not to look triumphant and barely succeeding.

"Would you like a cold drink?" she asked, leading the way to the kitchen. "I've got some things in the fridge."

"Nothing alcoholic, thanks. Mineral water will do."

"We're going out immediately after lunch, I'm afraid. Over to Sophia's. You do remember Sophia, don't you?" Charlotte added with a deliberate edge to her question.

Mackillen gave an awkward cough. On one of the very few occasions when he'd been invited over, he'd spent the better part of an evening telling Sophia in a stage whisper what nice tits she had. Caught between feeling flattered and outraged, Sophia had taken refuge by hanging on tightly to her husband's arm. In the end, the husband had thrown propriety to the winds by tossing a glass of Blish's best malt whiskey into Mackillen's face.

"The lawyer's wife. She's not still holding that against me, is she? It was over a year ago."

"Some things are difficult to forget, Giles."

"She was very pleased by the compliment," he said unrepentantly, adding, "At first, she was. That husband of hers probably stopped complimenting her ages ago. It made her feel good to see that a man found her attractive."

"You were talking to her breasts, Giles. All evening." They had by now entered the kitchen. "Amanda,

Mianna . . . this is Giles. An old friend of Daddy's and Mummy's."

He grinned at them. "Hullo."

Mianna pointed a piece of food at him.

"Back on the plate, Mianna," Charlotte commanded.

Mianna did as she was told with remarkable acquiescence.

Amanda surveyed him closely, not fooled by his apparent bonhomie.

"Hullo," she replied coolly. "Are you really my Daddy's friend?"

"Yes, of course," he replied, temporarily taken aback by the directness of the question. "I've known him for many years."

She gave him another serious look before concentrating once more on her lunch.

"Kids," he said lightly. "They don't beat about the bush, do they?"

"I'll get you that drink," Charlotte said, and went to the tall fridge to get a bottle of mineral water.

So easy, he thought.

The kitchen was the best of all places, even though the Mad Major had said the mike could be put anywhere and would still pick up conversations in all parts of the house. People tended to spend a lot of time in kitchens and talked a lot there. All he had to do was find a suitable place to leave the cassette.

He smiled at Charlotte as she handed him a tall glass of chilled water. "Thank you. Just what I need."

"You'll have to excuse me," she said. "I've got to see to the children."

"As I said . . . don't mind me. Do please go on. I'll have the drink and be on my way."

She relented slightly. "I'm sorry, Giles. I don't mean to be rude, but you can see for yourself."

"No need to apologize, Charlotte. I quite understand." He winked at Amanda, who did not wink back.

He took his time with the water, watching as she tended to the children and hating every moment of it. *He* should have been the one who had given her children—*white* children. But it was Blish who had been in there, inside of her, doing the things *he* wanted to, and it was Blish's brats she was looking after.

Mackillen seethed quietly. If he hadn't come to do the Mad Major's bidding, he would have taken rather more from Charlotte than just a glass of water. Her willing participation would not have been a matter for consideration.

But a very real fear of the crazy Russian had put an effective brake upon any lustful ideas Mackillen entertained about Charlotte. He kept smiling every time Amanda looked at him and casually looked about the kitchen, seeking out a likely place to hide the cassette.

Then he saw the perfect location. It was so obvious, he was surprised he hadn't noticed it before.

He finished his drink, then walked over to put the empty glass down near the fridge. There was a narrow slot between the right side of the fridge and a corner wall, with just enough room to put the cassette through. Once in place, it would not be detected for a very long time.

Charlotte was preoccupied with the children and was taking no notice of him. Quickly, he took the cassette out of his pocket and, keeping it hidden in his palm, slid his hand through the slot. The powerful magnet clamped the cassette to the side of the fridge.

Mackillen withdrew his hand, pleased with himself.

"I'd better be getting back," he said to her. "Thanks for the drink."

"What?" she said absently. "Oh. Yes. All right." She did not look round at him, but concentrated on wiping scraps of food from Mianna's hair. "A quick wash for you, young lady, before we go to Sophia's. Say good-bye to Giles."

"'Bye," Mianna piped.

"Good-bye," Amanda said at her most solemn.

"'Bye, children."

"Giles," Charlotte said, "would you mind seeing yourself out? I'm a bit tied up with this one . . . "

He gave her a smile he did not mean. "Of course. I'll call you about the dinner."

"Do that."

He went out feeling no regrets whatsoever. Blish would soon be receiving the attentions of the Mad Major. He wanted to shout his glee.

Perhaps Blish would be killed. Served him right for taking Charlotte. Who said there wasn't any justice?

Mackillen was completely unaware that Amanda had seen what he'd done.

In the car on the way to Sophia's, Amanda said, "Mummy, can I have the toy the man left?"

"What toy?"

"The one he left on the fridge."

Charlotte glanced in the rearview mirror. Both the children were safely strapped into their car seats. What was Amanda talking about? Mianna appeared to be dozing.

"Are you sure he left something on the fridge?"

"Yes, Mummy. I saw him. It was a little toy."

"I see. I'll have a look when we get back."

"Okay. Mummy?"

"Yes."

"Is he really, really a friend of Daddy's?"

"Yes. Why do you ask?"

"He's not very nice."

Charlotte found herself temporarily at a loss for words. "Out of the mouths of babes," she said at last.

"I'm not a baby," Amanda said haughtily.

"No, darling. You're not."

"Mianna's a baby."

Charlotte smiled to herself, and said nothing.

In his hotel room in Bonn, Blish checked his watch and decided Charlotte would be at Sophia's by now. They'd arranged that he'd call her there.

He was about to pick up the phone when he stopped himself. As with the Mercedes, Buntline had arranged this hotel, and by his own admission, the car was tagged. He could just as easily have arranged to have the phone bugged.

"Branko's made me paranoid," he muttered.

But he decided to play safe and left the room to make the call from one of the hotel booths downstairs. The receptionist booked him one of the four international cubicles near the desk and he entered to make the call to Sophia's house.

"Hullo, Sophia," he said when she'd answered.

"The traveling man," she said warmly. "I suppose

you want to speak to Charlie is your darling." Sophia tended to say things like that. "If you two ever break up, you know where I am."

"Behave, Sophia," Charlotte's voice said. "Put my man down." Sophia gave an exaggerated sigh and then Charlotte was speaking. "Hi, darling. Good trip?"

"Yes." What else could he say? "And how's your day?"

She understood what he meant. "Interesting."

"Oh?"

"Giles came round."

"*Giles?* What the devil . . . What did he want this time?"

"He just happened to be in the area and thought he'd stop by." She sounded as skeptical as Blish felt.

"Where you're concerned, Giles never 'just happens' to be doing anything."

"Amanda thinks she saw him put something on the fridge?"

"He what?"

"He put something on the fridge," Charlotte repeated. "At least, that's what Amanda says. She thinks it's some sort of toy."

Blish felt a strange prickling all along his skin. *I'm really getting paranoid*, he thought.

It could be nothing. Amanda might have imagined it all. On the other hand, why would Mackillen do something like that? To what purpose?

"You'll have to check," he told her. There was no other choice.

But what if it is some kind of bomb? He couldn't send Charlotte . . .

Get a grip on yourself, Blish. Giles Mackillen with a small bomb? That was really pushing it.

"You'll have to check," he repeated.

"Yes. It could be nothing. She might have imagined it."

"Possibly."

"I'll go. Give me about an hour, then call me at home."

"All right. Charlie?"

"Yes."

"When I call, remember what we discussed. Make no conversation. I'll ask you questions. Just answer yes or no."

"Okay."

"If there is something there, *don't touch it.*"

"Don't worry. I certainly won't."

"And Charlie . . . "

"Yes."

"Love you."

"I know."

They hung up together.

As he left the booth, the receptionist said, "Shall I put that on your bill, sir?"

He nodded. "Yes, please."

He went back up to his room, oblivious of the fact that the Porsche driver had kept him under observation throughout.

"Who is it?" he called in response to the knock on the door.

"Open up, Jordan."

Branko.

He went to the door and opened it, and stared at the gray-haired man in the smart linen suit.

"Where did you—" he began.

Branko put a finger to his lips. "Get your wallet and your jacket," he said in a low voice. "Your room could be all ears."

"Where are we going?" Blish whispered urgently.

"Just get your things!" Branko urged with a touch of impatience. He glanced quickly up and down the hotel corridor. "We can't stand out here—"

"But I've got to ring Charlie—"

"Call her from somewhere else. Hurry!"

Blish got his things, hurried out, and shut the door.

"Forget the lifts," Branko said, making for the stairs. "And keep the hotel key. We don't want the receptionist—and whoever else may be watching—to know you've gone out."

"You've gone gray now?" Blish observed as they hurried down from the sixth floor.

Branko grinned. "My distinguished look."

"Where did you spring from? And how did you know I was here?"

Branko gave another quick grin. "You're the easiest person in the world to follow. I've been with you since the airport."

"I'm not a bloody spy, you know. I don't spend my days dodging people tailing me."

Branko merely smiled. "It wouldn't hurt to learn. When we get down, you go first and take one of the taxis waiting in the rank. There's usually at least four there. Ask the driver to take you to the Friedensplatz Parkhaus. Got that?"

"Friedensplatz. Yes. What about you?"

"I'll be in another taxi. When you get to the car park, just wait by the entrance. I won't be long. I'll find you."

"I've got to call Charlie in an hour."

"Plenty of time."

Getting away from the hotel had been no problem. No one had appeared to take any particular interest.

The taxi stopped just before the entrance to the car park. Blish paid the driver and got out. He'd not seen Branko get into a second taxi and had no idea where the Russian had got to.

He kept thinking about what Buntline had said about Branko's activities. Buntline had told him not to trust Branko. But was Buntlinc himself any more trustworthy?

A powerful sound made him look round. A silver Porsche 911 Turbo with the BN index letters of the Bonn license plate was cruising toward him. Fat-wheeled, with a no-nonsense demeanor that practically shouted *move over*, it stopped next to him.

Branko's head popped out. "Get in!"

Blish stared at the car, then climbed into the low cabin that smelled richly of its black leather.

"My God, Branko!" he said as he clipped on his seat belt. "You don't do things by half, do you? A *Porsche 911?* Very low-key."

"Turbo," Branko said unrepentantly. "Don't forget the Turbo. Didn't you see that fantastic big spoiler on the tail?" He moved out into the traffic. "It all adds up to 408 bhp of hot metal. If you've got it, flaunt it. And I've got the money. Besides, there's a practical reason."

"Oh?" Blish appeared unconvinced, as what sounded like a squadron of aircraft preparing for takeoff grumbled deeply behind him. "And what happened to all those sneers about City types and their Porsches?"

"I still sneer at them," Branko said without a shred of remorse. "This is different. Most of them get their cars to impress, mainly women. 'Look at me . . . I'm successful,' they're shouting. They have no idea of the ethos of this machine. I *love* this car," he went on enthusiastically. "Automobile engineering at its peak. One of the things I love about the West. I've got it because it pleases *me*. I'm not interested in impressing others. Hear that sound! Like supercharged World War II fighters. There is nothing like it. Nothing at all. Glorious."

"I can hear. So what's the practical reason?"

"We may get chased," Branko said hopefully. "Four-wheel-drive *and* twin turbos. Top speed 295 kilometers an hour, give or take a kilometer or two, or 181 miles an hour, if you prefer. The brakes are like thrust reversers. It's just as good if it rains. We're ready for anybody."

"I'm not hoping for rain, and I'm not here for a high-speed chase, Branko."

"It could happen, whether you want it or not."

"I want not," Blish said, praying there wouldn't be any. "Where are we going?"

"Out for a drive, away from prying eyes and eavesdropping ears. Now tell me what has been happening since we last talked, beginning with why you changed your accommodation."

Blish hesitated, remembering what Buntline had told him. On the other hand, Buntline had also said to keep Branko's trust. The only way to do that with someone with such finely tuned instincts, Blish decided, was to keep back as little as was prudently possible.

"I had a visit from someone who made the changes."

"Buntline."

Blish looked sharply at his companion. "You *know* Buntline?"

"But of course. After all, we are in the same trade. He's one of yours."

"Thank God for that," Blish said with relief. "I wasn't too certain. I wondered whether he might be—you know—working for both sides."

"There are a few people like that," Branko remarked smoothly, "on your side of the fence, and on mine. I'm assuming they've put a tracking device on your car, as well as bugging it for sound. I'm almost certain your room and the telephone have been given the treatment as well."

"So you decided to come and get me."

"It makes sense, doesn't it? I *know* this car is clean. Whoever's watching the hotel can sit and stare at your Mercedes."

"They're after you, Branko."

"Everyone's after me. I'm Mr. Popularity. Anything else? Any other unusual occurrence?"

"Charlie had a strange visitor today. Giles Mackillen."

"I know he has this fixation about her, but what was strange about the visit?"

Blish sensed an extra alertness in Branko at the mention of Mackillen.

"According to Charlie," he continued, "my daughter Amanda saw Giles put something on the fridge. She thought it was a toy."

"What do you mean 'put something on the fridge'? Why a toy?"

Branko had spoken so quietly, his voice was almost overwhelmed by the leashed growl of the Porsche's engine. They were still in town, and cruising slowly with the traffic.

"You know those magnetic things you put on fridges . . ." Blish said. " . . . segments of plastic fruit, jokey signs . . . the stuff you can see in any group of students' shared digs . . . "

"I don't—"

"I'm not talking about you, Branko. But Charlie doesn't either. She's always hated the practice. So we've got one of the most pristine fridge surfaces you're ever likely to see, which is probably why, thank God, Amanda noticed. Giles apparently stuck something to the side of the fridge. There's a slot between it and a wall, and the space is just big enough to enable you to hide something in there."

"Giles," Branko murmured. "Of course. Does Charlie know what it looks like?"

"She didn't see at the time and is checking on it even as we speak. That's what I've got to ring her about. I'm terrified it might be a bomb. Though God knows where Giles would be able to get something as high-tech as that—"

"Not a bomb. The Mad Major gave it to him."

"What do you mean?"

"My major doesn't know for sure whether you and I have made contact," Branko was saying, speaking as if to himself. "But, wanting to cover all bets, he needed to listen in on your private conversations, even pick up snatches from your phone—which, by the way, could well be bugged by your own side. So how to do it? How to get one of his little eavesdroppers into your house? Enter Giles, who would sell anyone down the river, stage right."

"You're sure it's not a bomb?"

"That madman needs you alive. He wants to know where I am. If he kills you and you might have had the information, what good is that to him? He'll only kill you if he thinks you're in the way. Which, incidentally, you already are."

"Thanks for that cheering thought, Branko."

"Just being pragmatic."

"You and Buntline should set up shop together."

Branko smiled, but made no comment as he peeled off from the traffic to head south for the A656 autobahn.

"We'll find you a phone at an autobahn service station," he said. "You can call home from there. Unless Buntline has managed to get the Germans to bug every phone on every autobahn—which puts that idea well into the realms of the impossible—it will be a clean call. Just have plenty of change handy. Ask her if that thing looks like a thirty-five-millimeter film cassette."

"How would you know?"

"It's one of our favorite listening devices. We've got others, naturally; but this one is popular simply because everybody *expects* to see a roll of film about the house. It's also magnetic, and will easily stick to something like a fridge."

The road fed them onto the autobahn and the squadron behind Blish's left ear began their takeoff run as Branko gave the Porsche its head. The growl rose to a snarl. The squadron was launching into the air. The Porsche began to reel in the road as if on an endless takeoff, on a runway without limit. The horizon began to approach with telephoto rapidity. Other cars appeared to smear past as the turbocharged wheeled missile overtook them. The speed increased relentlessly, pinning Blish against the back of his seat.

"*Oooh mmyy Gaawwwdd!*" he exclaimed. "Branko! I've got a wife and kids! I want to see them again!"

"We're doing 250 kays," Branko told him cheerfully. "Going up to 260."

"I'm in a guided missile with a Russian lunatic," Blish said to himself. "For my sins." He shut his eyes.

Then a counterpressure was forcing him against his seat belt. Branko had hit the brakes. Blish opened his eyes, fully expecting to see an accident approaching at unmanageable speed.

But there was no traffic in front of them. They had slowed, remarkably, to a relatively crawling pace. He glanced behind. The following traffic was still a long way off, and didn't seem to be catching up. Then Blish realized they were still doing about 160 kilometers an hour and slowing.

"What was that for?" he asked.

"Just showing you how good the brakes are. We were at nearly 270 when I hit them. The car has perfect control."

"I had my eyes closed at the time," Blish said.

"Anyway, there's a stretch coming up that has a speed limit."

"Be thankful for small mercies."

Branko smiled.

At the hotel, the man with the blond crew cut went up to the receptionist.

"Herr Blish, please," he said to her in German.

She gave him her receptionist's smile, glanced behind, and saw that the key was not by its slot.

"He's in the hotel," she said. "Shall I try his room?"

"No need. I'll wait. I'll have a coffee. Thank you."

"Thank you, sir."

The man who was to captain the submarine lay on his cramped bunk, eyes wide open. Even though it had been some time since the general had been there, he still found it difficult to accept the deadly and monumental duplicity of the game that would be played upon the outside world, and upon the new Russia and its neighboring federation of states. The general was playing for very high stakes indeed.

The beauty of it was, no one except those involved with the project—and perhaps even a very few of those—knew of it.

The captain had no illusions. He fully realized that now he had actually seen the general and had refused to join the conspiracy, it was quite likely that there were plans to ensure he never spoke of it to anyone. Perhaps there had always been such an arrangement. Because he had not trusted the plotters from the very beginning—even before his shock discovery of the general's involvement—he had demanded, and received, half payment before accepting the mission.

Some of that money had been used to give his wife and family safe passage out of Russia, to a destination that was not on the exit documents. The ostensible holiday would become a permanent home somewhere else. More of the money had also been utilized in the purchase of their new home, where they would await his eventual arrival.

The captain knew that if he did not survive, his family would not be destitute, even if all they would get was the amount that had already been paid. But he'd taken precautions. He'd secreted some weaponry for use during the escape. If they tried to silence him here in the cavern, or on the way out, it would cost them very dearly.

The work on the submarine had now become less frantic. Final checks were being done, but, to all intents and purposes, the boat was mission-ready. The launch tubes were complete and the weapons loaded.

The nightmare was soon to begin.

Autobahnkreuz Meckenheim.

Blish saw the sign as Branko prepared to feed the Porsche into the filter for the A61 autobahn. Their route would then be taking them to the right in the direction of Bornheim, but they would not be going that far.

"There's a service station a few kays further up," Branko said. "You can make your call to Charlotte from there."

Eight kilometers later, they pulled off the autobahn and into the parking area of Peppenhoven service station near Rheinbach.

As he stopped the car, Branko said, "If she finds it, tell her she must *not* touch it."

"I've already warned her about that."

"Good. We might make a field man out of you yet."

"I doubt it."

Branko gave one of his smiles. "The pattern is so consistent."

"What pattern?"

"People who always say they'd never contemplate–under normal circumstances, of course—behaving in a manner they would find reprehensible, tend to be even more ruthless than a professional when the pressure is on. You're no different. Remember that. I think you should now make your call, or you'll be late."

As Blish began to climb out, Branko added, "It might be a good idea to get her to take the children and leave, until this is all over."

"Right away?"

"Immediately. Today. If it is a listening device—and I'm very sure it is—it won't take the Mad Major long to realize that one of the reasons he's not getting valuable information may be because the unit has been spotted. He'll then figure that perhaps someone has told you what it is. Who would that person be? Me. Guess what will happen next."

"I'm on my way," Blish said.

They had parked close to the building complex that housed the restaurant and other general services. Blish hurried up the short flight of steps. After a quick search, he found the telephones near the entrance and noted with relief that he could make an international call.

Charlotte answered at the first ring.

"Remember what I said," he prompted immediately.

"Oh yes."

Brilliant. She was spot on.

"Is it there?" he continued.

"Yes. Mm-hm."

He felt a chill descend upon him. *Giles Mackillen, ordered by the crazy Russian major, has actually bugged my house.* So much for friendship, even allowing for someone like Mackillen. Branko was certainly right about him. Mackillen would sell anyone.

"Is it a film cassette?" He was almost afraid of asking the question.

"Mm-hm. Yes."

Though the fact that he'd described the bugging device accurately brought some surprise into her voice, she was trying to make her replies sound as unstilted as possible.

"You're doing fine," he encouraged.

"Thanks."

"You haven't touched it."

"Nope."

"Good." He took a deep breath. "Are the kids with you?"

"No."

"Here comes the hard part." He paused. "Lothar."

There was a silence at the other end as she took in the full implications.

"Okay," she said lightly for the benefit of the eavesdropping cassette.

"I love you."

"Oh I know that." Pause. "Me too." Pause. "See you." She'd made it sound as if she'd been breaking in and out of a conversation.

They hung up together.

Please God, Blish thought as he returned to the car. *Keep them safe.*

Branko was standing near the Porsche, looking about him. Blish would not have been surprised if the Russian had started sniffing like a gun dog. There was a definable air of expectation about him.

Passersby, and the occupants of cars arriving and departing, gave the car admiring glances; but no one seemed to have an especial interest in its presence.

"Your call went off okay?" Branko asked as Blish joined him.

Blish nodded.

"And?"

"It's the cassette."

"The Mad Major's closing in," Branko said gravely. "Did you tell Charlotte to get out?"

"Yes."

"Well that's something. We're still ahead."

"I should be with them."

"You can't be for the moment, so accept the situation and concentrate on other things."

"I'm not like you, Branko."

"You may not be like me, but before this is over you may have to come close, to survive. Is the bolt-hole a safe one?"

"Very," Blish replied, his mind full of anxiety. "For the moment, anyway. Charlie thought it up. I never even knew it existed."

"Keep it to yourself. Don't tell me."

"I wasn't about to."

Branko's smile seemed to have an edge of steel in it. "You're learning fast."

"Now what?" Blish demanded.

"Now I take you back by a roundabout route, to flush out whoever might have decided to follow us, while I tell you about a few things I've found out. Get in."

The man with the blond crew cut had waited through two cups of coffee. An instinct made him go up to the receptionist once more. She remembered him and switched on the smile, more genuinely friendly this time.

"Perhaps you should try his room," he suggested.

"I'll do that," she said, and turned to her male colleague, who was at the switchboard. "Herr Blish's room, please—612."

The man at the switchboard tried several times, then shook his head. "There is no reply."

"He must either be in one of the bars, or the restaurants," she said to the crew cut, "or perhaps in the gymnasium. It is very popular with our guests. We have excellent equipment up there. I am sorry if you have missed your appointment. Shall I page him?"

"No, no." Crew cut glanced at his watch. "I think I am very early. I'll come back. Thank you."

He went out to a car at the far end of the hotel car park. He got in, took a small personal radio out of a pocket, and pressed a single digit.

"The Mercedes is still here," he said into it, "so he must be around somewhere. But I feel uneasy—"

"Mr. Buntline says have you tried the taxis?" the voice at the other end asked.

"Taxis? Why should I want to . . ." Crew cut paused, realization dawning. "Hold on. I'll call you." He switched off and got out of the car again.

He walked quickly to the cab rank and up to the first taxi.

"Did you or any of your friends take anyone into town recently?" he asked.

The driver looked him over and wasn't impressed. "Who wants to know?"

"Let's put it this way," Crew cut began in a hard voice. "If you try to be smart with me, you could have big trouble next time you want to renew your license."

The driver was still not impressed. His mouth turned down. "Government bureaucrats. A little power and you think you're God Almighty." He jerked a thumb backward. "Try Erwin Holbach. Three cars down. He took someone. Perhaps it was the person you are looking for."

"Thank *you*," Crew cut said sarcastically.

"Always glad to help," the driver said, watching as the blond man went over to the taxi he'd indicated. He looked as if he wanted to spit.

Crew cut was back in his car talking urgently into his radio. "He took a taxi into town. Friedensplatz."

"The Parkhaus near the Markt?" Buntline, speaking fluent German, had joined the conversation.

"Yes, sir."

"Anyone with him?"

"No, Mr. Buntline. He was alone."

"Did anyone else take a taxi into town about the same time?"

"Three other taxis took guests into town. A Japanese businessman, a French couple, and an American."

"What was the American like?"

"Beefy, about sixty. That's how the driver described him."

"And the French couple?" Buntline was inclined to dismiss the American as a possibility.

"Stylish. They looked as if they had real money, not just pretending, according to the driver of the taxi that took them. They were all over each other. Very sexy woman. He didn't think she was his wife. Taxi drivers are like that. He also thinks they were probably celebrating some sort of personal anniversary. He heard them talking in French. Although he doesn't really know the language, he recognized it easily enough."

"What would we do without gossipy cab drivers. Thank you." Buntline seemed unperturbed. "We'll simply have to wait for our man to return."

"He could be in danger."

"I doubt it, for now. Though that could well follow later," Buntline finished ominously. "Out."

Crew cut stared at his now-silent radio and gave a world-weary sigh.

They had been retracing their route along the A61. Branko spent most of the time in the fast lane, though at a relatively moderate speed. Even so, they were passing all traffic.

The Meckenheim junction came up once more, and this time Branko turned right, onto the short stretch of what remained of the A565. The autobahn ended, leading into the narrower national route that continued south, the 257 to Altenahr. There were bends in the road, some quite tight. Branko threw the Porsche into them with abandon. The car remained glued to the road.

Blish said, "There's no one chasing us, Branko."

"You're sure of that?"

"What do you mean—" Blish stared at him. "You're joking, of course."

"Sorry."

Blish glanced sharply back. "I don't see anyone."

"He's there."

"But how? I thought you said—"

"I said it might happen. Remember?"

"You *expected* this?"

"I expect many things. That way I don't get surprised." Branko kept glancing in the mirrors. "I know who did it. Only one person knows we're in this car."

"Who?"

"My contact. Cindy-Lou."

Blish looked at him, not sure whether to laugh or cry. "You work with a spy called *Cindy-Lou?*"

"Not her real name, of course. She's Russian, too, but an artist with languages and accents. She can be a Boston patrician, a tough New Yorker, a California babe, or a Southern belle. She's very, very good. She seems to like being Cindy-Lou. She can be a sexy Frenchwoman, too."

"Are any of you people stable?"

"Mostly." Branko was looking in the mirrors and slowing down.

"Why are you slowing down? I thought you wanted to get away."

"I want him to catch up."

"*What?*"

But Branko was concentrating on other matters. "Ah!" he said. "Here he comes. He's in a Mercedes 500SL and is driving too fast for these bends. He's going to lose it."

So saying, Branko sent the Porsche rocketing downhill. The awesome power made Blish fear that it was not only the Mercedes driver who was about to lose control. But the silver car, despite his terrors, clung formidably to the bends where another would long ago have catapulted itself into the scenery.

"Hah!" Branko shouted. "Look at him! He is weaving all over the place, trying to keep up."

Blish stared at the landscape rushing by at an insane speed, and wondered which fate was worse: being flattened by the lateral g-forces acting on the car, or being turned into a nervous wreck by Branko's driving.

What happened next would remain etched upon his mind for a long time. He saw it all with the unreal clarity that tends to occur during moments of extreme stress, when fragments of time seem to stretch forever.

They had come round a particularly tight bend and Branko appeared to slow down as another, shallower bend appeared. Blish thought it odd that Branko should do this instead of accelerating. He glanced behind and saw that the Mercedes, a dark-colored nemesis that gleamed malevolently, had gained considerably. Its driver had clearly believed he was catching up and, in his eagerness, had thrown caution to the winds.

Belatedly, Blish realized that it was precisely what Branko had been aiming for.

The authorities had sensibly put a panic exit on the bend, its entrance at the apex identified by intermittently positioned short, black-and-white and orange-and-black collapsible poles.

Blish was certain they were headed for the poles, despite the relative shallowness of the bend, for their speed was still frighteningly high. But the Porsche leeched itself past without drama. The squadron behind Blish's head seemed to be in the middle of an air battle as Branko worked through the gears.

The Mercedes was not so lucky. Already going far too fast for that particular section of the road and the driver's own ability, it went straight through the panic exit. Unfortunately, the road surface had abruptly changed from tarmac to loose chippings, which would probably have been effective in slowing it down under different circumstances. Instead, the laws of physics conspired to turn it into an instrument of destruction.

The rear wheels of the car spun furiously, raising a high column of dust. Then it began to swing wildly as its driver overcorrected. It slammed into the low barriers that bordered the slip road for a short distance, before flinging itself into the air and rolling over completely. It slammed back to earth with such force that its solidly constructed roof caved in partially with the fierceness of the impact. Miraculously, the passenger cabin was left relatively intact. The bouncing car heaved itself over one of the barriers and down a steep, but short incline, and into a small plantation of saplings. As it continued rolling, it decapitated one of the saplings, whose slender trunk had now become a spear.

The point of the sapling went through a window and impaled the driver, pinning him to his seat. He would die before anyone got to him.

Blish did not witness the ending sequences of the crash, for they were well away from the immediate area by the time the Mercedes had slammed down the steep bank.

Then he realized he'd been holding his breath.

The Porsche was cruising toward Altenahr.

"That was a bad accident back there," Branko said calmly.

Blish did not speak for some moments. "You . . . you led him into it," he said at last.

"What did you expect? Would you have preferred it if he had done it to us?"

"Perhaps he wouldn't have. They'd want to talk to you first."

"You wouldn't want to experience one of the Mad Major's interrogations, believe me. You'd pray for an accident. Well-done, Cindy-Lou," Branko added with satisfaction.

Blish looked at him. "*Well-done?* I thought you said—"

"I said I knew who had set them or him on my tail. I didn't say I was unhappy about it." Branko grinned. "We had to flush them out. See who was in Bonn. There'll almost certainly be more of them."

"Your contact has contact with your enemies?"

"There are many sides to Cindy-Lou."

"Do you trust her?"

"Of course not." Branko sounded as if the question barely merited a reply. "But we're useful to each other. Her people want the Mad Major stopped. I'll do that. They also need to know where the nuclear material's gone. That could be more difficult, but I'm working on it. I believe I may have something. As for

Cindy-Lou, she's supplied me with information that will be of great use to your own people."

"Isn't she playing a very dangerous game?"

"We're all playing a very dangerous game. You too."

"*Me?*"

"You're the lamb in all this. And you could get hurt."

"Well thank you, Branko!"

"You could also gain plenty."

"Will I survive long enough to enjoy my gains?" Blish asked sharply.

"We shall see. There's another aspect to my relationship with Cindy-Lou," Branko continued. "She is not very happy with the way things may turn out back home. I'll explain why later. Also . . ." Branko smiled. "I fuck well."

"Sex had to be in it somewhere."

"Sex is *always* in it," Branko emphasized, "as you ought to know. People who should know better continue to underestimate its power. It can work for you, or against you. What do you think is killing Mackillen? Sexual jealousy. He is prepared to ruin you because of it.

"Sex can bring down kings and kingdoms, ministers, presidents, and governments. Those who know how to use it have always got immense power. The beauty of it is, even someone on the lowest rung of society can bring down the most powerful. Just thinking about that gives me a charge."

"So you and—Cindy-Lou or whatever her real name is—are going to set up home together?"

Branko glanced across at Blish. "I didn't say that." He paused. "Then again . . . "

"There's all that money too, that you've got."

Branko said nothing for a while. They turned left off

the 257 and went slowly through Altenahr. Their new route was the 267, which would take them through the small vineyard towns and villages along the left bank of the Ahr.

"There is the money," Branko said.

They continued along the 267, through Ahrweiler and Bad Neuenahr, until the road once more became a motorway. It curved round to the right and fed itself into the A61 autobahn. They continued south. Branko drove the Porsche fast until, some kilometers later, he again turned off the autobahn and onto a narrow country road. They eventually came to a junction and Blish saw a sign leading to somewhere called Maria Laach.

The Laacher See was a deep natural lake about three kilometers across. What made it special was that it was the filled crater of an extinct volcano.

Branko turned right onto the new road, which bordered some poppy fields, toward Maria Laach. He obeyed the low speed limit, and less than ten minutes later, pulled into a car park by the lake. A surprising number of cars was parked there.

"This seems a popular place," Blish said as they got out. He looked about him, wondering if any of the cars present should cause them worry.

Branko noted his expression. "We're safe here. I chose this place deliberately. No possible eavesdropping. We're just another pair of tourists who've come to look at the lake."

"I keep thinking about whoever was in that Mercedes."

"Stop thinking about them or him. If it had been the

other way round, I can assure you they'd not be thinking about you. Let's walk away from the crowd." Branko pointed to a mound near the water's edge. "We can sit there and keep an eye on the car. And no one can sneak up on us."

They began walking toward the lake.

Across the road from the car park, Blish saw two buildings that struck him as incongruous. One was a monastery, the other a big low-lying hotel.

"This has the air of a spa town," he said to Branko as they walked. "I suppose the lake helps the impression."

"You're looking at the crater of a volcano."

Blish was surprised, but studying the landscape more closely now that he knew, it was easy to see. "Dormant? Or extinct?"

"I've always considered those terms irrelevant. Extinct volcanoes have been known to erupt. But I didn't bring you here to give you a geology lesson. I chose this place, however, to illustrate a point, among other things."

They had reached the mound and sat down.

"Look at all those people. They've come to admire the waters of the volcano—swim in it, sail on it. If it suddenly erupted, none of us would survive. But they're already sitting on a volcano, although they don't realize it. Even if at the moment it's some distance away from them, they're still very vulnerable to the aftermath of its explosion."

"You're talking about the Horsemen."

"Not just the Horsemen," Branko said. "I'm including the stolen nuclear material, because it is all part of it. Somewhere right now, unknown to these oblivious people, a submarine has been prepared to launch two nuclear weapons. They're small weapons, but given what they are, size hardly matters."

Branko paused, getting ready to drop his bombshell.

"I know who the Horsemen are," he said quietly.

"*You know them?*"

Branko nodded slowly.

"No wonder they're after you!" Blish said in a hushed voice.

"I told you I was popular."

"When did you find out?"

Branko gave a dry little laugh. "Cindy-Lou. They never realized that I didn't know their identities, but that someone close to them did."

"Cindy-Lou."

"The very same. She knows one of them personally. So you see, she can never go back. It's too late for her as well."

"She is, of course, the sleeper you mentioned before. The contact from Brussels."

Again, Branko nodded.

"I did wonder," Blish said. "But the name Cindy-Lou threw me when you first mentioned it."

"Because it sounds such a crazy name for a spy? It's perfect for that very reason. Now for the big prize," Branko continued. "The Horsemen are: Feliks Alexandrovitch Kurinin, general, formerly KGB, but really still in his old job—Russian. Valeri Ivanovitch Tikov, general, air force, serving with the *Russian* forces, though he's Ukrainian. Viktor Viktorovitch Selenko, formerly a naval commodore, now admiral—Russian. Igor Leonidovitch Garadze, general, army, and Georgian, but with a very strong Russian ancestry.

These are the four. But, there's a new factor. One of them—I have no idea which—has got greedy. He wants complete control of the new union. *He* is the one getting ready to launch those missiles."

The sense of shock was clearly in Blish's eyes. "Are you absolutely certain of this, Branko? If I go to Buntline with such information, the entire world is going to go on nuclear alert. Do you realize what we could be responsible for?"

"That's why I think we should do this more . . . circumspectly."

"What do you mean?"

"Buntline, you, and I should meet, at a place of my choosing. This has to be the absolute limit. No more people, or I vanish and leave your lot to sort out the mess *after* the event. Arrange for us to meet and I will hand over documents and tapes that will give him all he needs. I've even got a video of one of their meetings."

"My God. How . . . how were you, or . . . er Cindy-Lou, able to get hold of all this?"

"At great risk. That is all I can, or will tell you—or Buntline." Branko took another look at the people by the lake. "Look at them. If only they knew. Not so long ago, we drew up a scenario, based upon what has taken place since the so-called ending of the Cold War. The results chilled the blood of many of those present. It certainly chilled mine.

"They showed that given the current rise of petty nationalism, resurgent fascism, racist tendencies, and, most ominous of all, the apparent unwillingness or inability of the Western European countries to work for a common future together, war between those states one day has become a likely possibility. We couldn't believe you could be so stupid."

"I don't either. We'll never be that stupid. Your people must have distorted the way you looked at the trends—"

"Believe that if it gives you comfort. Look at what has happened to our own republics, and as for Yugoslavia—the Western nations have been so incredibly stupid, there is only one outcome. Eventually you will be forced to arm the Moslems, and, of course, there are plenty of those back home who will arm the Serbs. And then, we shall be back to a new Cold War.

"The West managed to throw away its valuable chances, and all because you were unable to keep out of the trap of nationalistic self-interest. Divided, you'll fall. One of the prime strategies of the Horsemen is the eventual disintegration of the Western European Union and, most important of all, the death of NATO. As for the UN, it is now such a laughingstock, it is practically irrelevant. The sheer incompetence and the screwups are mind-boggling."

Branko shrugged. "But don't take my word for it, if that makes you feel any better. Stupidity, after all, is part and parcel of the human condition. People are avoiding a thought that they already know is true: that the old Soviet Union, massively flawed as it was, actually performed a valuable task. It made people behave. It kept your Western nations *united*. It also kept all those nationalistic monsters in their cages. Now, they're all springing from their kennels like the dogs of plague that they are. Every idiot wants to flex his muscles.

"Part of me actually sympathizes with the Horsemen's wish to create a new Union. Unfortunately, the world has moved on—or gone into retrograde, which I believe is closer to the truth of the matter. If you're not all very careful, you'll find yourselves back in the nineteenth century. The trouble is, the gunboat now has nuclear weapons, and there are a lot of people out there with gunboats these days. Just look at what a bunch of lunatics or, more pertinently in this case, a wildly ambitious general, can do with one small submarine and two small weapons. If those things are fired—"

"Which, according to you," Blish interrupted, feeling poleaxed by Branko's vehemence, "could be launched at any time."

"It's a risk we must take. If we let panicky politicians get in on the act before these people are neutralized, we could have a nuclear war before you could yell bomb. This has to be done clandestinely. Buntline has his own channels to Moscow. He can use them. The Horsemen's cover will be blown, of course, and there'll be strenuous denials. But they'll want the same thing: to stop, or contain whatever is about to happen."

"I'll talk to Buntline," Blish said. "Get me back to Bonn."

Branko dropped Blish off in the Ückesdorf dis-trict of Bonn, where he picked up a taxi for the short ride back to his hotel. As he got out of the cab, he saw the blond crew cut heading toward him.

"We were very worried about you, Mr. Blish," the man said admonishingly in English. "Why did you leave the hotel?"

Blish stared at him. "I can't leave the hotel when I feel like it?"

The man looked confused. "Of course you can. I—"

"That's a relief. Tell Charles Buntline I need to talk to him very, very urgently. Now if it's all right with you, I'm going up to my room. He can reach me there."

"Yes. Yes, Mr. Blish. I . . . I will tell him . . . I—"

"Thank you," Blish said. He was about to continue on his way when he paused. "Tell me . . . are you here to help me? Or to follow me?"

"To help if you need me, Mr. Blish."

"Oh good. I just wanted to get that straight."

The phone rang just as he entered his room.

He picked it up. "That was quick."

"Is it important?" Buntline began immediately.

"It's sticky time," Blish told him. "Better come here. I'm sure you can find your way."

Blish hung up before Buntline could say anything more.

Half an hour later, a knock on the door made him call, "Who is it?"

"I'm here, Jordan," came Buntline's voice.

"That was quick too," Blish said as he opened the door. Crew cut was with Buntline. "I need to speak to you alone," he went on as they both entered.

"Kurt's here to remove a few things," Buntline said mildly, "then he'll wait downstairs."

Blish watched interestedly as the man named Kurt moved swiftly about the room, picking up small items from unlikely places.

"I suspected correctly, after all," Blish commented drily. "I'm certain I can make a formal complaint about this."

"You can—"

"But it won't do any good."

"Under the circumstances . . . no."

"Don't forget the phone," Blish said to Kurt. "I'm sure you've bugged that as well."

Kurt looked at both of them sheepishly before unscrewing the cover of the mouthpiece and taking something that looked like a headache pill out of it. He replaced the cover.

"Thank you, Kurt," Buntline said.

"Mr. Blish, Mr. Buntline," Kurt said politely, and went out.

"I assumed," Buntline began as the door shut, "that you wanted a private chat."

Blish stared at him for long seconds. "Even though I suspected it, I still can't believe you actually bugged my hotel room, including the phone."

"I wasn't bugging you *per se*."

"No. You were hoping to hear a conversation with Branko . . . *per se*. He's about to put you out of your misery. He wants to meet."

"So you were with him. Clever ruse."

"And it worked," Blish said unrepentantly. "What he has to say will make your hair stand on end. He wants just the three of us at the meeting. No tails. He can spot one at fifty miles. I make no apologies for the exaggeration."

"I see. And how do we do this?"

"You get into the Mercedes with me. We drive toward town along a particular route. He'll find us. If he spots anyone else, the meeting is instantly canceled. He simply won't appear. I'd suggest you agree. You wouldn't want to miss out on what he has for you. It really is sticky time."

Buntline did not waste time arguing. "Done," he said. "We'll start immediately. Soon enough for him?"

"He'll be waiting."

Blish had driven the Mercedes E320 northward into Bonn along the A565 and stayed on it to cross the Rhine, then joined the A59 autobahn going south. After about a kilometer he came off it, and joined the national route 56 to recross the Rhine via the Kennedybrücke. He then went left onto Adenauerallee, heading south once more, toward the district of Plittersdorf. Another left turn brought him into the Franz-Josef Strauss allee, taking them closer to the western bank of the river. A few more turns into side streets, then he was turning off into what looked like a dead end that would lead straight into the Rhine itself.

But there was a turning to the right onto a wide unpaved track that opened out into a derelict industrial site. He drove cautiously along a potholed surface. A double-roofed building covered with corrugated sheeting was on its last legs, standing like a tired old man, its sides shredded open.

Next to it was a long, low white building. This one had been gutted by fire, its interior blackened, its windows and doors smeared by upward plumes of petrified smoke. A prominent sign, itself blackened by smoke, carried the international no smoking logo. Someone had not taken heed.

Blish brought the car to a halt.

Buntline, who had remained commendably silent throughout, now said, "Is the guided tour over?" He looked about him alertly. "I do hope you haven't led us into an ambush, Jordan. This looks like the perfect place for one."

Both road and river traffic could be clearly heard, though the river could not be seen. A main road was beyond the buildings, partially hidden by a screen of tall trees.

"I took the route Branko gave me," Blish said. "This allowed him plenty of opportunities to check if we were being followed. I'm certain he's been trailing us throughout, making quite sure. He'll be here."

"I trust that your confidence will not prove to be misguided." Buntline had ordered Kurt to remain at the hotel.

Branko had insisted that Blish follow the prescribed route exactly. He'd also insisted that Blish say nothing to Buntline about the Porsche. He didn't want Buntline running a check on it, he'd said.

Blish was equally certain Branko would not come to this meeting in the Porsche. He heard a clicking and looked across. Buntline was holding a big automatic pistol and screwing a silencer onto it.

"A gun!" Blish said.

Buntline turned it over, inspecting it. "Why, so it is."

"He's coming to give you information," Blish said heatedly, "not to start a war with you."

"Being careful, old son. First law."

"Now look—"

"No. *You* look. I have rather a lot of respect for you, dear chum. You've handled what must be quite a hellish situation for you rather better than expected. But when it comes to *my* profession, I think you're somewhat out of the league in the advice department. This is my sort of job. Let me do it my way. Are we agreed on that?"

"Agreed," Blish said reluctantly after a while.

"I am on your side," Buntline added.

Blish said nothing.

They had been waiting patiently for about ten minutes when Buntline, glancing at his watch, said, "Nearly 1845 hours. No sign of your friend Branko."

"Perhaps he's spotted one of your people."

"That would have been a feat. I gave very strict orders. No one is following. At least, no one working with or for me."

"What about local German units?"

"This is closed down very tightly indeed. Those Germans working with me are the only ones in the know. I have total cooperation. No one will break the rules, or even bend them. If we have been followed, it's not by anyone connected with me."

"Then I've no idea what—Ah!"

"What? Where?"

"Over there. About the middle of the building."

From where they had parked, they had a clear view of one side of the fire-ravaged structure. There were six large and gaping, smoke-blackened rectangles where windows, or perhaps loading bays, had been. A seventh was a taller opening that looked as if it had once been an entrance used by lorries.

Branko was standing in the fourth opening from the left. There was a package in his left hand, held against his upper thigh. His right hand was in shadow.

"Well, well," Buntline began softly. "Lieutenant Colonel Pyotr Nikolaev, I presume."

"*Lieutenant colonel? Branko?* But I thought you said his real name was Diryov."

"I said *one* of his names. I wasn't sure it was Nikolaev, but now I am."

Still confused by this new addition to Branko's multifaceted identity, Blish said, "But how can you be sure?"

"I have a very old picture, taken in the Middle East. The likeness is not very good and only someone who'd seen him under the circumstances I have would have recognized him. He was in a khaki gabardine uniform at the time. To be fair, most people would not have made the connection.

"I never look at the faces at the outset. There are far more dependable body clues that cannot be totally disguised, if you do know what you're looking for. I am myself always conscious of this when I'm . . . er operating out of theater, and take my own rigorous precautions. I am as prone as the next person to the betrayals of my own body."

"Is Nikolaev his real name?"

"Who knows? To those really in the know, however, he's a legend."

"And to you?"

"I treat him with wary respect."

"He probably thinks the same of you."

Buntline smiled. "No doubt. Incidentally, a report came in about a Mercedes sports car going off the road to Altenahr rather spectacularly, and at a high rate of knots. Driver impaled to death. Foreign national. I don't suppose you had anything to do with it."

"Certainly not."

"I didn't think so," Buntline said evenly. "Well, let's see what he has to offer."

They got out of the Mercedes and began walking toward Branko. As they drew closer, Blish could see the outline of the shape in Branko's right hand, which was also at his side.

"*He's got a gun too!*" he whispered sharply to Buntline.

"Not totally unexpected," Buntline said calmly. "Not to worry. He's not going to shoot you."

"And you?"

"Not unless I give him cause. And I'm not about to do that."

They stopped just outside the opening. A strange mixture of smells, dominated by that of old smoke, came from the building.

"Mr. Buntline," Branko said.

"Charles, please, Colonel."

Branko barely reacted. "I see," he said quietly. "You are well informed, Charles. But let us stick to Branko."

"I'm happy with that. As to my being well informed, it was more a matter of luck."

"Luck. We all need that in our business. Sometimes it works for, sometimes against us."

"Yes, indeed."

Branko looked at Blish. "You followed the route exactly, Jordan. Thank you."

"Did it help?"

"Better than I'd hoped." Branko handed the thick, dark brown folder he was carrying to Buntline. "This will make your star meteoric, Charles," he said. The words held a smile, but there was no hint of one upon his lips. "However, I've handed you a nightmare. Among the details in there is information about a particular group who are biding their time in the new Russia. They're letting the course of events shape their own plans. For example, one of them said that the president's ill health is an ally. You can judge what they mean. How you attend to what's in that folder will make all the difference. There's no time to lose. But before we can leave here, we've got a problem."

"Ah," Buntline said, glancing down at the folder. "No free lunches then."

"I'm afraid not. We've been followed."

Buntline and Blish looked at him in surprise.

"I told my people—" Buntline began.

"They're not yours," Branko interrupted. "And they're *our* problem. I suggest we combine forces."

"I agree. How long have we got?"

"Any moment now."

Buntline passed the folder to Blish. "Guard this with your life. Find somewhere to conceal yourself and *stay* there. We'll be back."

"And if you're not?"

"Don't ask questions like that, Jordan."

"And if you're not?" Blish repeated.

Branko pulled out another gun, a small automatic, from under his jacket. "Then use this." He cocked it and offered it to Blish, who stared at it. "It looks small, but at close range it delivers a kick like a maddened horse."

"I'd take it," Buntline advised. As he spoke, there was the noise of a fast-approaching car. "Decision time," he added.

Blish took the gun.

Buntline and Branko split up and raced through the burned-out building as the car outside skidded to a halt. Doors opened and slammed. There was the padding sound of softly running feet.

Blish saw a large, cubelike container that had been placed in a charred corner, and he moved swiftly over to it. There was just enough room for him to squeeze in behind.

The next few minutes were like something out of a strange dream. In the burned-out hulk of the building he heard scurryings, sharp coughs, stifled screams, and thudding weights. There seemed to be no shouts, no low-voiced chatter. It was all done in an eerily mute manner that belied the slaughter that was being carried out around him.

He held on to the gun, wondering whether he'd be able to shoot someone who was holding one already pointed at him, and, if he did, whether he'd be able to do so in time to save himself.

He looked at the folder. If they killed both Branko and Buntline, they'd soon realize that he now had it and would certainly come looking for him. The information in that folder would ensure they killed him without compunction, in order to retrieve it.

In his mind's eye, he again saw the nightmare of Durleigh throwing his children into the nuclear cauldron.

Then there was an abrupt silence.

Blish waited, a film of moisture suddenly coating the hand that held the gun. It trembled slightly.

Get a grip! he admonished himself. *You'll have to shoot if they come. You've got to get the folder to London. You've got to go and find Charlie and the kids. You've got to—*

"Jordan! It's all over." *Branko! Alive.*

"A good team at work." *Buntline too.*

"Jordan?"

"Come on, old son," Buntline called. "This is not a trick."

Cautiously, Blish came out of his hiding place, making the barest of noises.

Buntline was just outside. He whirled at the sound, gun rising, then stopped himself.

"Smart," he said, "pointing the muzzle downward."

"Would you have fired?"

"We'll never know, will we?"

Branko came forward from the shadows. "And what about you, Jordan? Would you have shot at those men if we hadn't made it?"

"*I'll* never know."

Buntline took the folder. "Take charge of that, shall I?"

Blish passed the gun over to Branko. "You'd better take this, too." He lightly brushed patches of soot off his clothes, so as not to leave smears. "Those men?" he added.

"Charles will have to arrange for a cleanup squad for four items."

"Dead?"

"Doornails would be more alive," Buntline answered mildly with a straight face.

"You were right," Blish said to him. "Not my kind of league."

"If I may suggest," Branko said, "you two should return to London as quickly as you can. Jordan, when you get back, go after Charlotte and the kids. I have a feeling the Mad Major may be trying to get on their track." He looked at Buntline. "He'll need help."

Buntline nodded. "And you?"

"I have my own date with the major. One more thing. When the fancy takes him, the Mad Major sometimes likes to call his operatives by the names of the big cats. It's in keeping with his philosophy that they're fierce, relentless killers."

"And are they?" Blish asked.

"Oh yes. They're both those things. Some of them greatly enjoy killing. If you get one in your sights, don't think about it. Shoot."

"I'm not likely to have a gun."

Branko glanced at Buntline. "As I said . . . he'll need help." To Blish, he continued, "Don't be too sure that you won't shoot if the time should come, if there's a gun within reach."

Blish wasn't certain whether he would; but he remembered how he'd felt when he'd first realized Charlotte and the girls were at risk. He might hesitate to shoot to protect himself. But Charlie and the kids . . .

"Are those four men in there from the Mad Major?" he asked Branko.

Branko shook his head, but did not elaborate. "Catch you later." He turned to go.

"Branko?" Blish called.

Branko again turned to face him.

"How did they know you'd be here?"

Branko smiled, opened and closed a partially raised hand in farewell, then went back into the shadows of the burned building.

They watched him go.

"Come on, Jordan," Buntline said quietly. "Time we went to find your wife and children. I've got an executive jet waiting at Cologne airport."

The A458, Shropshire, England. The same day.

Charlotte was heading toward Much Wenlock, on the road from Bridgnorth.

Mindful of Blish's warning before he'd left for Europe that she should give no overt sign she was going further than either to the shops or to friends, she had been very careful not to make undue noise in the house as she'd prepared to leave.

It had been fortunate that the children had been at Sophia's at the time, as all they'd required had already been there. Thus, there'd been no need for her to load the car and so give the game away to whoever might have been keeping an eye on the house. Anything they would need later, she'd decided, could be purchased on the way.

She'd said nothing to Sophia, explaining the sudden departure by saying she was anxious about her mother and needed to visit her. She'd left a very confused friend behind.

Now as she approached Much Wenlock, she was surprised to find that her overriding emotion was not one of fear, but of anger. Her anger was directed at the people who had dared to invade her home with their obscene little microphone; at the wretched Giles Mackillen, who'd abused her hospitality under the guise of friendship; and anger, most of all, at those who had forced her to run, with her children, into hiding.

On the way up, she had stopped to phone the owners of the cottage to see if she'd be able to use it. To her relief, they had said yes. She had not relished the idea of perhaps having to search for a place, with two children made irritable by the long car journey.

She glanced into the back of the car. They were both asleep. They'd been very good, all things considered. At times, Amanda had amused her little sister by playing games with her. She couldn't bear the thought of anything happening to them.

When she'd made it to the cottage, the children

were tired and sleepy. She quickly prepared their dinner, then got them ready for bed. At about the time she'd got them settled down and was at last able to sit and think on her own about the situation in which she found herself, Blish was leaving his hotel to be driven to the airport by Kurt.

The Mad Major was not pleased with the news that had come in. He looked coldly at the man who had brought it.

"She has not returned?" he barked in Russian. "Are you sure?"

"Ocelot is still on station. Blish's wife has definitely not returned. It explains why we have not received anything from the mike since that phone call she received."

The Mad Major glared at him. "Must you always state the obvious?" Then the Mad Major paused thoughtfully. "Play me back that recording."

The man switched the digital recording on the small but powerful machine to PLAY. What came out was a sparklingly clear reproduction of Charlotte's voice.

"Oh yes . . . yes mm-hm . . . mm-hm yes . . . thanks . . . nope . . . no . . . . okay . . . oh I know that . . . me too . . . see you."

There followed various noises as she moved about the house, then the recording ended.

The man looked expectantly at his superior.

"There is something there," the Mad Major said. "Let's hear it again. And is this the best cleanup you can do? Can we hear nothing of what was said on the phone by the other person?"

"The one she used was too far from the unit. At first, it almost sounds as if she's making love to someone," his subordinate added, trying hard not to sound suggestive.

The Mad Major gave one of his bone-chilling stares. "Keep your mind on the task in hand," he snapped. "All right. Let's hear it."

Five replays later, the Mad Major was still convinced there was more to the apparently meaningless conversation.

"Let's hear it again," he ordered. At the end of that playback, he said, "Making love."

His subordinate looked alarmed. "Major, I was only—"

"It's all right, Puma. I am not to about to scold you. You may well have given us a clue. Let's have another replay, but stop when I tell you to. Begin."

"Oh yes . . ." the recording said.

"Stop! Hear the warmth in the voice," the Mad Major said. "But there's anxiety, too. Remember that warmth. Go on."

"Yes mm-hm . . . "

"Stop! She's agreeing to something, or confirming. Continue."

"Mm-hm yes . . . "

"Stop! Now she's reversed the response, but it's essentially the same thing. Again, she's agreeing or confirming. Next section."

"Thanks . . . nope . . . no . . . "

"Stop! Why thanks? And note how warm her voice gets. You were quite right, Puma. She *was* making love . . . to the man she's deeply in love with. Her husband. Blish phoned her. He speaks to her, prompting her so that she needs only to make the shortest of replies. As for 'nope' and 'no,' he's either asked her about something which she hasn't done, or isn't there. Take the next."

"Okay . . . "

"Stop! She's agreed to a suggestion he's made. Now the next."

"Oh I know that . . . "

"Stop! Just listen to that voice. She very pleased with something he's said, and is almost coy. A compliment, perhaps? Or is he telling her . . . he *loves* her? Let's have the last section."

"Me too . . . see you . . . "

"Stop! I think this confirms it. Note that final surge of warmth in the voice. He must have said 'I love you' to her. She tells him she knows it, then says the same to him. Then finally, 'see you.' Are they arranging to meet somewhere? I realize I have substituted what I think may have been said, but I am certain I am correct.

"Somehow, Blish discovered we had planted the microphone, and has got her to leave, taking the children. He's moving them out of harm's way. Now why would he do that?" The Mad Major's eyes glowed with a fury that bordered on the insane. But he remained controlled, and unnaturally calm. "There can be but one reason. He is in contact with *Diryov!* And Diryov told him about the microphone. I have no idea how that came about, but there is someone who can shed light upon it." The Mad Major's voice, for all his overt self-control, had risen to a snarl.

"Mackillen?"

"Yes!" The single word came out in a hiss.

"Do you think he warned them?"

"*Mackillen?*" The Mad Major's voice dripped contempt. "That poor excuse for a man would not have had the courage. No. He must have placed it in an exposed location, the moron. Blish and his wife are crazy about each other. We find the wife and we hold her. Blish will then have no choice but to tell us where Diryov is. Or we kill his wife and children." This strangely calm statement turned a threat into a coldly calculating promise.

"First, we must find her."

The Mad Major glared at Puma. "You really must try very hard not to state the obvious. Now let's pay Mr. Mackillen another visit. He'll be pleased to see us."

Puma smiled at the prospect. Had Mackillen been there to see it, it would have struck fear into the very core of his being.

Mackillen was enjoying a pint with colleagues outside a pub in Covent Garden. The warmth of the evening had caused most of the customers of the neighboring establishments to spill out onto the pavements and the blocked-off roads, mingling with each other. Mackillen was in intense conversation with a young woman whose eyes were glazing over either from boredom, or from a surfeit of drink. As he leaned ever closer, she moved slightly backward to put more space between them; but in the crush, there was nowhere for her to go.

She was beginning to look desperate when a man in a smart, lightweight suit and a strange smile tapped Mackillen on the shoulder.

"Mr. Mackillen!" the Mad Major said loudly to make himself heard.

Mackillen was brought up short, as if someone had yanked him by the neck. The young woman heaved a sigh of relief and quickly slipped away as Mackillen turned toward his persecutor.

"Let us talk where it is much quieter," the Mad Major said, taking him firmly by the arm.

Puma, on the edge of the crowd, smiled in his direction. He would have preferred it if Puma hadn't.

"My . . . drink," he protested. "My friends."

"Ah. Your friends. Where are they?"

"There," Mackillen said eagerly, pointing to four men and another young woman with faces made shiny by the heat, the booze, and the animated urgency of their conversation.

But any hopes he'd entertained of being saved from an audience with the Mad Major were soon dashed.

"I'm sorry I'm going to drag Giles away," the Mad Major said cheerfully as he went up to them, hauling a reluctant Mackillen with him. "He's handling a very personal portfolio for me, and I need to make some decisions tonight."

"Lucky sod," one of the friends remarked after quickly glancing at the Mad Major and deciding he was looking at a lot of money on the hoof. "Trust 'Killer' Mackillen to pick up a juicy sideline. Bet you get a fat commission, Giles. You'll make a killing."

"He will," the Mad Major said.

"Now we know where his next Porsche's coming from," another commented.

They all burst into laughter, as if this was the best joke they'd heard in years. They were still chortling as the Mad Major firmly led him away.

"Your friends do know you so well, Mr. Mackillen,"

he said as they neared the Jaguar XJR, which was parked a short distance away. "Please get in."

Mackillen climbed into the back. The Mad Major followed.

"Let's go," he ordered Puma, who had got in behind the wheel. "I am very disappointed," he continued to Mackillen as the Jaguar moved off with a smooth purr of its supercharged engine.

Mackillen looked timorously at his unwanted companion, his face twitching with uncertainty and fear. "I . . . I don't understand. What do you mean?"

"I mean you failed to do as I asked."

"But I didn't! I planted the mike!"

"Yes, yes. You did. Unfortunately, it was soon discovered. You must have chosen a bad location."

"But that's impossible! I put it in a very good position. It's on the side of the fridge, in a narrow space. It was well hidden. She never even saw me do it."

"That is difficult to believe. According to my men, she returned alone to the house, shortly after she had left with the children to go to the house of that friend you mentioned. She spent a very brief time inside and left again. While she was in the house, she had the briefest of telephone conversations with her husband. She hasn't been back since. How do you explain it?"

"I . . . I can't. I don't know what happened. She never saw me plant that cassette, I tell you!"

"Someone must have."

"I can't see how. I . . ." Mackillen's voice faded suddenly.

"Yes, Mr. Mackillen? You have remembered something?"

"But it's impossible . . ." Mackillen remarked softly.

"Let me be the judge of that."

"It must have been that brat—that daughter of hers. Hated me, that kid. She kept giving me those po-faced looks that kids sometimes do. How could a kid so young—"

"How old is this child?"

"Oh I don't know. Three . . . perhaps four . . . "

"Wise beyond her years," the Mad Major said coldly. "So you believe she must have seen you hide the cassette."

"It's the only explanation."

"It appears so."

To Mackillen, the Mad Major's sudden agreement was far more ominous than if he had shouted angrily at him.

"You will now appreciate why I need your services a little longer," the Mad Major went on. "I need to find Mrs. Blish, and you're going to help me. First, we shall go to her friend's house. You will take me there."

It was a command.

Mackillen went reluctantly up the short flight of steps and rang the doorbell. The Mad Major, following, paused a couple of steps down. There was a brief wait, then the pristine white door opened.

"Hullo."

"Oh. It's you Giles." Her tone of voice clearly indicated his presence was not a welcome one.

The Mad Major swiftly took control. He went up the remaining steps and beamed at her.

"Good evening. Sophia, isn't it?"

"Why, yes," she answered in surprise. "Do I know

you?" She could not place his accent and a puzzled frown creased her forehead.

"It is my misfortune that you do not. I am Thom Andersen," he continued, correctly dropping the 'd' in the name. "I'm Norwegian, and a colleague of Jordan's on the diplomatic circuit. He asked me to call upon him and Charlotte whenever I was in town. There's no one home and Giles suggested you might know . . ." He paused, looking helpless.

Sophia's forehead cleared. She was one of those people to whom all foreign accents were indistinguishable.

She smiled sympathetically. "I'm so sorry. You've missed them. Jordan's off abroad somewhere, and Charlotte went off to her parents' earlier today. Her mother's not too well."

The Mad Major put on his most disappointed face. "Oh well. Next time. Thank you very much." He began to make his way back down the steps.

"Look," she called. "I feel terrible. You've come all the way from Norway, only to miss them. Would you like to come in for a drink?"

He paused, and turned to smile up at her. "You are most kind, but Giles and I have some people to see. Perhaps next time?"

"We'll look forward to it."

"Thank you," the Mad Major said again, and went to wait for Mackillen by the car.

Just as Mackillen was about try to persuade Sophia to let him in, her husband called from within the house.

"Who is it, darling?" Footsteps sounded and Sophia's husband appeared, countenance immediately clouding over. "*Giles!* What do you bloody want?"

"Uh . . . nothing." Mackillen hurried back down.

"Depraved sod!" the husband growled, slamming the door.

The Mad Major smiled nastily as Mackillen got back into the car. "Such wonderful friends you have," he said as he entered and shut the door. "I'm glad you were not so foolish as to try to run inside. You would have forced me to kill all we found. All right, Puma. Let's go." As the Jaguar moved off, he continued to Mackillen, "You may now take me to her parents."

"Her parents! But you can't—"

"Developing a conscience, Mr. Mackillen? Please don't make me even more disappointed in you."

The Jaguar headed toward Surrey.

2045 hours.

It was still daylight when the Jaguar's fat wheels crunched up the drive to the Durleigh mansion. From a well-constructed hide, the watcher zeroed the long lens of his camera on the vehicle and recorded all those who got out. He noticed that a second car had accompanied the Jaguar, but had stopped further down the drive, well out of sight of the house. He then spoke into a radio.

"They must still be trying to find Diryov," the voice on the radio said.

"Shall I intervene?"

"No. What could you hope to do against all of them?"

"They might kill those people in there."

"That is not our affair. We want Diryov."

■ ■ ■

At the house, Mackillen went up to the door. Presently, it opened to his summons.

"My word," Brandon exclaimed in astonishment. "Mr. Mackillen! We haven't seen you around here for years." He looked at the Jaguar and the silent figure of the Mad Major. "Are you here to see Sir Richard? He isn't here, I'm afraid—"

"Sorry to barge in on you like this, Brandon," Mackillen said. "Actually, it's not Sir Richard we've come to see. This is Mr. Thom Andersen, a diplomatic colleague of Jordan's from Norway. He arrived in town unexpectedly and went to the Chelsea house. You see, there's been an open invitation from Jordan. Well, to cut a long story short, Jordan gave him my number, just in case of something like this. We went to Sophia's to look for Charlotte, but Sophia says she's here. And here we are."

Brandon, never having liked Mackillen, had listened to all this with stony attention.

"I'm afraid you've been misled, Mr. Mackillen. Miss Charlotte is not here. She hasn't been all day."

"*What?*" In his mounting anxiety, Mackillen lost control, putting Brandon instantly on guard. "But Sophia said Charlotte came here to see her mother, who's unwell."

"Lady Durleigh is her usual self," Brandon said stiffly, liking the situation less and less by the second. His eyes darted toward the still-silent figure of the Mad Major. "I'm afraid I cannot help you, gentlemen." He began to close the door.

The Mad Major had been losing patience. Despite

his weak leg, he moved swiftly to place himself in the doorway.

"I think not, Brandon," he said coldly, roughly shoving the older man aside. "We are coming in. And please, do not do anything foolish."

Then Brandon saw the gun.

The watcher did not see the third car.

There was plenty of urgent activity in the cavern. Over the past days high-value, easily transported equipment had been removed; but most would remain. Already, directional charges had been set, in preparation for the eventual destruction of everything within the underground chamber. The unique properties of the charges were such that the cavern would itself remain intact, so as not to trigger outside sensors by its explosive destruction. The equipment would simply collapse upon itself. This would give all those working on the project time to escape before the trajectory of the missiles would inevitably lead to the detection of the launch area. Many of the people had already left, giving the cavern, despite the activity, an air of having already been abandoned. It was an eerie scene, made even more so by the nature of the artificial lighting.

The submarine captain was topside, standing at the foot of the small ramp that led up to the vessel, surveying his surroundings dispassionately.

A scene from a technological hell, *he thought.*

Mercifully, he'd soon be well away from it and en route to his family. The plotters could all rot in the nightmare they had created, as far as he was concerned. He was retiring from this section of mankind.

The submarine, despite its relatively small size, still looked like a gleaming, dormant monster, the weaponry it now carried giving it a higher level of malevolence. The work had gone better than expected, and the date of the mission had been advanced.

A man he'd never seen before came up to him with a slim package in waterproof wrapping.

"Commander," the man greeted him, "your orders. Do not open them until you're under way. All targeting information is in there, and will take very little time to feed into the launch computers. When you return, this place will be empty and all charges set to go off at a specific time. It is vital that you and your crew are out of here before that happens. Though the explosions will be well contained, the directional blasts will be extremely hazardous. So don't hang around."

The commander nodded as he took the package. "Understood. And you are?"

The man looked at him coldly. "Good-bye, Commander." The man walked rapidly away.

"And the same to you," the commander muttered.

He turned the package over, studying it closely, but made no attempt to open it. As his hand shifted in the artificial glow of the lighting, he thought his skin had the typically sallow look of a submariner's without the benefits of the sunbeds of the big boats.

I need some sunshine, *he thought.*

Lady Durleigh was in her private study; but she was not alone. The first indication she'd had of something terrible entering into her life was the sudden slamming of the door coming open, and Brandon being pushed into the room, to be followed by two strangers and Giles Mackillen.

That had been half an hour ago.

She was now lying back on her deeply upholstered, reclining chair, as if at the dentist. Her face was puffy, and, though tears had been forced out of her eyes, the swellings had nothing to do with tears. The Mad Major had carried out some of the activities for which he was infamously known.

Brandon, tightly held in a neck grip by Puma, was struggling ineffectually to escape in order to go to her aid. He tried to speak, but only strangled raspings came out of his mouth.

"Let him breathe, Puma," the Mad Major ordered conversationally, not looking round. His attention was fully upon the hapless woman in his clutches.

Puma complied and Brandon cried hoarsely, "Leave her alone, for God's sake, you monster! She can't tell you anything!"

The Mad Major still did not look round. "Can you?" He didn't seem to mind being called a monster.

"No! I've already told you I have no idea where Mrs. Blish went. She *never* came here! How many times—"

"As many as necessary until I get the information I want." The Mad Major slapped Emily Durleigh hard across her already-bruised face with the back of his hand. Pinpricks of blood sprang out of the cracks of the swollen skin, leaving thin trails as the hand swept across. He wiped his hand with a pure white handkerchief, causing bright red blotches to appear upon it.

"Oh Emily," Brandon said brokenly. "I'm so sorry—"

"Do you hear, Puma? Another one in love. This manservant has been in love with his master's wife all his life. Typically in a bourgeois society such as this, he suffered, in silence, the humiliation of seeing the woman he loved bedded by another." The Mad Major made a sound of disgust. "Where is your dignity, man?" he snapped at Brandon, still without turning round. He hit Emily Durleigh once more.

Brandon gave a moan of very real pain. The Mad Major ignored him, concentrating on her.

"You may think this is painful," the Mad Major said to his victim solicitously, "but I assure you it is quite pleasant when compared to what I *can* do to you. Why don't you simply tell me where Charlotte has gone? I am running out of patience, and time is marching on. Come on, Emily. Tell me what I want to know."

"But . . . but," she began tearfully in a weak voice. "I've . . . I've already . . . said. I have . . . no idea. She never rang . . . to tell me. I'm . . . I'm worried . . . about her."

"So am I. Don't you see? We can help each other. You tell me, and I'll find her for both of us."

"But—if I don't know—"

"*You must know!*"

The sudden yell was accompanied by the heaviest blow yet. His fist slammed against her cheekbone. It made a sickening noise.

"Oh no, no!" Brandon cried heartrendingly. "Oh please, leave her alone!"

At last, tolerance gone, the Mad Major rounded upon him. "*Shut up!* If you do not, I shall have Puma silence you for good!"

Mackillen, who had been cowering in a corner throughout, now found he couldn't bear to watch. At first, he had been horribly fascinated; but now, the sight of the bloodied face was making him ill.

The Mad Major returned to his work. "Tell me where she is, Emily, and I won't hurt you anymore. That's a promise. It will be all over."

She was sobbing weakly, bewildered and very scared. "But I really . . . have no . . . idea—"

"*Do you people believe I am bluffing?*" he roared suddenly.

Then, without warning, he drew his automatic and shot Mackillen twice.

The crack of the unexpected gunshots seemed to hang in the room. Mackillen's eyes, widened in shock and disbelief, were staring down at the red blossoms that had appeared on his chest. Already dying, he desperately tried to wipe away at them with his hands. The initially frantic movements began to slow down until they stopped altogether, as his body toppled forward to fall heavily. His right leg drew itself up in a last reflex. Then he was still. No sound had come out of him.

Even Puma was taken by surprise. Brandon stared at the body, not wanting to believe what had occurred.

"Perhaps now," the Mad Major said, "you will both take me seriously. *Where is Charlotte, Emily?*" he barked.

But something strange had happened. It could have been the shock of the casual nature of the killing, or it could have been a sudden memory of earlier beatings. Whichever cause had been the trigger, Emily Durleigh had retreated into her past and seemed to be babbling.

"The cottage," she mumbled, the words running into each other. "I'll have to go to the cottage. He won't find me there. I can't tell Brandon. Dear, dear, Brandon. Richard might try to get it out of him . . . "

"She's lost her mind—" Puma began.

The Mad Major raised an imperious hand to stop him.

Brandon was staring at the abused wreck on the chair, unable to comprehend what she was talking about.

"What does she mean?" the Mad Major asked him. "What cottage?"

"I . . . I don't know. Perhaps she has gone back to her childhood."

"She mentioned your name and the name of her husband. That is not her childhood, is it?"

"No."

"Then . . . what . . . does . . . she . . . *mean?*" the Mad Major demanded exasperatedly.

"I don't—"

"*Shut up!*" The Mad Major was once more listening intently to Emily Durleigh, whose voice had now grown perceptibly weaker. Once again, she was talking about a cottage.

"The cottage. Must get to the cottage. Must get Charlotte away."

The Mad Major was staring at her with heightened interest; then he turned to Brandon.

"She's talking about that cottage again, Brandon," he said in a deceptively reasonable voice. "She seems to have retreated into an old memory. Does that mean anything to you? Why would she take Charlotte away? And where to?"

"Her husband, Sir Richard," Brandon commenced with reluctance, "frequently used to attack her during the early years of their marriage—"

"And you, the man who loved her, stood by and let that happen?"

"You don't understand—"

"I understand perfectly. He was your master. You loved above your station."

The calculated insult made Brandon stiffen.

"Would you like to hit me, Brandon?"

"*Yes!*" Brandon shouted.

"At least you've got some spirit left. Not that it will do you any good." The Mad Major leaned closer to Emily Durleigh, then whispered in her ear, "Tell me where you took Charlotte, Emily."

"Much . . . "

"Much?" The Mad Major frowned, certain he was going up another blind alley.

"Much Wenlock," she said.

After that, it was easy.

■ ■ ■

"All right, Puma," the Mad Major said. "You can let him go."

He'd got all the directions he needed out of Emily Durleigh. She was still babbling, still unaware of what she had done.

Brandon rushed over to her, cradling the battered face and trying to wipe the blood away.

"Emily, my love," he said gently and kissed her on the forehead.

He was still cradling her when the Mad Major shot them both.

"Let's move," the Mad Major said. "We've got a long way to go. Drive as fast as you dare. The others will have to keep up. But watch out for policemen. We don't want their interest."

"And if they do show interest?"

"They may not live to regret it. There are two kinds of policemen," he went on. "Unarmed ones, and targets."

He laughed as they hurried outside, leaving the three bodies where they lay, and got into the XJR. The laugh made even Puma shiver. Puma turned the car round quickly while the Mad Major got out a map to plot the fastest route that would take them as directly across country as was practicable, using the motorways wherever possible.

The Jaguar hurtled down the drive, scattering gravel like grapeshot from its wheels. As it went past, the second car turned to follow, keeping pace.

The third car, waiting beyond the drive and hidden by tall hedges in an overgrown turning point, allowed them to travel some distance before trailing them.

The watcher in the hide noted that only two men had returned to the Jaguar. He reported this over his radio, and that both cars had gone.

He was told to stay put.

The hatches were secure. Everything was ready. The moment had arrived. The captain looked at his nominal second-in-command. Both men exchanged neutral glances. Each understood fully what they were about to do.

The captain took a deep breath, then uttered the most fateful words of his life.

"Dive the boat! Dive! Dive!"

The minisubmarine, free of its moorings, began to sink.

The Lynx battlefield helicopter was beating its way toward Shropshire. On board, in addition to the crew, were Blish, Buntline, and three other men. These men were heavily armed and in black combat gear. Buntline had omitted to introduce them. They also wore black, hoodlike balaclava helmets. Each carried a cut-down assault rifle with night sight, at least one automatic pistol—one had two—and what seemed like a selection of grenades. They also carried big knives.

Blish stared out at the darkened landscape, watching, as pinpoints of light and, sometimes, great clusters of illumination from interconnecting towns and villages slid past to one side beneath them. Sometimes, they crossed great swaths of darkness, broken only by a solitary twinkle. On other occasions, the glow of a town would appear on the horizon, never to materialize as, bypassing it, they skimmed their way into the night.

The executive jet from Cologne had landed at a military airfield, where a car had been waiting to take them to a building just off Whitehall. Buntline had disappeared for a while to dispose of Branko's folder and to set up the mission to rescue or protect Charlotte and the children.

He had eventually returned to say that the material in the folder was the biggest and hottest coup ever and that clandestine operations were being mounted to try and neutralize the Horsemen. Buntline was not sure whether everything would be in place in time. It was touch and go, but many intelligence services had gone on the alert. Everyone had agreed this was preferable to going public.

Buntline's department had wanted Blish to be available for debriefing, but Blish's own immediate concerns were for his family and he'd wanted to talk to no one until he was quite certain his wife and children were safe. He was therefore pleased that Buntline had given that priority. Besides, there was more than enough in Branko's folder to keep Buntline's department and its international allies happy or worried for months, and perhaps even years.

They had returned to the military airfield, where the helicopter, the armed men, and the change of clothing had been waiting. Now, as the Lynx whipped its way toward Wenlock Edge, he prayed they would be in time.

"We'll make it," Buntline's voice said in his ear.

Like Buntline, he wore a flight helmet. He made no

comment. *I hope so*, he thought, not allowing himself to think of the worst-case scenario.

This scenario, according to Buntline, would be to arrive and find that Charlotte and the children were either dead or held hostage. Buntline had actually said that the hostage scenario was the very worst of two already-bad options. If they were dead, there was nothing that could be done except to hunt down the perpetrators.

If they were alive and held hostage, knowing they were living and breathing and that your subsequent actions could be responsible for their deaths, was a far more horrific set of circumstances.

Buntline might well be able to make such clinical judgments, Blish now thought. They weren't his wife and kids down there, and at risk.

Moscow, 0300 local.

Captain Lirionova stared at her screen and gave a sharp intake of breath.

She had taken a few hours' break and, having left the computer to autonomously conduct some specific searches, had returned to check if anything of interest had been found. She had called up the various results, and the implications of one had so terrified her, she was now unsure of what she should do.

She stared at it, very much afraid of alerting the general. After about five minutes of agonizing, she contacted his private residence, convincing him of the need for his presence, without giving any details over the phone.

He would be with her in an hour, he said.

An hour, she thought as she put down the phone, would already be too late.

It had probably already been too late before the first of the searches had begun.

Then she realized that her entire body was shaking.

The Lynx made its first landing on a flat section of a dismantled railway track, low down on the western slope of the Edge. From there, it was roughly one and a half kilometers eastward in a straight line to the cottage. The men in black got out swiftly, to begin making their way up the ridge through the dark of the woodland. They would then make their way down the opposite slope, to approach the cottage from three directions.

The site of the landing had been deliberately chosen. The sound of the Lynx would have been masked by the Edge, and anyone hostile waiting at the cottage should not have heard it.

The aircraft lifted off again and, taking a roundabout route, made its second landing. This time it was in a field some two kilometers southwest of the cottage. From there, it was virtually level ground in a direct line to the village.

Buntline had found boots and a field jacket for Blish. In the shirt and trousers he'd worn on the flight from Cologne, he set out with Buntline on the two-kilometer trek to the cottage. Buntline was armed, carrying both an automatic pistol and a Heckler and Koch submachine gun. Attached to his left ear, and invisible in the dark, was the single headphone with throat mike, connected to the secure datalink unit in a breast pocket of his field jacket.

They walked in silence, each occupied with his own thoughts.

Buntline's men made it to the village while Blish and Buntline were still on their way.

The men carried out a very careful reconnaissance of the area, moving closer with each circuit until they were at the cottage itself. They took their time, using their sights to check that no one was waiting in ambush inside. Satisfied that the area was clean, they settled down to wait for Buntline and Blish.

When they were still a good four hundred meters out, Buntline called a halt.

"Bossman. We're coming in," he said.

"Roger, Bossman," came a voice on the headphone. "Area clear."

"Don't want to get shot by our own side, do we?" he said to Blish. "You'll be pleased to know we've beaten the opposition. There's no one waiting for us. Your wife's car is there."

"Oh thank God," Blish said, the relief washing over him in a great wave. Then he paused. "*What if they've already been and taken them?*" he added in a fierce, anxious whisper, as if expecting ears in the night to be listening.

"No go. No extra tracks. Your wife's car is the only one to have gone there."

"They could have approached on foot. Just like us."

"I do understand your anxiety but believe me, my people have sanitized the area. No one is in there except your family."

"Have your men checked?"

"They're waiting for us. How do you think your wife and children would react if suddenly confronted by three armed men in black, in the middle of the night?"

"Of course you're right."

"Of course I'm right," Buntline agreed. "Now let's pick up the pace."

A hundred meters out, Buntline stopped once more. "Bossman coming in."

"Roger, Bossman."

"One of them will have a night sight on us, just to make sure," Buntline said as they continued walking. "After all, we could have been ambushed, with an impostor in our place. In case you think that's unlikely, I can assure you such things do happen. I know of one case where two people on a mission got briefly separated. One was ambushed and his place taken by an impostor, who bluffed his way long enough to take out the second man."

"It happened to your people?"

"No. I was the impostor."

"Lesson appreciated."

They called their way in all the way to the cottage until Blish was startled to see a shape suddenly appear beside him.

"Still clear?" Buntline asked of the shape softly.

"Yes, sir."

"All right. Thank you."

The shape melted away.

"Your show now, Jordan," Buntline said. "Knock on the door. We'll be watching."

"What if your men are wrong and those people *are* inside?"

"You're about to find out."

"That makes me feel really secure," Blish said. "Just tell them to shoot *past* me, not *at* me." He walked toward the door of the cottage.

He knocked. No response.

He knocked again. Still nothing. If Charlotte were in there, she would not answer a knock on the door of a detached cottage in the middle of the night, in a tiny community in darkest Shropshire. But she'd certainly be awake now, listening in trepidation, with the kids in the bedroom with her.

Then he remembered. "Charlie! It's Lothar!"

"Lothar?" came an amused whisper next to him in the dark.

"A long story."

A light had come on.

"Lothar appears to have succeeded," Buntline said drily.

Another light was switched on, this time on the ground floor. There was the clicking of at least two locks, then the sound of bolts being drawn. Then the door opened. Light flooded out, stabbing the night.

Only Blish stood there, feeling naked, Buntline having slipped back into the shadows. The others, Blish knew, would be at strategic points near the cottage.

Then, as Charlotte stood before him, a great welcoming smile on her face, her arms opening wide to embrace him, several things seemed to happen in a confusing jumble.

"*Out of the light!*" someone cried sharply, close by.

Charlotte's face changing from happiness to fear.

A familiar coughing sound that he'd heard only a few hours before in Germany.

A brief cry that sounded like a night creature caught by a predator.

A heavy weight slamming into his back, hurling him into the cottage.

The sharp cry of his name from Charlotte.

A child crying, "*Mummy!*" from upstairs.

The door slamming shut.

Charlotte saying in a voice made squeaky by fear for his safety, "*Jordan!* Are you all right?" and trying to decide where her first attentions should go.

A voice saying, "I'm okay." His own.

Charlotte running up the stairs.

A voice saying, "*Kill the light!*" Not his own.

Blish realized he'd not been injured, but that someone was lying on the floor of the cottage. One of the men in black.

"The light!" the man said again. "Kill it!"

Blish crawled over to the light switch, then tried to reach it from the floor. It was just beyond his outstretched fingers. He'd have to risk propping himself on his elbow. He did so and quickly flipped the switch. The room plunged into darkness.

"Thank God for that!" the man on the floor said.

But there was more light. Upstairs. A series of blows, like pebbles hitting, slammed at the cottage.

"The bastards are shooting through in the hope of hitting someone," the man in black said. "Tell her to douse that light."

"Charlie, turn off the light!" Blish called. "And don't move about, for God's sake!"

There was a brief pause, then the light went out.

"What's going on, Mummy?" Amanda.

"Shhh!" Blish heard Charlotte say.

There was a slight gasp over to his right. Had the man been hit?

"Are you hurt?" Blish asked.

"My pride certainly is," came the reply. "When I jumped to push you out of the light, I hit the doorjamb with my elbow. Bloody silly thing to do. I must have bruised it pretty badly. I can't use the arm at the moment. That was so damned clumsy, a recruit couldn't have done worse."

Blish knew Buntline's man was being hard on himself.

"You may well have saved my life," he said. "Thank you."

"All in the service," the other said, remarkably cheerfully. "I spotted a movement and acted. I wasn't sure we had bandits out there. Not so soon, anyway. We'd had that area cleaned just before you arrived. They must have been behind us, and just in front of you. They made themselves the jam in the middle."

"So what do we do?"

"We sit tight. Bossman and the others will be doing a little hunting just now."

The man's rhythm of speech made Blish say, "Edinburgh?"

A chuckle came out of the dark. "Spot on. Have you any idea how long I've been out of that town?"

"How long?"

"Most of my life. Still has a hold on me, though."

"As Bossman didn't introduce us," Blish said, "and it seems as if we're going to be in here for a while, may I call you Edinburgh?"

"Shorten it. Edin will do."

"Edin it is. So what do you think's going on out there?"

"Something pretty fierce."

■ ■ ■

The Mad Major seethed in quiet rage. They had made good time, frequently exceeding the speed limits by considerable margins. No police had come near. They had left the cars just off a road a kilometer away to the east of the village, and had made their way on foot to the cottage. Once, they'd heard a helicopter, but as it hadn't come near, had given it no further thought.

The Mad Major swore to himself. It had been a stupid error of judgment. Now it seemed Blish had protection for his family. No matter. He would still get to that cottage.

The Mad Major meant it.

"Here."

Blish felt the metallic shape that was being pushed into his hand. An automatic.

"Take it!" Edin insisted. "It's a nine millimeter, Uzi automatic pistol. It's cocked and ready to go. All you've got to do when the time comes is pull the trigger. It's got a hell of a punch. One of my favorites. But don't worry. I've got my backup."

So he'd been the one with the two pistols.

Blish hesitated.

"Take it, man! My elbow's not too good. You never know how the deck's stacked. You might need to have this handy. That's your wife and kids up there, and if one or more of those bastards get in, you'll have to make one of the toughest decisions of your life."

Blish made a rueful noise.

"I was that funny?" Edin asked.

"Not so long ago, someone said much the same thing to me."

"Sounds like he knew what he was on about."

"He does."

"Well? Are you going to take this shooter, or what?"

Blish felt his hand close about the gun. "I hope I don't have to use it."

"We all do. But sometimes, you don't have the choice."

One of Buntline's men had Puma in his sights. The scope gave the scene a greenish tinge. Puma was partially hidden by a tree up a steep incline, behind thc cottage.

Buntline's man waited patiently.

Then Puma began to move. He was good and only exposed himself for a fleeting second, but it was enough. The assault rifle coughed.

The shot was clean and took Puma at the base of the skull. Puma fell forward without a sound. Buntline's man immediately began to shift position.

Then something tore through the scope, shattering it. The second bullet hit him fully in the chest.

He was flung backward.

"Shit," he said softly.

Then a new blackness took hold of him.

The Mad Major made his way to the body. The faint greenish glow of the scope had been enough of an aiming point.

He moved on.

■ ■ ■

"I can't hear anything out there," Blish said.

"Things are happening," Edin told him. "Believe me. By the way, I hope your wife hasn't left any windows open. It's a warm night. She might have thought it a good idea."

Blish felt his blood go cold. "I'd better—"

The grip of a strong hand stopped him. "Listen."

Blish listened, but could hear nothing. "I can't—"

The hand gripped him again. "Someone outside," Edin whispered so softly, Blish had to strain to hear. "Close."

Edin began to move. Blish sensed rather than heard any actual movement.

He gripped the pistol and propped himself against the low wall that divided the kitchen/dinette from the sitting room. That way, he faced the back door, leaving the front to Edin.

There you are, Branko, he thought. *I've got a gun in my hand now.*

Moscow, the same time.

Kurinin entered the office and looked at the pale face of Captain Lirionova. She was not at her machine.

"You appear to have seen a ghost, Captain. Is it that serious?"

She nodded, at first not trusting herself to speak.

"I'm waiting, Captain."

"Comrade General," she began hesitantly, "you asked me to approach the problem from different angles. I have done so. I tried all avenues, but got nowhere. In the end, almost in desperation, I decided to check the senior noncommissioned officers. I wasn't sure what I would find. I discovered that a senior sergeant, Aleksandr Politimov, had gone missing."

"Missing? How?"

"That was just it, General. There was no record of what had happened. At first, I thought that perhaps he'd been posted to a special unit and records of his movement were in a secure file. I have access to those files. No Politimov. I then checked the last unit he was assigned to. It was not to a unit but to the staff of a senior officer, on special duty."

The captain paused, looking increasingly unsure of herself.

"Continue," Kurinin ordered.

"I checked the sergeant's specialty. He was a diving instructor. I . . . I checked the senior officer's records for special courses recently taken. He had recently undergone, and passed, a diving course."

"What point are you making?" Kurinin's eyes seemed to peer into her very soul.

"The course was not recorded according to procedure, General. I only discovered it by coming across a requisition for air tanks. It was for the senior officer, long after he had passed the course. This officer's duties do not require him to have the diving proficiency of a specialist. I . . . I don't know what to make of it, General. Sergeant Politimov seems to have vanished without trace while still assigned to this officer, yet the fact was not reported. But . . . here is the name of the officer in question."

She went to her desk, and brought up the name on the computer. She stood up again quickly, as if her chair had suddenly become too hot.

Kurinin went up to the machine and peered at the

highlighted name. He remained absolutely still for several seconds. Then he straightened and went out without another word.

Lirionova stared at the name.

General Igor Leonidovitch Garadze. One of the Horsemen.

The submarine was on its way to its launch position, which it would reach in one hour. The targets had been programmed into the missiles. All that now remained was to reach position, and launch.

The captain studied the faces of his companions in the small conning tower. He wondered what they were thinking. Were they counting the ways in which they would spend their generous remuneration?

When he had unsealed the target coordinates, he'd at first thought the general and his cohorts had gone insane. But there was a kind of logic to it. The general would get the power he craved, and the world would blame a rebel republic, which could then be severely punished. A couple of cities would be poisoned for generations. The missiles might themselves even be shot down.

He would not put it past the general to have rigged up antimissile batteries to shoot the things down and claim the credit. Either way, there was going to be chaos. And then . . .

Enter the general. Savior.

The Mad Major had found Puma's body. Using a low-light torch, he'd briefly shone the reddish glow upon the shattered head and face. Someone would pay.

At the back of the cottage, the rising ground came quite close to the windows of one of the smaller bedrooms. This was empty, but when she had arrived, Charlotte had opened the windows in all the bedrooms to allow fresh air to circulate. She had shut them all again, but the one close to where the Mad Major was now standing had always fitted badly, and had never been secure.

The Mad Major, balancing precariously and working swiftly so as not to be caught while he was so vulnerable, discovered to his delight that he could work the catch free. Within seconds, he had quietly entered the cottage. Despite his leg, he seemed able to move with terrifying capability.

He checked out the bedroom, then moved to the second. Also empty. He came to the master bedroom.

Astonishing, he thought. An old house whose floorboards didn't creak at night.

He opened the door silently. The red light glowed upon Charlotte and the two children.

"How nice to meet you at last, Mrs. Blish."

"I heard something!" Blish said in a low whisper.

"So did I. A voice. Shit. Someone's got in!" Edin kept his own voice low, too. He moved again, back toward Blish. He peered upward, straining to see in the gloom.

"Oh God—" Blish started to say.

"Don't! Don't move, and don't do anything stupid. If you go rushing up there, he'll nail you before you've gone two feet. Then what good would you be to your wife and kids? We've got to play this right. Time to break radio silence. Alpha Three to Bossman," Edin said as softly as possible into his unit.

"Go ahead."

"We have an intruder."

There was no exclamation, just the barest of pauses.

"Where?"

"Upstairs."

"Hostages?"

"Almost certainly."

"On our way. Job's all done out here."

"Caution."

"Understood."

"They've cleaned up out there," Edin said to Blish in his low whisper. "On their way back now."

"They'll be too late! I've got to do something!"

The hand was again gripping him, holding him back. "What you'll do is get killed. Your family doesn't need a dead hero who's been stupid. We do this properly. We wait."

"Mummy, who's that man?" came Amanda's voice suddenly. "What's he want?"

"*No!*" Edin hissed as Blish had begun to move.

"Are you down there, Mr. Blish?" came a strange, chilling voice from above.

"Leave it!" Edin hissed once more. "He's goading you into doing something stupid."

"Let me go!"

"*No!* Not unless you get your senses back. And while I'm busy holding on to you, I can't do my own job properly. Which is it to be?"

"Are you there, Mr. Blish?" came the unnerving voice with the distinctive accent, from the upper dark. "I have beautiful company. A beautiful woman, and two beautiful children. The children want their daddy, I think."

"Daddy?" came Amanda's voice. "Are you here, Daddy?"

"Oh God, oh God!" Blish whispered.

Edin's grip was still formidable. There was no way of getting free without a lot of noise, despite the other man's weakened elbow.

"Where's my daddy?" he heard his daughter ask.

"Did you hear, Mr. Blish? In case you're wondering who I am, perhaps you've heard of the Mad Major. Does that silence mean no? Or yes? You and your friend Branko have caused me considerable problems, Mr. Blish. I have a very great dislike for those who cause me problems. I become quite enraged, and I take severe punitive action.

"For example," the Mad Major went on, "I was forced to get the information about this place from your wife's mother—"

"Oh no!" came a sudden wail from Charlotte.

"Oh I'm afraid so," the Mad Major said loudly enough for Blish to hear. "She did not survive the experience, I'm sorry to say. Neither did her manservant."

This time there was a loud cry of anguish from Charlotte. "You murdering—" she began to shout.

The sound of a blow stopped her in mid-sentence.

"*Mummy!*" Amanda screamed.

Mianna began to cry.

Blish tried to get up.

"Jesus, man!" Edin hissed at him, hanging on. "Use your head! If he'd wanted to kill them, he'd have done so by now. He wants something. That's your bargaining chip. Now cool it. Relax."

Blish was breathing as quietly as he could, but there was a great heat behind his eyes. He discovered he was gripping the gun tightly. He also realized something quite shocking. He was ready to use it.

After a while, he relaxed. "Where the hell are the others?" he asked impatiently.

"They're out there. They know the situation. Talk to him."

"*What? The children will hear my voice and—*"

"Exactly. It will distract him. He must be alone up there. I don't care how good he is. He can't concentrate on all of us at once, especially in the dark. Go on. Talk."

"What do you want, Major?" Blish called suddenly.

"*Daddy!*"

"Oh, Jordan!"

Both Charlotte and Amanda spoke together.

"*Quiet!*" the Mad Major roared.

There was instant silence from above, broken by a terrified whimpering from Mianna.

"Silence that child or I'll do it for you!" the Mad Major ordered.

"Shh, darling," came Charlotte's voice softly.

"So you are down there, Mr. Blish," came from the dark above. "Good try. Hoping to swamp me, were you? I've used that trick myself on occasion."

"Shit!" Edin whispered.

"What I want, Mr. Blish, is your friend. He has a great sum of money that belongs to me. He betrayed my trust. Tell me where he is. Your family will go free, and I shall be on my way."

"Free? Like my mother-in-law and Brandon?"

Blish wondered what had happened to Durleigh. Nothing ever happened to people like Durleigh.

"That was unfortunate."

Blish felt movement. Edin had let him go. But Edin was shifting position.

"What are you *doing?*" Blish whispered at him.

"I know sods like that. He *will* kill them when he's ready. Trouble is, that could be at any time. He has no intention of letting them go. I'm giving it to you bluntly. No point doing otherwise. If you know what's in store, you can act."

"For God's sake! You've just told me not to do anything!"

"You, no. Me, yes."

"But the others . . . and . . . and your elbow . . . "

"I don't need my elbow to walk. The others will be making their way here. He doesn't know that."

As if he'd listened in on the conversation, the Mad Major said, "I'm assuming you have colleagues outside. If they move against this house, your family will be killed."

A shocked gasp came from above. Charlotte.

"Shit!" Edin said again. He spoke urgently into his radio. "Alpha Three to Bossmann. Do *not*, repeat do *not*, attempt rescue. Hold."

"Shit!" Edin swore for a third time. "It's down to you and me," he added.

"It always was."

Blish was astonished to find he had now become quite calm. Perhaps it was because the situation had at last become clear. It was up to him to save his family. As Edin had predicted earlier, the time had come when choice had been removed from the equation.

"Yes," Edin was saying. "But there's only one thing worse than an amateur."

"What's that?"

"An amateur with an emotional stake. But that might help."

"Mr. Blish! You've been quiet."

"Your pal's getting lonely. Talk to him," Edin advised as he continued. "He's toying with you, but go on. Talk."

"How do I know you'll keep to your word?" Blish called to the Mad Major.

"You don't. But then, I hold all the cards. Three of them. You really should have kept out of matters that did not concern you, Mr. Blish. You would not be here tonight, had you done so."

"I did not choose. I was chosen."

Blish's eyes had grown sufficiently accustomed to the gloom to enable him to make out a moving shape.

Edin was heading up the stairs.

"Like greatness, you had it thrust upon you," the Mad Major suggested.

"Something of that order. Yes."

This is a crazy conversation, Blish thought.

"Then as with greatness, you must accommodate it accordingly. I need to know the whereabouts of your friend. The choice is between that and the lives of your family."

Blish paused deliberately before replying. Edin was making good progress.

Perhaps the Mad Major was not aware there was a second person downstairs.

Edin had been very quiet. Even when he had spoken, his voice had only just carried to Blish, and now, as he moved, there was no sound at all.

"I was with him in Germany," Blish now said.

"Germany? When?"

"Yester—"

Suddenly, Blish was interrupted by the double sound of two sharp coughs, followed by the heavy crash of a body falling down the stairs. It stopped abruptly.

"That was very stupid, Mr. Blish!" the Mad Major shouted.

Edin. He'd got Edin!

The terrifying thought whirled through Blish's mind. He was now alone with a clinically insane, highly professional killer who held his family hostage in a darkened house in the middle of nowhere. If an equally, professionally skilled practitioner like the man he'd known only as Edin had been taken, what chance could he possibly have?

"Mr. Blish! Have you got any more of those people down there with you?"

"No," Blish answered in a shocked voice. It was not an act.

"I can't hear you!"

"No, I said!" The tremor in his voice was even more pronounced, the louder he spoke.

"Daddy!"

"Shut that child up!" the Mad Major snarled.

Blish heard the soothing tones of Charlotte as she tried to comfort Amanda.

She sounded so calm now, he thought, as she spoke to their daughter. It was clearly for the sake of the children; but he wondered for how long she'd be able to keep up the facade.

"Come up, Mr. Blish. I want to see you. And I do hope you haven't lied to me about your other colleagues."

"I haven't."

"Then please come up."

Blish stood up slowly. Holding the pistol behind his back and unsure of what he would do, he began to make his way toward the stairs. He reached them and began to climb. There was a small landing halfway up, where Edin's body lay. As he reached the landing, he felt two distinct taps on an ankle.

He paused. He must have brushed against part of the body. No. There were the taps again.

"Close your eyes." The words were so softly spoken, he nearly missed them.

Edin was alive!

Close his eyes? What did Edin mean?

"Hurry, Mr. Blish! I do not like to be kept waiting!"

"I'm . . . I'm trying to get past the . . . body."

"Don't pass the time of night with it. Keep moving!"

Blish continued upward in the dark. Trusting Edin, he shut his eyes as he reached the top.

"And there you are," the Mad Major said.

The top landing was suddenly flooded with light as the Mad Major flicked the switch.

And Blish understood what Edin had meant. He would have been temporarily blinded by the sudden illumination. As it transpired, his eyes adjusted themselves more quickly to the sudden change when he opened them. But something else had happened too.

As soon as Amanda saw him, she yelled, "*Daddy, Daddy!*"

The Mad Major had positioned himself so that he covered both the top landing and the bedroom where Charlotte and the kids cowered on the floor. His back was toward the open door of another bedroom. Amanda's sudden yell made him turn fleetingly toward her.

At that moment, Blish brought the gun up.

This slight disadvantage, to someone of the Mad Major's caliber, was of no consequence against a rank novice in the close combat stakes like Blish. There was no way in which Blish would have been able to shoot first.

Two coughs spat sharply. The Mad Major reared on his toes, seemingly wanting to stretch forever. His eyes grew round with surprise and disbelief as he stared at Blish.

"You . . ." he began. "You . . . how?" He tried to bring his own gun to bear upon Blish.

A third cough sounded.

The Mad Major's dying body staggered. The gun fell out of fingers that opened slowly, like the petals of a flower sensing a new day. He took a couple of steps toward Blish, who kept watching him, the Uzi unfired.

The Mad Major stood there, glaring at Blish, unable to talk, the latent fury within him refusing to let him die. Then, suddenly, the body collapsed and fell heavily to the floor. It didn't move again.

Neither Charlotte, nor the children, who had watched it all, made the slightest sound. They simply stared at the body, then at Blish.

Edin, Blish thought with a rising sense of joy and relief. *Edin had got the Mad Major.*

Then Amanda broke the spell by shouting, "*Daddy, Daddy!*" Freed from Charlotte's protective embrace, she rushed toward him. "Have you come for us, Daddy?"

"Hullo, sweetheart," he said, and, putting the gun down, got to his knees to scoop her close. "Yes, I have. I have."

Charlotte came to him with Mianna and they held

on tightly to each other. There was a slight bruising on her cheek where the Mad Major had hit her.

He kissed it tenderly.

"Oh Jordan," was all she could say, her tears streaming.

Still holding on to his family, he turned to glance down the stairs. "Thanks, Edin," he called.

There was no reply.

"Just a moment," he said gently to Charlotte. "That man just saved our lives. Let me check on him." He made his way back down. Edin did not appear to have moved. "Edin? It's all over. You got him. Edin! Better call the others on your radio and let them know."

After what seemed like forever, there was a soft groan.

"It's done, Edin," Blish said. "Pretty good shooting."

"I . . . I agree," came the tired voice. "Never . . . never thought you had . . . it in you."

"*Me?* I didn't—" Blish paused. "If not you . . . who?"

But Edin had passed out again.

Blish took the headphone and throat mike from the unconscious body. "Bossman, it's over."

"Where's Alpha Three?" came Buntline's startled voice.

"Wounded. Don't know how bad. I haven't moved him."

"Everyone else okay?"

"Yes. No other casualties. The chief assassin's dead."

"We'll be right with you. Well done."

"But I didn't—"

But Buntline had switched off.

So who had killed the Mad Major?

Moscow, 0350 local.

Kurinin had made countless calls on the ultrasecure line in his office. Specialist units all over the Federation had been put on alert. Some would be able to move at a moment's notice.

Grim-faced, he made one more call.

"Tikov," came the firm voice in his ear. The air force general immediately knew the caller's identity. No one else had access to that particular line.

"Put the special Su-35 fighter units on alert," Kurinin said. "Have them armed with the new R-77 missile."

The long-range rocket/ramjet R-77 air-to-air missile was so new, it was uncertain whether funding would be available for its continuing full development. The

Horsemen, however, had stocks of their own to arm the big, twin-engine, highly maneuverable fighter.

"Is it time?" Tikov asked, his voice sharp with expectancy.

"It's something else. Hold them ready."

"Acknowledged."

They broke the connection.

As Kurinin put the phone down, he reflected upon the scale of Garadze's betrayal. Throughout history, such people had brought untold destruction and suffering upon their fellowmen, in the pursuit of power for themselves.

"I do not want power simply for myself," he said into the room. "I want order returned to the Union."

But Garadze had seen fit to jeopardize all that.

Kurinin felt the betrayal all the more keenly. Garadze was one of his closest friends. It was a highly personal betrayal.

In the computer room, Lirionova was staring at something that had come unbidden upon the screen. First, with a sudden beep, the screen had gone black, to be followed by a broad blue band that lay horizontally across it.

The blue band was now expanding until it filled the entire screen. Then red letters began to appear, in English.

Someone had hacked into the terminal. She could not believe it. Was it a member of the invisible organization she'd accidentally discovered? She read the astonishing message as it came through.

HORSEMEN COMPROMISED. ONE MEMBER

INITIATING NUCLEAR STRIKE TO INFLUENCE WORLD EVENTS. A REBEL REPUBLIC WILL BE MADE SCAPEGOAT. INTERNATIONAL COOPERATION IS NECESSARY IN ORDER TO DIFFUSE THIS THREAT SENSITIVELY. VARIOUS ORGANIZATIONS ON ALERT. CONTACT CODES FOLLOW. ENDS.

Paling, she reached for the phone.

Kurinin entered the room almost at a run.

"No identity of origin?" he asked her as he read the message.

"None, General. I have the contact codes on file. Although I've been searching for this submarine commander, I—I still cannot believe they would—A *nuclear* strike! It's insane."

"There are times when the lust for power destroys reason," he said, voice made harsh by the thought of Garadze's betrayal. "I will admit that I am ruthless in my drive to create a new Union; but I would not betray a comrade, much less a friend."

Kurinin's eyes were cold as he spoke. He looked at her, and she shivered.

"I am assuming that no one else has seen this message."

"No . . . no one, Comrade General."

"Good. Wipe it."

She immediately did so.

"Captain," he went on, "your performance has been exemplary and selfless. You deserve a proper acknowledgment of this. I shall recommend that you be promoted to major."

"Thank you, General!"

"But be warned. The world tonight is a most dangerous place. Over the next few days, many things will be happening. There will be plenty of jockeying for position. The Horsemen ideal may have to be modified if it is to survive. We have been damaged, but not eliminated. I would like to know that I can count upon you in the future."

Her eyes did not waver. "You can, Comrade General."

The submarine had arrived at its launch station. It lay silent on the bottom.

"Begin countdown!" the captain ordered.

On the launch console, the launch crewman rapidly tapped in the code for the first missile. He tapped in the code for the second. Digital numerals began the countdown. They reached zero within a nanosecond of each other. A Klaxon sounded.

"Countdown complete. Systems green!"

"Launch One!"

The crewman pressed the launch button.

"One launched!"

The boat rocked slightly. A great rush of air sounded above them and the water bubbled furiously. Then a roaring sound followed.

"Launch Two!"

The crewman hit the companion button.

"Two launched!"

The boat rocked again and the second rush of air heralded a repeat performance.

"Both airborne and on target!" the crewman called.

"Prime charges," the captain next ordered. "Then abandon ship! Let's get out of here!"

■ ■ ■

Hastily repositioned satellites picked up the launches almost immediately. High-priority, secure communications networks hummed with activity. Trajectories were analyzed, predictions made, likely targets assessed, antimissile batteries put on immediate readiness, the launch site identified and targeted for a possible retaliatory strike.

Those in the know held their breaths as two of Pandora's children, carrying their megadeath cargo, headed for destinations as yet unknown.

The alarm howled its warning to one of the detachments of the area antimissile regiment, one that happened to lie in the path of the first missile. The crews locked on target and fired a huge salvo in order to overwhelm the low-flying weapon.

Several lost the lock because of the extremely low altitude at which the target flew.

But one succeeded.

The early dawn of the new day was lit up by a new sun as the mini cruise missile exploded. The airburst billowed outward and began to form into the familiar, dreaded mushroom. The missile took its revenge upon its killers by vaporizing all beneath it. The antimissile detachment ceased to exist. When its sister units failed to make contact with it after seeing the cloud in the distance, no one wanted to fire at the second, expected missile.

The second missile, however, had veered off in another direction.

It was heading toward a city.

■ ■ ■

Four Su-35s, each with a full complement of R-77 missiles, roared down the runway and leapt into a near-vertical climb for altitude. They gained height rapidly and, on full afterburners, headed on an interception course for the second cruise missile. They split into two combat pairs, each pilot hoping his missile would get the kill while they were still a long way away from the resulting nuclear explosion.

They got the missile on their long-range radars when it was just one hundred kilometers from its target city, which had no local air or missile defense.

All four aircraft got a perfect lock-on. Each fired a single R-77, conserving weapon load in case of a miss. They were careful to remain at a reasonable distance.

One R-77 plowed into high ground. Another, for some reason, ignored the nuclear missile completely. The third and fourth scored direct hits simultaneously.

A second mushroom blossomed over the Russian landscape. This time, a large area of forest was turned to cinder and another patch of ground poisoned.

The aircraft returned to report mission success.

The submarine destroyed itself just as the retaliatory strike arrived. The missiles that rained down were not nuclear-tipped and all they hit was an already-disintegrated boat.

The submarine commander and his crew made it back to the cavern exactly as they had practiced and found the place as deserted at they had been warned it would be.

Dripping in their wet suits, they stared at the place in which they had lived for all those long periods that had seemed like years. But now they could enjoy their money.

"Let's move it!" their captain ordered. "This place is set to blow."

They picked up replacement air tanks, hurried toward their escape route, and sank into the subterranean channel that would eventually take them to the other side of the mountain.

When they had left the water for good, the sub commander retrieved his secret hoard of weapons.

"Insurance," he said, and armed them.

They never made it.

They were still a kilometer from the exit when explosions, behind and ahead of them, sealed them in. They had walked into their tomb.

A day later, General Garadze entered his staff car, secure in the knowledge that no one knew of his treachery.

As the driver turned the ignition, the car exploded.

Both the general and his driver were killed.

The south bank of the Thames, London, a week later.

Blish walked slowly along the terrace of the Royal Festival Hall. He stopped and leaned against the railing. He watched a river boat heading downstream toward Greenwich. There were many people aboard. He could hear music. A party perhaps.

"I thought you'd be in South America, or somewhere like that by now."

"I'll be there," Branko said, "or somewhere like it, sometime."

It was the first time they'd seen each other since Germany.

"My folder was of use, then?" Branko went on.

"*Of use!* Listen, they'll be poring over its contents for years. As for that video . . . The main thing, however, is that the weapons were stopped in time."

"And the Horsemen?"

"From what little Buntline has told me, its seems as if a little weeding out is going on over there."

"That's putting it mildly. It's a secret civil war." Branko smiled suddenly. "So . . . you would have used a gun, after all."

Blish stared at him. "It was you, wasn't it? *You* killed the Mad Major. I've asked all of the Buntline people who were there. None of them did it. And I know it wasn't me. No one's made a gun yet that can shoot without firing."

"You're alive, and your family's alive. And you were spared from killing your first human being. That's all that matters. But now you also know just how far you're prepared to go." Branko paused. "How are things at the FO these days?"

Blish gave an amused smile. "The PUS seems to think I have promise, after all."

"Praise indeed. Be careful. He might think you've got a taste for this kind of life."

"Forget it," Blish said, seeing again the terrified faces of his children, and the bruise left by the Mad Major upon Charlotte's cheek. And Emily and Brandon dead.

Branko looked out upon the river.

"If you say so. Be always on the watch, Jordan," he went on quietly. "This is a fine country. Guard it well. But there's an acid eating away at its heart and an emptiness I haven't seen before in the faces of your people. Something's been taken from them. Disaffection is ripe ground for the demagogue. I come from a land that knows this only too well. Do not be complacent. You are not immune. Be on the watch," Branko repeated. "Always."

A silence fell between them, each reluctant to say the words of parting.

"So . . . are you going to jump into my car one fine morning, ten or twelve years from now?"

"Who knows?" Branko replied mysteriously. "You'll have a teenage daughter by then."

"God. Yes. Can you believe it? Me. Father of a teenage young woman. I still *feel* like a teenager."

"Don't we all?"

"And what are you going to do with all that money?"

"Enjoy it!" Branko said with a grin. "Is there anything else to do with money?"

"The root of all evil," Blish warned lightly.

Branko laughed. "That's what the puritanical rich say to keep the dispossessed in their place while *they* pick the sweet fruit at the top of the tree. I'm neither puritanical, nor dispossessed."

"You're a complex man, Branko."

"In this complex world, that's a safe thing to be. I'm truly sorry about Charlotte's mother and, of course, Brandon," Branko added soberly. "They should not have gone like that."

"That bastard father of hers," Blish said with sudden venom. "Do you know he was actually screwing his bit on the side while his wife was being murdered? It never happens to the bad ones, does it?"

"Sometimes, it does. He doesn't have a home anymore, does he?"

"Not the mansion. No. It's ours now. Emily had a will that Durleigh never knew about. She said things in it that exposed him to the daylight."

"There. You see? Sometimes it comes right. And now, old friend, a Russian bear hug. Yes?"

"Yes."

They slapped each other's backs, then parted. Branko walked quickly away, then stopped and turned round.

"Perhaps not as long as ten years."

He grinned and walked on.

ENDING

South America.

The helicopter clattered its way above the rich canopy, dipping suddenly as it came upon the vast waters of the huge river. It skimmed above the surface, then banked left to follow the course of a tributary that was itself bigger than the rivers of many other countries. It kept going until a clearing came into view. A big white house stood in beautifully landscaped grounds that went right down to the water. A rich plantation covered a large area beyond the grounds. A white motorboat was moored at a small pier.

The helicopter swooped down and landed on the

perfectly kept lawn. Its blades whup-whupped idly, but the pilot did not cut the engines.

Two men in pale suits got out and hurried swiftly toward the house. A woman in her late thirties, or perhaps early forties, came out on the veranda. Her complexion was not that of someone who had spent her life in such climes. She seemed a little puzzled by the presence of the helicopter.

The men went up to her and said something which terrified her. She tried to run into the house. They pulled out automatics and shot her in the back. They then went into the house. More shots followed. When they came out, a fair-haired young boy of about ten, in the company of an Indian boy of about the same age, was running toward the helicopter.

There was no fear upon the boys' faces. They simply wanted to see the machine at close range. They had obviously been playing by the river. The fair-haired boy was carrying a toy submarine.

The men came up to them.

"What is your name?" one of the men asked the fair-haired boy in a language that was familiar, but not of South America. The boy told him.

The man shot the boy, then, for good measure, shot the astonished Indian boy as well.

The killers climbed back into the helicopter. It rose, a giant, noisy, predatory insect, and went back the way it had come.

Watching the neat plantation recede, one of the men said, "That's the whole of the bastard's family gone."

"Nice piece of real estate to go to waste though."

"Who gives a shit. A whole city nearly paid for it with its life."

When the helicopter approached the airstrip it had come from, a man beyond the perimeter raised a tubelike item to his shoulder. He put an eye to a sight that showed a pulsing diamond neatly framing the helicopter.

He squeezed the trigger.

A flaming streak headed for the aircraft. It hit the helicopter squarely and consumed it in a ball of flame.

The man then put the launcher down, swiftly wrapped a spiral of what looked like white tape around it, and left it there.

Then he quickly got out of the area.

A little later, the launcher began to disintegrate.

Born in Dominica, **Julian Jay Savarin** was educated in Britain and took a degree in history before serving in the Royal Air Force. Mr. Savarin lives in England and is the author of *Lynx*, *Hammerhead*, *Warhawk*, *Trophy*, *Target Down!*, *Wolf Run*, *Windshear*, *Naja*, *The Quiraing List*, *Villiger*, *Water Hole*, *Pale Flyer*, *MacAllister's Run*, and *Horsemen in the Shadows*.